"For whom is it well, for whom is it well?
There is no one for whom it is well."

Chinua Achebe, *Things Fall Apart*, 1958

CW01500767

For Ivan
1988—2007
You took a bit of us when you left.
Rest easy, my Angel.

PROMISES

PROMISES

A Novel

Goretti Kyomuhendo

Catalyst Press

Published by Catalyst Press
www.catalystpress.org

In North America, this book is distributed by Consortium
Book Sales & Distribution, a division of Ingram. Phone: 612/746-2600
cbsdinfo@ingramcontent.com
www.cbsd.com

In South Africa, Namibia, and Botswana, this book is distributed by
Protea Distribution. For information, email orders@proteadistribution.
co.za.

First edition, first printing
1 3 5 7 9 8 6 4 2

Printed in Uganda by:
Honey Badger Ltd
www.honeybadgerprinting.com

ISBN 978-1-960803-22-1
Library of Congress Control Number: 2024951885

PART ONE
2007

Kampala

1

It should have been their wedding day. A simple, but formal ceremony at the Registry Office, with two witnesses. Then they would settle into their forever-after. The white wedding would follow later, they had agreed three years back, when they had their traditional kwanjula ceremony.

Instead, Kagaba spent most of the day with a travel agent, who was trying to get him a cheaper air ticket to the UK. Ajuna spent hers at home, plowing through a pile of undergraduate essays.

The traditional ceremony had depleted their finances—Ajuna's, to be precise—since Kagaba was still unemployed. They were now in a desperate situation. They needed to find at least three hundred pounds more in four days' time for Kagaba's travel. How had they come to this?

Today, Ajuna marshaled her not-so-good cooking skills to prepare Kagaba's favorite food: matooke and smoked fish in groundnut sauce, with steamed dodo on the side. He declined her offer of a late lunch, saying he didn't feel like eating or drinking anything, and headed straight to the bedroom.

After a while Ajuna followed him. He had undressed to his underpants, his shirt and jeans strewn on the floor. Ajuna picked up his clothes, folded and laid them out on the cane chair at the foot of the bed. Was he already asleep? Straightened out on the bed facing the wall, his tall frame extended to the base of the bed, his feet touching the chair.

Ajuna stripped off her kitenge wrapper, the only garment

covering her body, and stretched out beside him. She slipped her hand inside his underwear, pressed her breasts against his smooth back and placed her leg between his. Kagaba always made the first move, but over the past few weeks, Ajuna had grown bold. Kagaba stirred, gently pushed her hand away. "I can't, Ajuna ... a headache."

She nibbled at his earlobe and placed her hand on his warm thigh.

"Ajuna ..."

She massaged his nape, teasing the curly hairs covering his lower neck. The rest of his hair was not like that. It was dense and deep black but not curly. A current coursed through her body.

"You provocative thing," Kagaba muttered, pulling in his legs, moving his torso away from hers.

"What did you say?" She burrowed her head into his furry chest, kissing his shoulders.

"Go away." His eyes remained closed. She tried to stimulate him once more, in vain. She got up, sat on the bed and watched him sleep. For a moment, she wondered what the day would have been like had they got married. She wondered what the future held. When they had set today as their wedding day about five months back, she would never have imagined anything disrupting their plans; least of all, Kagaba's leaving for the UK. But here they were—planning for a departure instead of celebrating.

She covered her nakedness with the wrapper and padded to the kitchen, the cold cement under her bare feet soothing away her rejection. The laundry was still lying in the baskets near the washing machine under the sink, which was also full to the brim with unwashed dishes. She had expected the cleaning woman to come in today; she might still make it; it wasn't evening yet.

She moved to the living room, the throbbing between her legs receding. The coffee table had turned into a dressing table: a comb, a tin of hair oil, a jar of Vaseline, a book she had been reading the previous day. On the floor, more students' essays lay in a heap, unmarked. On the couch, her laptop was still open. About twenty emails sat sullenly in her inbox. She needed to find the courage to tackle her domestic mess. Right now, she felt unmoored.

She picked up one of the essays and skimmed through the first three pages. The opening quote was borrowed from William Adams's *Green Development: Environment and Sustainability in the Third World.* There was no citation at the bottom of the page. She turned to the last page, searching for the bibliography. None. She looked at the name on the first page: Nansikombi Margaret. It was impossible to know who she was in a class of a hundred and thirty students. Yet, the administration expected her to give attention to each student in addition to other administrative roles.

Her own research assignment had gone two weeks past its deadline. She now doubted her wisdom in starting on her PhD so soon after finishing her master's degree. Her salary was inadequate; she was still living in the tiny one-bedroomed apartment offered by the university. Her man was leaving— before their marriage.

Two hours later Kagaba was out of bed; she heard him flush the toilet.

"The cleaning woman didn't come in today," she explained by way of an apology for the mess in the living room when he joined her.

Kagaba did not respond. He sat down on the narrow sofa— the only furniture they managed to squeeze into the small living room.

"My Thursday schedule is killing me, Kagaba," she moaned. "Two lectures before midday, then workshops up to eight in the evening. By Friday, when I don't have to teach, I am too exhausted to think of cleaning."

"You keep saying you will sack the cleaner, but you never do," Kagaba finally spoke, but from his tone, she deduced that the cleaning woman's ineptitude and the dirty apartment was not what he wanted to talk about. They should be talking about the complications of his imminent departure for the UK.

"Ajuna, you know that if I had a job, I would not be leaving. You know it has been three years of looking." He spoke as if talking to someone else who did not know these facts. He stood up abruptly and went to the kitchen, returning with a glass of water.

"Why did I even bother with a master's? Uh? What good is a man with no job, no money?"

"Don't say that!" She stood up, took his hand and led him back to the sofa. "You're still everything any woman would wish for."

He said nothing as he drank the water.

She stroked his hands, soft as ever, and snuggled closer. After three years, he still made the butterflies in her stomach flutter.

"I'm not getting any younger," Kagaba said eventually.

"Come on! Twenty-eight is not ancient. There's still plenty of time to turn things around. And the UK will offer more prospects."

"My father says, 'He who enters a forest with an axe cannot fail to get firewood.'"

"He's right, Kagaba. You're well equipped. A solid, postgraduate qualification in Economics is not something to be sniffed at."

"Sometimes I wish I had specialized in Accounting."

"Economics offers a wider range of opportunities. Marketing, investment; these sectors are more developed in the UK."

"You think so?"

She stood up. They had been through this discussion before. There was nothing more for her to add. She picked up her laptop and moved to the dining table; but instead of going to her emails she picked up her phone to call Kalayi, her younger sister. This is something she had been putting off for a while. But it had to be done now. They were running out of time. She planned to convince Kalayi to ask her rich boyfriend to lend them some money toward Kagaba's air ticket.

The pressure to find the money for Kagaba's trip was killing her. Alex, the shrewd entrepreneur who made a living "aiding" people planning to escape the throes of poverty in Uganda, had made it clear: "You cannot afford to miss this chance." A graduation ceremony in the UK had been used as Kagaba's excuse to obtain the visa. And it was happening in four days' time.

Kagaba's phone rang as Ajuna began to dial Kalayi's number.

"It's Kato," Kagaba announced. Kato was his childhood friend who had married Kagaba's sister, Ama, a nurse. Kato had promised to "find" some money from the British-funded Aloe Vera company where he was manager. Kagaba would refund the money as soon as he got a job in the UK. He moved to the bamboo tree shed at the front of the apartment, where there was a better network connection.

As Ajuna waited, she served herself the food that was still on the dining table without warming it in the microwave first and started eating. She could not explain this sudden love affair with food. She was conscious of her height. If she piled a lot of fat onto her miniature stature, she would look like a mushroom. Was it true that women gained weight with age? She was thirty-one.

"Has he got the money?" Ajuna asked as Kagaba came through the door.

"Well, yes and no."

"What do you mean?"

"He didn't get all of it. We need to find more money."

"We'll find a way," she spoke with more confidence than she felt. She began dialing Kalayi's number again but thought better of it. She would call her first thing in the morning. She didn't want to deal with that now, knowing how Kalayi might react.

"Please, honey, eat some food," she said to Kagaba, but he shook his head. Tension lines had creased his forehead. The stress was taking its toll. He said he was going to meet Kato at a Kafunda to get the money, and he might return late, given how crazy the traffic jam got on Friday evenings. If Ajuna had her way, she would not have involved Kato in their plans to find the money for the air ticket. His corrupt ways troubled her. She watched Kagaba walk away with a sense of loss. In just a flash, so much had changed between them.

When Kagaba first moved in with her after their kwanjula, life was blissful. She had just graduated with a distinction for her master's and bought her first car. It gave her immense pleasure when she returned home to find Kagaba waiting for her every evening.

But failure to find a job was beginning to frustrate him and mar their happiness. At times, he acted irrationally, testing her patience to the limit. One time, after a disagreement, she had exploded, "This is my house, and that's my car!"

She had regretted the words immediately and apologized, but Kagaba had packed his bags and left. It took the intervention of his sister, Ama, to bring them together again.

She was drained as she retired to bed, but she still struggled to sleep. Today was supposed to be special. Momentous. She shouldn't be going to bed alone.

During the night, she heard Kagaba unlock the front door and by the time he walked into the bedroom, she was wide awake and watched him as he undressed and slid into bed beside her. His hands found her breasts through the nylon nightdress. She felt his hot breath on her ears, and turned to face him, bringing her mouth to connect with his. Her hands located his stiffness, and she snuggled closer.

"I love you, baby," he breathed into her ear, "I love you so very much."

2

In the UK, if everything went as planned, Kagaba would be staying with Musana, Kato's older brother, who had agreed to show him the ropes as he settled in the new country. Although he had been living in the UK for a long time, Musana was still "sorting out his papers," which meant that he was unable to return to Uganda for visits.

The little that Ajuna knew about Musana, she had gathered from Ama, who called him a delinquent. It was rumored that before leaving for the UK, Musana stole millions of shillings from his employer, Shell. When the money ran out, his wife abandoned him and their two children to Kato and Ama, and returned to her homeland, Rwanda.

"Musana just called," Kagaba said when Ajuna joined him at the dining table. He was eating his breakfast before setting off for the travel agent's.

She waited.

"He's pushing me to confirm my travel date. I think he's getting impatient."

"Tell him we're still trying to find the—"

"He's aware," Kagaba interrupted. "He mentioned getting a day off from his job to fetch me from the airport. And about my job ..."

"Yes?" Ajuna looked up. Musana had assured Kagaba that finding a job in the UK with his level of qualifications wouldn't be hard. Musana had friends who knew friends in the right places. The pay would be excellent.

"We're still on track," Kagaba beamed, his shoulders sliding back in a relaxed posture.

"That's great, honey." Ajuna hugged him. He enfolded her in his large arms, planting several kisses on her forehead.

"Wait. Are you alright? Your head feels hot."

"I'll be fine," Ajuna dismissed his concern. She had woken up feeling queasy, her joints aching, her ears ringing. She did not want to mention it to Kagaba, knowing he had a lot on his mind.

"It's probably the flu," Kagaba offered, "Take some Panadol, drink plenty of water, and lie in for the day. By evening, you'll be ..." he made the victory sign.

But Ajuna did not have the luxury of shutting out the world, not with Kagaba's impending journey. She needed to speak with Kalayi. She called her to come to the apartment, since she could not go to town to meet her as she had earlier planned.

Kalayi arrived later in the evening after clocking off from work. She found Ajuna lying listlessly on the sofa, browsing through an old newspaper. She offered an alternative diagnosis. "It's the stress over Kagaba's trip. Is that what you wanted to speak to me about?"

"Yes."

"What about it? Hasn't Ama's husband stolen enough money from his office to buy the ticket?"

"Kato? He did not steal the money, Kalayi. It's a loan, and Kagaba will refund it as soon as he gets a job in the UK." She did not want to get into a discussion of Kato's deceitfulness, not now.

"Well, then, what's the problem?" Kalayi was her usual buoyant self: matter-of-fact, loud.

"We need some more money. What Kato got is not enough. We need at least three hundred pounds more."

"And you expect me to provide it? Have you forgotten that I don't have a proper job? And that I earn peanuts? And that I'm still on probation, nine months after I started working? I have no appointment letter, no—"

"Please, Kalayi, don't shout. My head is aching. And that's not what I meant—"

"No, let me finish," Kalayi raised her voice, vexed.

Ajuna let her go on because she needed to humor her.

"Our stupid bookshop manager," Kalayi continued, "has now introduced The Customer Care Creed, and they expect all the employees to recite it *every bloody fucking morning*! It goes like this." Kalayi stood up and flattened her hands against her sides, as if she was about to sing the national anthem.

"I, Kalayi, swear that I will treat the customers of this bookshop with respect. That I will smile whenever I see a customer, and keep the customer happy at all times … And so much more bullshit," she sat down heavily.

"Is this really true, or are you exaggerating a little?" Ajuna hoped she sounded concerned enough.

"Cross my heart. This is the latest disgraceful requirement by my silly manager. She seems to derive pleasure from humiliating us. When I tell people that these are Ugandans mistreating fellow Ugandans, they don't believe me. They ask me, 'Are you sure your employers are not Indians?'"

Ajuna looked at her sister sympathetically, pitying her. She had been complaining about her vile employers for ages, but she did not have many options. After completing her A levels, Kalayi had refused to take up the teaching diploma course she was offered on government sponsorship. She reasoned that their elder brother, Jimmy, had failed to find a job five years after studying the same course and now worked as a driver. She wanted to privately pursue a business course instead, which she claimed had better job prospects.

But their father was neither willing nor able to pay for it. She accused him of destroying her dreams. Their mother, as usual, took Kalayi's side, which angered their father. He gave her an ultimatum: either she takes up the offered course or leaves his house.

Ajuna would have chipped in to pay for the course, but she

was already paying school fees for their two orphaned nephews, on top of meeting the medication costs for their diabetic father.

She invited Kalayi to move in with her, hoping to persuade her to take up the teaching diploma. But two months later, she had failed to convince her to go for the course. Given their opposite personalities and the fact that they shared the same bed—there was no space to fit another—they did not get on well.

"I cannot complain enough," Kalayi was still talking. "One of these days, I will throw their stupid uniform in their faces and walk away."

"You have to be patient." Ajuna knew she had to tread carefully. Kalayi could be unreasonable when angry, and today, she needed her in a good mood because of what she was about to ask her.

"I'm serious," Kalayi threatened, her eyes burning. "God knows how much more I can take." Kalayi calmed down a little, and Ajuna relaxed, hoping she had managed to persuade her to keep her job, at least for another few months.

Ajuna steeled her nerves. "Can you get a soft loan from your boyfriend?" She expected Kalayi to explode, but her anger had waned.

"Samuel? I'll talk to him. I'm meeting him tonight. He's taking me out to this new restaurant in Kololo. It's kawa! And as for Samuel, he is so … ooooo wonderful. You should—"

"Tell him we'll repay him as soon as Kagaba gets a job in the UK," Ajuna added quickly, now that Kalayi was melting.

"I'm sure he won't mind. Samuel has no money issues. But you seem anxious about something else, sis? Are you worried you'll lose your prince once he's gone?"

"Of course not. I'm just concerned that he will … that he will … find it hard to make it in a foreign country. Isn't that valid enough?"

"Are you not worried that a sharp-sharp kyana will snatch him? He's so handsome and as calm as a monk. He won't survive those women in the UK."

"I trust him, Kalayi."

"How long does he plan to stay in the UK?"

"We're not sure, not yet. He will see how things work out after he's settled in. But the plan is for him to come back after he's made some money and set up a consultancy to do with business management."

"Well, everything seems to be sorted out then."

"Yes."

Before she left to go meet her wealthy lover, Kalayi agreed to Ajuna's request to tidy up the apartment, but not before delivering a harangue on how she would soon start charging for her services. Why could Ajuna not simply fire the irresponsible, inefficient worker? She moved about in the kitchen, bedroom, bathroom, and living room with an admirable agility and efficiency, a sunny smile lighting her face.

"I could work for you, you know, and perhaps you'd pay and treat me better than my current employers."

Ajuna smiled. Kalayi can be benign when she chooses to, she thought. She was still her warm-hearted, kid sister, despite her misgivings. She remembered the events after she had told Kalayi to move out, following the disagreement over her refusal to take up the diploma course. A quiver ran through her body. She had hoped she had got over that traumatic episode.

Ajuna was still thinking about Kalayi when she heard a knock at the front door. It was Ama. She had not called her. She wondered why she was visiting after eight in the evening, but Ama immediately explained. "I spoke to Kagaba this morning and he said you were not feeling well. I thought I'd come to check on how you're doing." She examined Ajuna, feeling her pulse and forehead. "You have malaria," she declared. "Why don't you come to the clinic tomorrow so we can do a blood test?"

"Kalayi thinks it might be stress," Ajuna hazarded, knowing this might offend Ama, who never liked being challenged on a medical matter.

"Nonsense, stressed over what? Kagaba's trip?"

Ajuna nodded.

Ama did not comment, which surprised Ajuna, but she remained hovering over Ajuna. Every so often, Ajuna was uncertain how to deal with Ama. In some ways, Ama and Kalayi were similar. They were both short-tempered, high-energy people. But whereas Kalayi was open-minded, Ama could be annoyingly old-fashioned.

Ama was the first person among Kagaba's family that Ajuna had met, soon after their love affair started. She was reluctant to make her a friend. She came across as overbearing. She worried she could easily take over her life if she let her. But she was wrong. Beneath the armor of self-confidence, Ajuna had discovered warmth and generosity; and Ama's exceptional closeness to Kagaba, even when they did not share the same mother, warmed Ajuna toward her future sister-in-law.

At first, Kagaba's excellent cooking skills were a mystery to Ajuna until Ama explained. In the absence of Kagaba's birth mother, he had been raised by their aunt—Ssenga Jovia—their father's younger sister. Kagaba shared a unique bond with her.

"How was your shift?" Ajuna asked.

"The usual," Ama replied, exhaling. "That hospital has gone to the dogs, kabisa. And to think that it's the whole country's referral hospital. There are too many patients, too few nurses, and even fewer doctors. They work us like donkeys and pay us nothing. If I wasn't working part-time at the private clinic in the evenings, I don't know if I would be able to afford sanitary towels."

The bit about not affording pads was an exaggeration. Ama's husband, Kato, made enough money for the both of them. He made the money not as project manager of the Aloe Vera company but from altering accounts ledgers, supplying fake receipts and invoices to auditors, and from kickbacks and commissions from the project's clients.

"I have brought some money for Kagaba's trip." Ama slid an envelope into Ajuna's hands, surreptitiously, as if she was worried someone was watching.

"Oh, we didn't expect this? Kato has already ..."

Ama waved away her protestations. "It's not that much. Besides, Kagaba will need some extra cash as he settles in a new country. I should be leaving now," she said, standing up.

"About the money, we can't, I mean, the loans are already too much."

"No worries, Ajuna, I don't expect to be paid back. Kagaba is my kid brother. I would do anything for him. You must come to the clinic tomorrow," she added, sounding like a doctor. "And don't stress too much over Kagaba's trip, everything will work out fine."

Monday morning, Ajuna woke up feeling upbeat despite a persistent headache. She decided to pop into her office to do a bit of administration work and clear her desk. She debated whether to drive or just use the shortcut from her flat to Senate Building, where her office was located. She hated using the shortcut, though. The small path was always littered with rubbish, because there was no proper refuse-collecting system at the university, so tenants just deposited their waste anywhere. But since it was not too hot, the fifteen-minute walk might do her good.

Students were back for the new semester and because studies hadn't gotten underway, many were loitering about, or lying in the grass, basking in the warm sun outside Senate Building. The once green-green grass had turned into a pale shade of brown. Of late, the battering from the sharp sun was relentless.

To her left, St. Andrew's Chapel parking lot was full—perhaps a funeral service was underway. She would avoid the shortcut that passed through the lot. She turned back and sloped down the hill, past the canteen. This route would take her an extra ten minutes. She walked fast, the sun was getting hotter, but she could already see Senate Building ahead.

Her mind flipped back to the day she first met Kagaba. It was at Senate Building, on a rainy, windy May morning. The university was engulfed in end-of-year exam fever. She was dashing from a lecture to a meeting when it started raining. She decided to brave it; after all, she had an umbrella.

But the fierce wind rendered the umbrella useless and by the time she arrived at Senate Building she was drenched. She shoved aside the horde of students queuing to go through the metal detector, jumping the second layer of security. But the security man called her back. "Madam, please, you have to go through that machine as well, and please place your handbag in the tray, do you have keys in your pocket?"

As she stood waiting for the lift, she realized how wet her clothes and shoes were; her hair was a mess, with droplets of water dripping down her face. She couldn't go to the meeting like this. She would go back to the apartment and change; the downpour had stopped. She arrived home panting from the brisk walk but couldn't find her house keys. She turned her handbag inside out, removed all the papers and books from the tote bag slung over her shoulder; nothing.

"Hello."

She jumped. The man was standing right behind her, in the narrow opening to her apartment. The first thing she noticed when she turned to look at him was how tall he was. He seemed to be looking down at her. "Hello?"

"Your keys, you left them at the security machine," he held out the bunch for her to take.

"Oh, thank you, thank you so much." She felt like a fool, standing there in her wet clothes, the man staring at her with a bemused smile. How had he known where she lived? Was he one of the students she had shoved in her haste to get through the security layers? He must have followed her to the apartment.

"Are you a student?" she asked, not looking at him.

"Yes, final year, Economics department."

"How old are you? Sorry, I didn't ... what's your name?"

He grinned, flashing the whitest set of teeth, and said, "Twenty-five. My name is Kagaba."

It had started raining again. Still mortified by what had possessed her to ask such a personal question, she fumbled for something to say to appease him. "Come inside. Would you like some tea?"

He was gazing at her with the shyness of a boy, smiling. A fleeting weakness threatened to buckle her legs. She breathed in, struggling to maintain her composure, then opened the door. But he remained standing in the passageway. She said she was going inside to change. He replied that he'd wait for the rain to stop, and then rush back to Senate Building, as he had an exam that day. She started to close the door behind her but was unsure whether it might look like she was being rude. He looked vulnerable, standing there on his own. Because of his towering height, he did not look twenty-five. She would put him at twenty-eight, same age as her.

Their next encounter, a few months after the university had closed for end-of-year holidays, was not a coincidence. That same year, in December, they were engaged and married in a kwanjula ceremony.

As she worked she remembered she owed Jane a call. Jane was her best friend and colleague at the university. She taught statistics at the Business School, about three miles from the main campus, where Ajuna taught. She phoned to let her know that she was in the office finishing off her admin. Jane promised to drop by on her way home.

Ajuna needed to unburden herself. She thought back to what they had already gone through to get Kagaba to the UK.

Kagaba got his visa the traditional, Ugandan way; with the help of Alex, the astute businessman introduced to him by

Musana. From obtaining forged bank statements and invitation letters from "relatives" abroad, to bogus birth and marriage certificates of non-existent children and spouses, Alex did it all.

Alex had identified a bona fide university graduate of ACCA, who was traveling to the UK for his graduation at the University of Greenwich. The university allowed him to invite up to four relatives, as long as they could prove that they could afford travel and accommodation expenses.

For Kagaba's name to be appended on the "relatives" list, Alex had charged one thousand pounds, which Kato "borrowed" from his office. At that point, Kagaba became the graduand's eldest brother.

But that was not all. To make Kagaba's application water-tight, Ajuna paid Alex an amount large enough to buy a plot of land in Kampala so he could obtain a bank statement that supported Kagaba's new status as a successful aloe vera farmer. On top, Kagaba needed a marriage certificate, and two children's birth certificates that showed he was already a father. In his new passport, Kagaba was made thirty-five years old to fit his new identity.

As well as all this, Kagaba needed to show proof that he had booked and confirmed accommodation in London; in this case, at a B&B close to the University of Greenwich, the same accommodation that the other three "relatives" had already confirmed. He could not use Musana's address because Musana was still without papers. The seven-day stay at the B&B—the period they had applied to stay in the UK—cost over five hundred pounds.

There was no way Ajuna could have afforded it all on her meager lecturer's salary, which she already shared with the rest of her family, and she had taken a soft loan from Jane, which Kagaba would repay after getting a job in the UK.

Mercifully, Kagaba's application, together with the three other "relatives" were approved by the UK embassy. And from that moment, there was no turning back, having invested so much into the process already.

"All this bothers me," she said to Jane when she arrived.

"What bothers you?" Jane dabbed at her face with a hanky. Ajuna's tiny office was stuffy with heat and lack of space. She had recently added an extra desk for Dr. Tindi, a fellow lecturer in the Geography department who had returned from his studies in Cambridge. He had not been allocated an office yet because of a disagreement with the head of the department. The whole thing was turning acrimonious, and Ajuna had offered to share her airless, cubicle-like office while Dr. Tindi sorted out his woes with the head.

"Everything bothers me," Ajuna replied. "The forgeries, the money we're investing. Sometimes I wonder if it's all worth the effort. Suppose Kagaba is found out on arrival at Heathrow and is deported? Suppose the graduation ceremony is canceled, or postponed, as always happens here? Then there will be no reason for the group to travel to the UK. I would die if that happened. That man, Alex, made us cancel our wedding so as not to miss this so-called graduation!

"And I still have doubts about that man, Musana, being Kagaba's host in the UK. Much as his schemes got Kagaba the visa, he is still of doubtful character. I don't think he's dependable. He's assured us Kagaba will find a job immediately. But suppose … How shall we repay the loans?" Ajuna had never been involved in any forgeries before and perhaps that was her greatest discomfort about the whole phony process.

Jane said nothing for a while and Ajuna felt grateful for that. That's one of the qualities she liked most about her friend. She was realistic without being cynical, a pessimist in a way that Ajuna liked. If Jane felt she had no valid advice to offer, she would rather not say anything than blurt out meaningless, empty-sounding phrases. As a friend, she was indispensable.

Ajuna and Jane had attended the same secondary school and later university, and had remained very close since. Their bond was like that of sisters; perhaps because Jane did not have a sister.

Jane's father was a retired High Court judge, her mother a former civil administrator; both high-status jobs that had allowed them to cater for their four children's needs without going through the usual hassles many Ugandan families had to deal with. Now Jane's three brothers lived abroad and worked in high-profile, well-paid jobs. They took care of any financial family needs. Because Jane did not have to look after her aging parents or extended family, she normally had some spare cash at hand to bail Ajuna out in times of financial hardship.

"Isn't it a little too late for regrets?" Jane asked.

"I guess so."

"Something else is bothering you, Ajuna." It was a statement.

"Yes. All this money we have sunk into Kagaba's trip. Honestly, I …"

"You are worried about what Kagaba's departure will mean to your relationship," Jane persisted.

Ajuna sighed. Jane was right, as always. If she were to place her worries in hierarchy, sustaining a long-distance relationship would take first position. Would she survive Kagaba's absence? In the past three years, their love had grown thicker than blood. Would he come back to her? They should have got married first.

Jane stood up, pulled the only empty chair in the office closer to Ajuna's desk. She took her hand. "Ajuna, you have to trust that Kagaba will do the right thing."

"I hear you, Jane. I can't turn the clock back now."

After Jane left, Ajuna closed the door and sat without moving for some time. As she stood up to leave, a spell of nausea hit her, and she thought she was going to vomit all over her writing desk. She clasped the desk and fought off the urge to throw up.

She should have listened to Ama and gone for the malaria

test. She had been under a lot of pressure these past three months; not sleeping well and working too hard, which could have compromised her immunity.

3

Ssenga Jovia made Kagaba miss his flight. Two days before the departure date, Ama informed him that their father's sister was traveling to the city the following day to see him off.

"She can't come," Kagaba fumed, as he narrated the news. "She's never been to the city, or anywhere, for that matter. Her health is not good, and we can't afford any more financial obligations at this time. She might require a hospital; who will pay the bills? And how will she finance the trip? I'm going to call my father and ask him to stop her."

"Tomas is coming with her," Kagaba told Ajuna later in the day, after he had spoken to his father.

"Who's Tomas?"

"You don't remember Tomas? You've met him before, Ajuna; he's our cousin who has lived with us since I was a child. His father is my father's and Ssenga Jovia's younger brother. My father said there's nothing he can do to stop them. Ssenga Jovia sold some of her pigs to raise enough money for transport. Ama will fetch them from the bus park and accommodate them."

He sounded resigned. The mental pressure of organizing the trip had stolen his natural calm.

"I think it will be alright," Ajuna tried to reassure him. After all, Ssenga Jovia seemed to have thought of everything. According to Ajuna, it seemed Ssenga Jovia and Tomas were going to extra lengths to come to Kampala, but it was not her place to point that out. Was it really necessary for two people to come all the way from the village to see Kagaba off? If it were his father, it would have made more sense, but why his aunt and cousin?

It had been agreed that Kagaba's father would carry Ssenga Jovia on his bicycle to the bus park, and make sure they boarded the right vehicle. Tomas, who would have to walk the three miles to the bus park, would set off earlier, at the crack of dawn. He would carry Ssenga Jovia's big bag on his head, too.

The day for Kagaba's departure dawned. His flight was at 9.35 pm, aboard British Airways. Alex had told Kagaba that he would meet the rest of the group, the "relatives" of the graduand, at the airport.

The group included a young woman purporting to be the graduand's wife, but who was going to join her real husband in the UK.

The other was a man in his late fifties recently retrenched from his job as a banker. After failing to secure other employment, his children had been thrown out of school, and his house was repossessed. He decided to try his luck in the UK. He used his retrenchment package to finance his trip. He was masquerading as the graduand's father.

The third was a child of seven years. She was going to be reunited with her parents, who had left her behind when she was just a year old. For the purpose of obtaining a visa, she had pretended to be the graduand and his "wife's" daughter. Her parents in the UK had paid for the trip.

Ajuna wondered how they would play the purported family connections—the graduand, the wife and their daughter— having only met for the first time at the airport. Her fear was that if one was caught, the rest of them would be found out. And how would Kagaba, acting as the graduand's older brother, fit in?

No one in the group had ever traveled abroad before, and their assurance that they would make it to the UK lay in their solidarity of traveling together.

Ssenga Jovia and Tomas were supposed to arrive by noon. Ama was anxious to be at the bus park to receive them, fearing that they might get overwhelmed by the rush and indifference of the city. She had woken up early to prepare a "small" meal for her brother before he embarked on his sojourn to a foreign land.

"It's only for the immediate family, a few close friends and my colleagues from hospital," she argued when Ajuna expressed reservation about the timing.

"It will be a late-ish lunch, about 3 pm, after I've picked up Ssenga Jovia and Tomas. After eating, we shall drive straight to the airport."

Ajuna was not convinced. It meant squeezing in extra time to drive to Ama's house. Kagaba was frazzled by the journey's preparations, and Ajuna was anxious to get to the airport early enough for Kagaba to get acquainted with his travel companions. Besides, Ajuna knew the get-together wouldn't be as small or as brief as Ama wanted her to believe.

Kato had hired a video man to record the event, and Ajuna was told to bring along at least three colleagues from university. Kalayi and her boyfriend, Samuel, were also invited. That was already twenty people, if you included Ama and Kato's four children, friends and other family members. Ajuna invited Jane and Dr. Tindi, but only Jane eventually made it. Dr. Tindi said he had to deal with a family crisis.

There was no point reasoning with an overly excited Ama, who was eager to show off her kid brother about to depart for the UK. And so, Kagaba finished packing and they arrived at Ama's house just as she was about to set off for the bus park to pick up Ssenga Jovia and her escort.

It took Ama almost two hours to establish that Ssenga Jovia and her companion had not traveled, after all. By then, it was almost two in the afternoon. She called her father, after failing to locate the duo at the busy bus park. Her father filled her in: Firstly, Ssenga Jovia wanted Kagaba to postpone his departure, because she had to give him a special parting present. Also, he needed her total blessings. Ssenga Jovia was planning to travel to the city the next day. At the moment, Ssenga Jovia and Tomas were at the police station in Hoima.

As it turned out, Ssenga Jovia had got into a scuffle with the bus conductor because he wanted to keep her big, black bag in the boot, where all other luggage was. Ssenga Jovia wouldn't hear of it. She argued that the bag contained very important things. She insisted on carrying it on her lap. The conductor argued that the bag was taking up space that could have been occupied by another passenger. A fight ensured and the two were kicked off the bus.

Ssenga Jovia insisted on laying charges. She got an apology, a full refund of their tickets, and a few shillings to treat the scrapes inflicted during the scuffle.

Ama laughed off the impossible demand to postpone Kagaba's journey and headed straight back home, hoping to beat the early afternoon traffic in time to serve her guests. But by 4 pm she was still stuck in the jam; that's the time they should have been heading to the airport. She called Ajuna and said if she wasn't home in an hour, they should just head for the airport without her. That's what happened in the end.

Ajuna noticed the mix-up with the handbags while they were already at the airport. In haste to rush off to the bus park to pick up Ssenga Jovia and Tomas, Ama had picked up Ajuna's handbag, which was the same Chinese fake leather make and color as hers. Both bags were placed on the dining table, where Ajuna had deposited hers when they arrived at Ama's house.

Kagaba's passport, ticket and other travel papers were all in Ajuna's missing bag. He could not trust his tired mind to remember all the documents he needed for his travel, and so they had agreed that Ajuna keep the documents and hand them over to him at the airport.

Ajuna's frantic call came as Ama arrived back at the house.

It was two hours before the flight took off. Ama figured she might just make the twenty-eight-mile journey to the airport if she drove like a mad woman. But she did not make it. The highway was clogged with evening traffic, and taxi drivers made the situation worse by jumping the queue and honking like crazy men, which caused more distress to other fellow road users.

Fortunately, British Airways operated three direct flights out of Uganda each week. The next was in two days. The following day, they went to the airline's offices to have Kagaba re-booked, and paid the fine for having missed his flight, which ate further into his meager pocket money.

Ssenga Jovia did not make it to the city that time either. Her high blood pressure had shot up following the stress she had endured at the hands of the rude bus conductor.

The handbag mix-up—how could she not have noticed she wasn't carrying her handbag all the way to the airport? Ama should have seen that she was carrying the wrong handbag— but she said she was too distracted to notice. Then Ssenga Jovia's fight with the bus conductor—why would she opt to carry a huge travel bag on her lap, instead of placing it in the boot?

Ajuna questioned whether she should have read more into these incidents.

London

1

Welcome to Heathrow Airport. Life is a curve. Where are you on it? The sign was emblazoned on a mounted, rotating billboard. Kagaba pondered how he would answer the question. Perhaps he was at the middle of life's curve. He was twenty-eight years old, and the life expectancy for Ugandan men was about fifty-six. Women lived a little longer, were expected to die just shy of their sixtieth birthday.

Or was he at the start of life's curve? Wasn't he coming to the UK for a fresh start?

"Look at these roads! Can we ever achieve this level of development back home? Not in a thousand years. When I first came to this country, I had to learn to drive on a pothole-free road. See how many lanes there are."

Kagaba counted four lanes on either side of the motorway. Musana talked fast and loud, not giving him a chance to respond. They were driving out of Heathrow, and Musana had brought a heavy jacket for him to wear on the trip from the airport, but it smelt of dirt and booze and cigarettes, and he could not bring himself to wear it. Besides, he was not used to sharing clothes.

"I'm fine," he had lied, pulling his light jumper closer to his shoulders.

"It's only October anyway, and *real* winter is not yet here, when temperatures can drop to two degrees," Musana concurred, adding that the forecast for the day was eleven degrees Celsius and for autumn, that was quite okay. The passenger who sat next to him on the plane had said as much, warning that Kagaba would have to buy a heavier coat for the approaching winter; otherwise, the cold would make him sick. Kagaba had explained that he had never been to the UK before, or Europe, or America, and had never experienced winter, never seen snow.

"Living in a new place can be tough at the beginning," the passenger said, trying to make conversation. "I live in Aberdeen. It's cold as a tomb, especially when the winds begin blowing in from the North Sea; and it rains at least once every day. I'm not Scottish. I was born and raised in London, but I work for an oil company in Aberdeen and the money's good. That's why I tolerate the cold. But I still have to escape to a warmer climate every now and then. I loved your country very much. I can't understand why anyone would want to leave such a beautiful place. The temperatures are excellent, the people are friendly and warm, the fruits and vegetables fresh; though I can't say much for the food. It was a bit too bland for my taste."

He spoke in a throaty voice, pulling at his thick moustache. Kagaba did not know which of the questions or statements to respond to.

"And what are you coming to do in the UK?" the man prompted.

"To work."

"Ah!" The non-Scottish man sounded impressed and turned to take a better look at him. Kagaba slouched further into his seat.

"Which company?"

"I studied Economics at university. I'll be looking at jobs within investment, finance and marketing sectors." He wanted to add that he had a master's; he was well equipped, as his father would put it. "My brother-in-law will help," he said. "I'll be staying with him at the beginning."

"Oh," he seemed to have lost interest after learning Kagaba was not an expatriate like himself. He reclined his chair further away from him, and only started talking when a stewardess stopped by their seats to offer them delicious-smelling food. Kagaba shook his head when asked to choose between chicken and beef.

"Are you vegetarian, then? To say the truth, I haven't met many Africans who are," the man chuckled. "You guys surely love your meat."

Kagaba smiled, hesitating whether to divulge the truth or to simply lie and say he wasn't interested in the food. "I don't have money to pay for it," he relinquished when the man kept pushing.

"It's free. Oh, for goodness' sake! Look, you paid for it already when you paid for the ticket."

He tried the food. It did not taste like chicken at all and the portions were like a child's. He had eaten very little in the past two days. After he had missed his flight and the opportunity to travel with the graduand's team, panic had set in and food was the last thing on his mind.

Musana was still talking, his voice meshing with the early afternoon traffic. It was a gray, misted day. Raindrops tapped on the windscreen, making a sound like chickens pecking millet from dust.

"After I drop you off at the house, I'll go straight to work. I swapped my night shift so I could pick you up. If you had come two days ago as planned, this wouldn't have happened. I couldn't ask for another day off today. You shouldn't have missed your flight." His tone was sharp, and Kagaba stole a nervous glance at his host.

"Nsonyiwa, Ssebo," he said in Luganda. He was already missing the language, the lingua franca of Kampala.

"No need to apologize. You're here now and that's what matters," Musana spoke like a British man, and Kagaba found it hard to follow what he was saying. He was almost unrecognizable from the mental image Kagaba had of him; he had last seen him about eight years before. His face was smoother and fatter and his resemblance to his younger brother, Kato, had diminished over the years.

Musana was dressed in a worn-out leather jacket and wrinkled, black trousers. His shoes looked like they had not been cleaned in a long time. Kagaba was wearing a plain, two-button navy suit, a blue polyester shirt and tie, and he hadn't expected to stand out in the cheap attire but that's how he felt, like he was superior to Musana, a man who had been living in the UK for so long. The carpets and seat covers of his white Corona were tattered and scattered with empty cans of food and beer, and smelt like sour milk. Even Ajuna's second-hand Sprinter was in better shape.

His stomach grumbled; his hands trembled in the chilly air. Musana said he was saving fuel by not switching on the heating in the car.

"I shouldn't have brought the damn car. We should have used the Heathrow Express. It takes only fifteen minutes to Paddington and under an hour from there to Deptford. That's where I live."

The cars ahead were not moving at all.

"This is freaking me out!" Musana yelled, his eyelids fluttering. He banged his head on the steering wheel. "Fuck. We should have used the train. I shouldn't have listened to Kato. What does my brother know about rush hour in London? But he insisted that I pick you up because you had carried a lot of food stuff." He laughed mirthlessly. "I hope you haven't brought yams and sweet potatoes. No one has time or gas to cook such heavy carbohydrates. We only cook light meals. You understand what I mean?"

Kagaba thought of all the bother that Ama and Ajuna had gone through to prepare all sorts of Ugandan food for him to carry to the UK: millet flour for making porridge, cassava flour for making kalo, peeled matooke, dried mushrooms, pounded groundnuts, smoked tilapia wrapped in several layers of foil so its pungent smell wouldn't escape into the aircraft. The cow-ghee had been confiscated at Heathrow because animal products were prohibited from entering the UK. He had paid a fine for excess baggage, which nearly finished his pocket money.

They should not have bothered. Where would he put all the food? Throw it away? He did not have any friends in the UK yet. Did Musana have any friends they could share it with? Like Ajuna did when she was sent food from the village?

Musana continued cursing as the traffic on the M25 remained static, and Kagaba busied himself by looking out of the window at the unfolding landscape. This must be farmland, considering the crops, white sheep, and fat black cows on the neatly demarcated plots. The trees were stunted and blackened, with no sign of leaves on their thin branches.

Musana rumbled on about how he was not going to make it to work on time, whether he should just call in and cancel his shift; but that would mean losing a day's wage which, given his dire circumstances, he could not afford.

The cars ahead budged a little and Musana pressed on the accelerator with more force than was required. The car leapt forward, ramming into the one in front. Kagaba jerked forward, hitting the dashboard. He didn't realize he was screaming. Musana was holding on tightly to the steering wheel when he seemed to comprehend what had happened. "Holy shit," he sucked his teeth, banged his balled fists on the wheel.

"My M.O.T. expired last month. Do you know what that means?"

Kagaba did not.

"It means I don't want to be caught in this mess," Musana shouted.

The occupant of the car he had rammed into had stopped and traffic was piling up behind them. She maneuvered out of the lane onto the shoulder of the highway and stopped. Musana did the same and parked behind the woman's new-looking Jaguar. He jumped out of the car just as the woman began to disembark from hers. She looked elderly, probably in her sixties or so.

"You've knocked my car," the woman said, speaking slowly, like Musana was a child.

"Madam, I'm sorry, but at least it's not serious, it's only a small dent," Musana had switched from being grumpy to being extremely cheerful and nice. He was even smiling. The woman did not speak immediately. Kagaba got out of the car and followed Musana as he examined the damage to the woman's car. The biting cold nipped at his face and he started to retreat to the car. But then the woman said, "I'm going to call the police."

"Madam, please, I don't think that's necessary, I will call my insurance company and everything will be sorted. This is really a small matter." Musana sounded alarmed by the mention of the police, his eyes darting, glancing over his shoulder.

"I will call the police," she insisted, now sounding angry. She said she wanted to have a witness to the "accident" who would corroborate her story when it came to dealing with the insurance people. Musana said she could take a picture of the damage, which she could then show to her insurers, but the woman said her phone did not take pictures; it was only for making calls. She got out her phone from her handbag and began punching numbers.

Musana's next move left Kagaba astounded. He dropped to his knees, right there on the motorway, not caring about the wet tarmac and the drivers throwing him furtive, confused glances.

"Please, madam, take pity on me, on us," he waved toward Kagaba's direction. "My brother here is coming from Uganda, and he carried bad news about my father … I wasn't paying attention and I—" He had dropped the British accent.

"Please get off the road; stand up!" The woman sounded and looked distressed. "It's dangerous. And I have already called the police. I will explain to them … please get up off your knees."

Slowly, like a defeated man, Musana rose to his feet, his black trousers dripping with water, a bit of wetness in his eyes.

The police arrived quickly, and after briefly interviewing the woman and taking down some notes and pictures of the dent, they let them go. Musana's sour mood returned the moment he got back behind the wheel; cursing the woman for the unnecessary trouble: "The police can start asking for papers instead of M.O.T., she could have got me into a lot of trouble."

A prominent signpost announced their arrival in Kent: *Welcome to Kent, the Garden of England*, and after another thirty minutes, they veered off the motorway and entered a residential area. The roads in this part were not as wide or neatly paved, but were all clearly marked with noticeable signage: *Abbey Road, Rainsborough Avenue, Reginald Close …*

Rows upon rows of brown-bricked, storied houses greeted them. The houses were dilapidated, unlike the ones Kagaba had seen in movies. They had no terraces, no swimming pools and no white children riding bicycles on paved sidewalks. They all looked identical: same size, same white window frames, semi-detached, the chimneys rising to the sky like spires. Did the British have only one architect?

Musana kept on driving as the streets became narrower, dirtier, and, finally, they reached their destination. He parked on the street with two of the tires resting on the curb, like the other house owners had done. There was barely enough space left between his car and the one behind it.

He jumped out of the car. "Let me show you to our flat," he called Kagaba to follow him. "I'm sure you'll be fine. The house might feel colder because we avoid switching on the central heating in daytime because of high energy costs these days. But you can make yourself a hot choc. You understand what I mean?

"This is your set of keys," he continued, breathing fast, "this one opens the front door, and this silver one opens the door to our flat. I have to run now." He spoke while already moving out of the room, and Kagaba remained standing at the landing. "Get the suitcases from the car and bring them inside," he shouted as he ran down the stairs.

Kagaba went back to the car to collect the heavy suitcases. It took him nearly twenty minutes to heave the luggage up the stairs and into their small room. The effort left him exhausted. The "apartment" was housed in a two-bedroomed house. He surveyed the house, finding the toilet and shower, which shared one space. The second bedroom, at the extreme end of the narrow passage, was closed.

He sat on the bed and ate the takeaway they had bought on their way from the airport.

"I'm in the UK!" he wanted to announce. "Greener pastures await me: a job, money, and other promises." He wanted to call Ajuna and let her know. But his phone's battery was flat. He checked in his rucksack for the charger, but it wasn't there. He prayed he hadn't forgotten it in Uganda. In any case, Musana had promised to call on his behalf.

Although it was just after five in the evening, it looked as though it was night already; like when they had been on the plane, floating on dark, nighttime clouds. He snuggled inside the covers, memories of the tortuous journey temporarily erased from his mind. He closed his eyes and waited for sleep.

2

Kagaba woke feeling disoriented. He rubbed sleep from his eyes and let them rove, taking in his surroundings. It was a small room, about twelve by nine feet, with a single window that did not open. Only a tiny vent at the top was half-open. The drapes were dark and thick; the netting white, the bed medium-sized, the duvet a drab green. He sniffed the moldy, pervasive smell that enveloped the room and sneezed.

The floor was carpeted with a brown-black rug, its color fading, giving it an almost unrecognizable shade. By the wall, below the window, was a mattress strewn with tumbled sheets and blankets. A built-in closet stood in the corner with two suitcases placed on top, half-open, clothes spilling out, like they had been dumped there in a hurry. A reading table, an old computer and a small television were the only other appliances in the room.

Where was Musana?

He heard the shower run. That must be him. He wondered what time he had returned last night, or could it have been early this morning? Was it just a day since he had last seen Ajuna? It felt like eternity. How long had he been living in the UK now? His watch was still reading Ugandan time: 9 am. That would make it six in the morning in the UK. Was it possible he had been sleeping for that long?

The shower had stopped running but Musana did not come out. He would have to interrupt him to take a pee. As he was about to knock, the door opened into his face and he almost collided with a burly man, a small towel wrapped around his lower body.

"Hi," he said without looking at Kagaba, in a manner suggesting he was unsurprised by his presence; like he had expected to come out of the bathroom and find another man standing in the hallway waiting to use the loo.

Kagaba stared at the stranger in amazement. His hair was a color between red and orange, bright hot, like it would smolder at the ignition of a match. It wasn't wet. He must have showered without washing his head. His shoulders were broad, his chest and arms covered in more layers of red hair. He strolled past Kagaba, opened the door of the second bedroom and banged it shut.

Kagaba entered the bathroom. It was dirty and wet and smelt of male odor. The toilet's seams were stained yellow, the cover floppy. The sink was wide and white, scattered with a few toothbrushes. An oval-shaped mirror hung on torn wallpaper. It was broken at the top, so that when he looked into it, it cut off half of his head. Kagaba was surprised he had missed all these details on his arrival, yet he had used the toilet.

Later, he heard a door open, a key turn, and another door open and close. Whatever had happened to Musana?

Kagaba went to the kitchen downstairs, made himself a cup of tea, and found some bread in the top rack of the fridge. He was famished and wished he could have a warm, solid meal. He thought of the food in the two suitcases and his insides churned.

By mid-afternoon, he was ravenously hungry. He unpacked the food and cut off a large chunk of tilapia, which he sprinkled with salt and a generous spread of groundnut paste. As he ate, he surveyed the kitchen. It was the largest part of the house. A dresser filled with plates and glasses stood on one side of the wall, and on the other, a small dining table with two chairs. The washing machine and dishwasher were fixed below the small sink next to the cooker. He looked at the large windows again. The glass was thick, just like the bedroom windows. He tried to figure out what it was about these windows that was so unfamiliar.

Then his eye caught a mouse trap, tucked away in the space between the wall and the fridge. Had it not been for its familiar, shiny black color, he would have missed it.

Mice in London! He remembered what Ssenga Jovia used to say about rats having ears that listen to human conversations. Whenever she planned to lay a trap for them, she would warn everybody not to breathe a word about it.

"The rats will hear you," she would say, "and they will avoid eating the poisoned food. Rats are as vindictive as their enemies, the cats. Once a rat learns that you plan to kill it, it will sneak up to your bed while you're asleep and take its revenge. It might chew off part of your toe or, worse still, gouge out your eyes. If you annoy a cat, it will waylay you in the corridors and pounce on you as you go to bed. Be careful! Don't say anything."

He wondered if the rodents in London behaved the same way as those in Ssenga Jovia's house.

Nowadays, she complained that there was a new breed of rat that came from Bulaaya, meaning the UK, hiding in the same containers transporting second-hand mivumba. "They are deadly," Ssenga Jovia said. "They are tiny like this, and they've eaten all my shoes; even when I try to kill them, the poison doesn't work on them. Their bodies are already hardened with chemicals they put in these mivumba clothing."

He finished his meal. It had left a bitter, raw taste in his mouth and he went to the bathroom to rinse it out. Where the heck was Musana? Suppose something terrible had happened to him, an accident, death even. He had no way of contacting him. He had checked all the suitcases but failed to locate his phone charger. What will happen to him then? How would he find a job, money, food? How would he repay the loans he had accumulated back home? Had Musana managed to phone Ajuna, as he had promised, to let her know that he had arrived safely? She would be sick with worry by now.

He closed his eyes and pictured Ajuna's face, furrowed with anxiety, like the first time they met at her doorstep. He was right behind her when she noticed him, and he could see she was scared. But before then, he had watched her walk away from the security check point in front of Senate Building, forgetting to take her keys. He was about to catch up with her at the lift when she turned and rushed out of the building.

She was walking at supersonic speed, impressive for such a short person, and it was difficult to keep up with her. He trailed her, observing her round bottom and projecting hips. She swung her short legs like she was on a march, her wet hair bouncing up and down. Her serious demeanor contrasted with the feminine gentleness with which she cradled her bags. He found all of it endearing.

And then he was standing just a step behind her at the doorway of her home. He wanted to reach out and touch her hand, just to reassure her. Afterwards, he could not stop thinking about her.

He couldn't stop thinking about her now. Was she thinking about him as well? Missing him? He opened his eyes.

The house had turned chilly, and he decided to go back to bed. The dirty-smelling jacket Musana had offered him earlier was lying on the rumpled mattress and he draped it over his quivering shoulders.

Evening fell.

Where on earth was Musana?

Darkness began to approach, and the room grew chillier. He made another cup of tea and took it back with him upstairs. The hot liquid burned its way down his throat before settling into his rumbling stomach. He felt some relief. Yellow light flickered into the room from the street, and his attention was caught by the wide window from where the light was streaming in, imagining what lurked outside. Instantly, he understood what was different about these windows. They were not secured with burglar proofing like the ones back home. He felt a bit of panic. And as if to confirm his fears, a sound, undefinable at first, but soon it became clear that someone was opening the front door. He was off the bed and heading for the door before he could think of what he was doing.

It was the red-haired man. He was coming up the stairs. "Hi," he said when he saw Kagaba, not waiting for a reply.

"Good evening, sir," Kagaba said to him, his pounding heart settling.

"Huh?"

"May I ask something?" Kagaba continued, seizing the opportunity. "I was wondering if you knew where Musana was."

"Excuse me?"

"I mean, my brother-in-law, the guy who lives in this room … the one who picked me up from the airport. Do you know where he is? Do you know where he works? What time does he usually come back home?"

A startled flicker was the only expression that appeared on the man's broad face. Kagaba tried again, gesturing widely to try to make his point.

"Sorry, I'm not sure I'm following what you're saying." He didn't sound rude but confused. He opened the door to his room and entered. Kagaba heard a latch fall, a key turn, and the man's voice on the phone.

Desperate situations call for desperate interventions, his Economics professor used to say. He knocked on the man's door and was surprised when he opened it.

He said the first thing that came to his mind. "Where can I get some food?"

"Food?"

"Yes."

The red-haired man hesitated and, for a split second, seemed unsure whether to retreat into his room or answer his question, but said, "There's a place called Deptford Mini Supermarket …"

"Supermarket?" Kagaba repeated the only word he caught. "Where's that?"

"Four blocks from here, take the first right, then do a left …" With that, the man shut his door again.

Four blocks, Kagaba pondered. He would risk it. He had some money. He opened the front door and a flap of cold air rose to his face, forcing him to step back into the house to get a warmer cardigan. He let himself out again and emerged on a brightly lit street. After scanning the column of identical houses; he saw the white-and-black sign at the corner of the street reading. *Deptford Lane*. He memorized it.

Take the first right. After a few feet, he came to the end of the street. *Do a left*. That led him into a narrow, dimly lit alleyway strewn with empty beer cans, plastic bags overflowing with rubbish, and dog shit; the walls covered with graffiti.

When he came to the end of the alley, he was surprised by the sudden open space that greeted him. At the end of the open street there was a pharmacy, a car rental and a closed food kiosk. A little ahead he saw a signpost with large blue lettering announcing Deptford Market, but the stalls were empty. The vendors must have closed for the night. He did not see any supermarket.

Wind blew at his face and his eyes teemed with tears. He turned and walked back to the house. Once inside, he sat on the landing, his mind in turmoil, wondering how he was going to communicate with the outside world without a functioning phone. A profound sense of sadness overcame him. When the tears started dropping, he did not try to stop them. The sobs were silent at first, but he soon lost control of his emotions and his body shook, like he was being yanked back and forth by an invisible force.

He had not cried like this since he was a little boy of six or seven when his father had first taken him to boarding school.

Ssenga Jovia did not accompany them that day. It was a weekday, that's what he could remember—a Tuesday, perhaps, and it was in the afternoon. The whole thing seemed to have been planned in a great hurry. His father had told him about the plans to move him to a boarding school. "In two days," he had answered, when he asked when.

But Ssenga Jovia had spent the whole weekend preparing his clothes and bedding, and roasted groundnuts and pumpkin seeds for snacks. She sewed his name on his uniform shirts and shorts and engraved his red pair of sleepers with his initials using the tip of a knife. His excitement was total: he jumped about the living room, bounced on his bed, beamed, laughed as he watched her pack everything in the green metal suitcase his father had bought in town. The idea of going off to boarding school made him feel like a grown-up about to begin a new, independent life.

They should have left earlier that Tuesday morning, but Ssenga Jovia insisted he eat some food first, which she had woken up very early to prepare. He didn't know she had slaughtered a whole chicken! And she served him the juiciest chunks of meat, normally reserved for visitors, an indication of the importance of his departure to a new school. His father did not eat; he looked unhappy and tense and was impatient for them to set off.

When they arrived at the school, his father parked his bicycle in the tarmacked yard and told him to wait there and keep watch over the suitcase, mattress, and a yellow jerrycan still secured to the carrier. Kagaba had ridden perched on the bar.

His father was gone for a while. Kagaba used the time to observe the school surroundings: the grass was neatly trimmed and the compound clean. There was hardly any sound, though he could see a few boys walking fast to a big building, dressed in their smart white shirts and blue shorts and ties. Some looked like men, while others were about his age, or a little older.

His father returned with a black folder, his name written on it in large letters. "Let's go," he said urgently as he unstrapped the mattress and suitcase from the bicycle. An older boy hurried to them and helped carry the stuff to the big building.

From that time, everything moved fast. He was told to follow the boy who had helped them carry his belongings. But he did not move. He did not want to be here anymore. He wanted to return to his old school, and to Ssenga Jovia. He began to cry. His father tried to soothe him, but he clung to his trousers as he mounted his bicycle. He began riding off. He followed him; when he increased speed, he did too, breaking into a run.

They reached a high iron gate, which he didn't remember seeing when they first arrived. A huge sign, reading *St Aloysius Boys Primary Boarding School, Hoima*, glared at him, daring him to go through the gate.

All this time, his father didn't turn to look at him; when he was about to go through the strong gate, he turned. His eyes were moist. Before he was let through by the gateman, he grabbed Kagaba and hugged him close to his body. And then he was gone.

The feeling of abandonment Kagaba had felt that day twenty years ago now bubbled up from deep inside him. He was once again that little, unloved, unwanted boy, betrayed by the one person who was supposed to love and protect him: his father.

Where the blue blazes was Musana? Why had he betrayed him? The resentment building up in his heart made him worry that he might hate Musana for life.

He stopped crying when he sensed someone standing in front of him. It was the redhead, extending his hand toward him. "I'm Sean," he said. "What's your name?"

He said nothing for a few moments, but the man kept his hand hanging in the space that divided them.

"What's your name?" he spoke slowly.

He told him.

"I'm afraid you'll have to spell it for me."

He did, and when Sean pronounced it, the sound bounced off his lips, hard and dry. "You're cold, Kagaba," he said, when he shook his hand. "I'll switch on the boiler." When Sean returned, he sat on the step with him. "Did you get some food?"

Kagaba was not hungry anymore. His thoughts had returned to Ajuna, whom he worried Musana had failed to contact. She must by now be sick with worry, not knowing whether he had arrived safely.

"I would like to make a call," he announced to Sean.

"Eh?"

"A call," he demonstrated with his fingers.

"Oh! A call," he drew out the "a" and "l's.

"I want to let my people back home know I arrived safely. Where can I make a call?"

"A call," Sean repeated. "Do you have a phone?"

"The battery is flat. I forgot my charger. And I need to buy airtime."

"Here, you can use my phone."

He dialed Ajuna's number, and an automated voice replied, "Sorry but you do not have sufficient funds to make this call." He handed the phone back to Sean, explaining that there was not enough money to make an international call.

"Where are you calling?" Sean asked.

"Uganda."

Sean blinked, roughed his red hair with his chunky fingers. "Uganda, Africa."

"Oh, I see. I'll go to the shops and top up. I'll be right back."

"What?"

Sean repeated what he had said, speaking guardedly.

"I can send an SMS instead," Kagaba pronounced each word as clearly as he could so Sean could understand him. Sean handed him the phone again.

Arrived safely, wil kol later when get fone. Kagaba.

He waited a few minutes before a reply came through.

Ajuna in hosp. kol asap. Kalayi.

"Is everything alright?" Sean was looking at him intently.

"No. My fiancée back home is in hospital. I have to call immediately!"

"Do you have her number? Sorry, that was a stupid question. Listen, I'll run to the shops and top up. I'll be right back."

Ajuna, sick! She was fine only a few days ago. Sick with what? Had they been trying to contact him through Musana?

When Sean returned, he dialed Ajuna's number again.

"The number you're calling is busy. Please try again later," said the automated voice.

Kalayi. He should call Kalayi. He started dialing, his fingers moving with stunted action as he soon realized that he could not remember all of it. Ama, surely Ama would know about Ajuna being in hospital.

A woman speaking in a language he could not readily identify as English answered, demanding to know who was calling her number. "Ama, I want to speak to Ama," Kagaba shouted. "Wrong number," the angry voice on the other side of the line snapped, and the line went limp.

He was trembling. Sean sat down beside him and placed his arm over his shoulders. "Are the lines busy? Do you need some help?"

He shook his head, took a deep breath and dialed Ajuna's number again. Kalayi answered.

"Kagaba, where the heck have you been? We've been trying to reach you. Why didn't you call as you promised, what happened—"

"Kalayi, I borrowed this phone, how's—"

"Ajuna is unwell," she cut him off. "She fainted; she's now in hospital but she's improving—"

"Can I speak to her, please!"

"She's on bed rest. The doctor put her on total bed rest. I'll let her know you called."

A click and the line went dead.

"What's the matter with your fiancée?" Sean sounded alarmed.

"She fainted," Kagaba muttered. He had stood up during his conversation with Kalayi. "She fainted," he repeated.

"Is she going to be alright? Sit down," Sean gently led him to the bedroom and made him sit on the bed. "I'll make you a hot choc. It will calm your nerves."

All energy was ebbing away from his body like pressure being let out of a tire. When Sean returned with a mug of steaming hot chocolate, he took it with unsteady hands, but did not take a sip immediately. It was too hot. Sean took it from him and placed it on the floor.

"Do you want to be left alone?"

He wanted to speak to Ajuna, or Kalayi, or his father, or Ssenga Jovia. He wanted to talk, not to be left alone.

"I'm sure she will be alright." Sean's tone was reassuring. "Look, I have to run now. I'm meeting a few blokes at ten, and we're going clubbing. Tomorrow is a bank holiday. Keep the phone so you can talk to your family. I have two phones, actually, so I don't really need that. There's some food in the fridge and you can have it when you feel like eating. And if you need to talk," he threw his big hands into the air, "here's my number." He handed him a piece of paper. "Call me any time."

About an hour later, Kagaba sent another message to Kalayi's phone.

How's Ajuna? What happened?

A reply came back shortly. *Who's this?*

Kagaba. p'se lem no how Ajuna is

Beta. Mite leave hosp 2moro

But what happened?

After about twenty minutes there was still no reply. His watch was reading 9 pm, which would make it midnight in Uganda, and about twenty-four hours since his arrival in the UK—and since Musana's disappearance.

3

The rest of the night passed quietly. Kagaba drifted in and out of fitful sleep, his mind a field of disjointed dreams, hallucinating between two places. The dreams carried him back to Uganda, and he saw Ajuna lying in a hospital bed swathed in white, surgical sheets, tubes coming in and going out of various parts of her body, her face contorted in unbearable pain. Then visions of Musana's mangled body trapped under a massive trailer flashed through his mind.

Morning did not bring relief. From the window, the day looked somber. No flicker of sunshine permeated the heavy drapes. No warmth. No sound. A few people were walking up and down the street, silently, like zombies. The streets in Kampala would be buzzing with noise and human traffic at this time of the morning.

Kagaba wondered how he was going to spend the day. He avoided dozing off in case the dreams attacked him again. Instead, he contemplated his new life in London—a joyless, cold city. A city that did not smile. A city that did not welcome visitors. He missed the warmth of Uganda already.

A desire to speak with Ssenga Jovia overwhelmed him. She would dispel his fears. When his father had dumped him in boarding school, it was Ssenga Jovia who rescued him. "It's turning him into a very shy person," she argued with his father. "What he needs is love, so he can grow into a confident young man able to defend himself." His father finally relented.

In time, sleep took over. He opened his eyes to find Musana had resurfaced. He must have let himself in quietly—or perhaps he had stopped listening for footfall on the stairs, a knock, or the sound of a key turning.

Musana looked disheveled. His eyes were flaming red; his shoulders slouching into his short frame. He kicked off his drenched boots soiled with black mud and massaged his toes through the smelly heavy-duty socks. Then he seemed to notice the heavy cardigan weighing down his weary shoulders and discarded it on the floor.

"This job." He clicked his tongue and scratched at his unkempt hair under a blue cap. "I was sent to work in Cambridge, which is a long way from here. Six straight shifts—in this fucking weather! The guy supposed to take over never turned up."

He lit a cigarette and took deep drags, like one enjoying a well-cooked meal. Musana worked as a security guard, he revealed. Earning a mere two and a half pounds an hour—just a quarter of the minimum wage. His employer was not registered with the authorities. He only recruited illegals like Musana, who could take anything.

"So, how have you been? I can see you managed alright," he pointed at the half-finished plate of food Sean had offered Kagaba the previous night. "Smart fellow. That's the way to go in this country. It can get pretty tough unless one learns how to be resourceful.

"We have to talk," he continued, "we need to discuss stuff—rent, bills, jobs; you understand what I mean?" Before Kagaba could respond, he went on, "But let me first get some shuteye." Musana slumped down on the mattress on the floor and climbed under the blankets.

Kagaba swiped at the cloud of smoke before speaking.

"Ajuna is in hospital."

"Who?"

"Ajuna"

"Who's that?"

"My ...wi ... my fiancée, my woman back home."

"The one who teaches at the university? I'm sorry to hear that. Is it serious?"

"Yes. She fainted. I spoke to her sister this morning. She said Ajuna was still very weak."

"She'll be alright," Musana's eyes were already closed. He buried his face deeper into the pillows. "Let me catch some sleep. We'll talk later."

For a long time, Kagaba listened to Musana's rumbling snoring, his mouth open, drool trickling at the corners of his mouth as snot escaped from his wide, flaring nostrils. He breathed heavily, making choking sounds, which frightened Kagaba.

As he watched him, he noticed Musana's premature baldness. He looked much older than Kato, yet they were only a few years apart. Musana could not be more than thirty-two. Who was this man? Would he find him a job? Would he assist him to settle in London? Would they ever become friends? He did not like Musana's cynicism and roughness. He did not fancy living with him in the dire, filthy conditions of this room.

Kagaba made a promise to himself: his first paycheck would go toward finding his own place. A decent, habitable two-roomed apartment, which he could turn into a proper home. Where Ajuna would visit him one day.

Outside, it was raining—a steady, unhurried downpour— the kind that goes on forever. Then he heard a familiar whistle and felt some relief. He jumped off the bed and opened the door.

"Hi," Sean said cheerfully. He put his head in through the door and saw Musana. He retreated, murmuring that he had not meant to intrude. Kagaba followed him to the kitchen downstairs.

"So, your brother's back?" Sean asked, pointing upstairs.

"He's actually my brother-in-law. His brother is married to my sister. He came back this afternoon. How was your … your outing?" He did not feel like discussing Musana.

"Great. I spent the night at a friend's. How's your fiancée?"

"I spoke with her sister this morning and she said Ajuna is still under bed rest. But I need to speak to her if I can buy a card." He had earlier found his way to the nearby shops but when he told the sales lady that he wanted to buy airtime, she didn't understand what he was talking about.

"No worries," Sean said. "I bought you a phone card. I also brought some takeaway. Would you like to join me?"

"Yes, thank you so much. You've been so kind to me."

They ate at the kitchen table and, afterwards, Kagaba dialed Ajuna's number. He was so relieved to hear her voice when she finally answered that tears pricked his eyes.

"I'm fine," Ajuna kept saying when he pressed her to find out about her health. "I was discharged and I'm home now. They took blood and urine samples for tests. I'll go back tomorrow to see the doctor. I guess it was just the fatigue and stress of organizing your trip. I only needed a good rest and was kept in hospital for observation."

She was more concerned about him and how he was faring. Was it very cold? Did he have enough warm clothing? How was Musana treating him? Did they live in a nice house, and did Musana own a big car? Would he help him find a job soon?

He tried to allay her concerns. No point in discussing his hardships. That might stress her further. Rather, he inquired about Ama, Kato, Kalayi, Ssenga Jovia, his father, and step-mother. Ajuna laughed and said, "You've only been gone three days, not three months. Everything is still as you left it."

After they hung up, he felt a hollowness in his stomach. He missed Ajuna so much. He wanted to hold her in his arms and make love to her perfect, petite body.

He woke up early the next morning so Sean could take him to a shopping mall to buy another phone card. Musana was already gone, and he did not know when he would see him again. They took a bus, and the ride took nearly an hour.

He had expected a huge shopping mall and neon lights advertising flashy designer goods, but the shopping center turned out to be a cluster of shops selling cheap, plastic wares, African women's hair pomades and Halal meat. Internet cafés and Western Union signs were everywhere. One big shop sold different brands of palm oil only, from Sierra Leone, Nigeria, Senegal, and Ghana. Part of the street had been cordoned off to accommodate stalls of second-hand clothing, fresh vegetables, plantain and potatoes. Most of the vendors were Asians and Africans, who were enticing passers-by to come and buy from their stalls as all the T-shirts were now reduced to one pound.

"Is this London?" he asked Sean, unable to hide his disappointment. Sean laughed before answering. "This is London, yes, south-east London, to be precise, but perhaps what you mean is Central London? That's about ten miles from here. I'll take you to visit 'London' on my day off next week."

He bought the phone card from an internet café and Sean said he had to rush off to catch the train to work. He showed him which bus to take back home—the number 180. It seemed simple enough. He would disembark at the Deptford Islamic Centre after counting four stops and then take the second left, and turn left again, after the T-junction. Their house was only a short distance from the bus stop, No. 16 on Abbey Road.

But the bus took a different route due to roadworks. He got home by some stroke of luck. A woman on the bus offered to walk him to the bus stop, close to their house, after he had asked her for directions.

"Thank you very much," he said to the woman.

"Ssi Nnyo," she answered, dismissing his gratitude.

"How did you know I was Ugandan?"

She smiled as she began walking away, "From your nose, and the texture of your skin."

"Nnyabo," he called after her, excited to have met a fellow

Ugandan so easily and unexpectedly, "please give me your number. I would like us to stay in touch."

But the woman was already on her way and simply waved to him.

He called Ajuna the moment he got inside, anxious to know the results of the tests. Before they could exchange greetings, Ajuna said, "I'm pregnant."

"What!" A surge of unsteadiness swept through his body. He wobbled to a chair but did not sit; placing both his hands on its sides.

"I don't know how it happened ... I mean ... I'm on the pill ... I must have missed a dose."

"Are you sure, Ajuna?" A bare whisper, he couldn't even hear himself. The word "pregnant" floated in the room, before growing fangs and clutching at his throat.

"Twelve weeks."

"Ajuna," his voice contracted.

He gave up trying to say anything more.

4

As the weight of the situation sunk in, Kagaba understood that he could not sit around and wait for the office job Musana had promised him. What he needed right now was a stable source of income to take care of his imminent responsibilities. He asked Sean to help him find a job. Any job.

"Can you drive?" Sean asked him. "Can you read a map?"

He had learned to drive Ajuna's car. Sean took him to meet his boss at a courier company. If he got the job, he would be allocated a company car to begin with, which he would use to deliver parcels in an area assigned to him by his supervisor. Depending on the weather, and how hard he was willing to work, he could deliver anything between one hundred to one hundred and fifty parcels a day.

He would be paid about a pound a drop. He made a mental calculation and converted the money into Ugandan shillings: He would be earning about half a million Ugandan shillings; *in a mere day*. Half the monthly salary Ajuna earned as a university lecturer.

His palms were sweating. He could pay off his debts in the first year, pay for his education in the UK, build a house back home, buy Ajuna a new car, a motorcycle for his father, two Friesian cows for Ssenga Jovia so she would never lack milk, fly to Uganda to be present for the birth of his baby. And marry Ajuna in church, in a big, white wedding.

He wasn't quite sure about map reading. But Sean said the office would give him a Sat Nav, which worked as a digital map. He was unsure if he would be competent enough to drive on the roads in London. They were wider, busier; most probably the traffic laws were different to the ones in Uganda. But he would practice and learn and become better with time.

He had already decided that he would not tell Ajuna about being a delivery man. This was not what he had come to the UK to do. In any case, he did not want to cause her any more stress in her condition. He would wait until Musana delivered on the office one he had promised.

On their way to the courier office in Greenhithe, Sean told him a story about a Nigerian man who used to work there a few years back. He first worked as a courier, and later took a part-time course, graduating with an MBA. A year later, he was promoted to Operations Manager and continued to prosper, buying two houses and a Mercedes.

One day, the police came looking for him. He was charged with credit-card fraud. He had used his position as a senior manager to glean off vital information from credit cards that were entrusted in his care. After extracting what he needed, he would reseal the parcels and hand them over to the couriers to deliver to their rightful owners. He would then sell the information to a gang of thieves for hefty sums of money.

"So there's a lack of empathy toward Nigerians at my office," Sean concluded his story. "But you're not Nigerian, and there shouldn't be a problem."

The office was not as he had expected. It was a kind of warehouse, and the manager, a woman, was seated in a small, partitioned room at the back. Sean led him through stacks of parcels to the manager's office. When she saw them, she smiled without effort and said, "Is this your friend you told me about? Come in. I'm afraid there's only one chair." She spoke comfortingly, and Kagaba relaxed, his initial fears of failing to impress her soothed by her gentle manner. Sean excused himself, saying he was going to start mapping.

The manager asked him a few routine questions; how long

he had been living in the UK and if he had a valid driving permit, which she asked to see.

"Ah, I can see it's a Ugandan permit. But that's alright. You're allowed to use it for the first six months until you get a British one."

Then she asked for his passport.

"But you have no right to work in the UK." The gentle tone was gone. "Look. You're here as a mere visitor, and your visa expires in six months. I thought I had made this clear to Sean. He assured me that you were not like, well, not like ..." she tripped on her words, shifted her eyes. "We can't employ you. We'd be risking a fine of ten thousand pounds. The Home Office is very strict these days." She breathed heavily, like she was struggling to compose herself. Kagaba remained frozen in his chair, unable to defend himself.

"If you want to work in this country legally, you'd have to apply for a work permit." She touched his hand lightly. "I don't know how you can go about obtaining a work permit—it's fairly complicated."

"I'm very sorry," Sean said afterwards, over and over, like it was his fault.

In the days that followed, Kagaba hardly left the house. He wanted to be alone to ponder his situation. Ajuna pregnant! He tried to keep the news at bay as best he could while he figured out what to do about his predicament.

"Do you doubt it's yours?" Ajuna retorted when he quizzed how she could get pregnant while on the pill. "Just say if you want to deny the responsibility."

"I don't doubt you, Ajuna, I completely trust you. And I love you, as you already know. It's just the timing, but—"

"But what?"

She threatened to cut him off.

By the end of his first month in London, he had used up most of his money on phone cards to speak to Ajuna, to reassure her, to maintain contact. She must know how much he wanted to be a father; they had discussed it several times. He longed to create his own family, a perfect family of Daddy, Mummy, and Children. He had no memory of his own mother. He did not want his children to grow up feeling the void that had consumed his own childhood; the confusion, the embarrassment of not being able to provide an answer to a simple question: "Who is your mother? What is her name?" He wanted to be a present father, not an absent, penniless, jobless one.

Kagaba fell into a routine. In the mornings, after a breakfast of toast and tea, occasionally with a boiled egg and fruit, he would leave the house to get some fresh air, and idle away the time in a nearby park if it wasn't too cold. November had ushered in a cold spell. He would observe small children screeching with joy as their mothers pushed them on different sorts of swings and slides, the images reminding him that he was soon to be a father. He would stay out until late afternoon, skipping lunch, and later take the 180 bus to Deptford Shopping Centre to loiter around the shops.

One time, he saw a job vacancy sign outside the KFC window: *Waiters Required Apply Within.* He dashed inside and talked with one of the staff behind the counter. "You need to speak to the manager," the man told him without looking at him, impatient to serve the next customer. Another staff member directed him to the manager's office, but a small note on her office door indicated she had stepped out for ten minutes. He would check again tomorrow, he told himself, not feeling as confident as he had when he first entered the KFC. Suppose the manager asked to see his passport? Suppose she called the police? He did not know the requirements for applying for a work permit. Sean had said he had no clue. He would have to consult Musana.

In the evenings, if Sean returned early, he would bring a takeaway which they shared as they watched TV and drank beer in his room. Or Kagaba would cook rice and the beans he had brought from Uganda, or make groundnut sauce.

Sean had a sister called Emily, who worked for a charity that "supported African causes." Sean reckoned Emily would be happy to meet Kagaba because she was "genuinely interested in African issues." He said their family was originally from Ireland, but his grandparents had migrated to England many years ago.

Sean was surprised to learn that Kagaba was a university graduate with two degrees. He said school hadn't been his thing. When he turned sixteen, he quit. He said Emily was the brainy one and had about four or even five degrees. Kagaba noted the bitterness that stole into Sean's tone whenever he talked about his sister, and he wondered what had caused the tension.

Every once in a while, when Sean had a day off and the weather wasn't so unkind, he would take Kagaba on a tour of Central London. They had visited Trafalgar Square, and he had hoped to feed the pigeons with bread crumbs as he had seen tourists do on TV, but the pigeons were not around. They had also gone to the London Eye, but it was too expensive to ride in its high-tech glass capsules. He had taken pictures though, pretending to be boarding one of the capsules. He later sent one to Ajuna.

Ajuna had responded with excitement at seeing Kagaba "enjoying life in London," commenting on how great and happy he looked. Kagaba did not tell her how hard it was finding a job, or how unhelpful Musana was. "Everything is fine. We're just working out a few details here and there," he assured her when they talked.

It was when he spoke to Ama that he failed to mask his true sentiments. "I'm fine," he would lie, but Ama was not fooled.

"Listen. Musana is not doing you a favor. I look after his undisciplined children; what does he pay me for it? Nothing. *Noooothing!* Their mother claims she left the children in their uncle's care. That's rubbish. Does Kato even know what these kids eat, or how they sleep? When they fall sick, who takes them to hospital? Who picks them up from school? And what do I get for all this labor? Not even a scarf, not a handbag, not a pair of shoes. He thinks his brother married some kind of slave, eei? He should never forget that you are my brother, and that he owes me."

Kagaba knew that wasn't the whole truth. Musana regularly sent money to Kato as a contribution toward his children's upkeep, including their tuition. He sometimes went with Musana to the shopping center for Musana to use the Western Union and for him to buy a telephone card.

Kagaba began to suspect that Kato didn't pass the money to Ama, but he did not want to get entangled in the issue. It was a delicate situation to navigate. If he told Ama the truth, she would confront Kato, which might lead to a rift in their marriage. If he told Musana about his suspicions of Kato, that may cause a fall-out between the two brothers.

He owed his stay in London to Musana; Musana held the key to the promise of a better future.

Every time Kagaba thought about the job-hunting blues he had endured, a tremor of trepidation coursed through him. After completing his master's in Economics and Management Science, he had applied for several jobs as a market research analyst. As an Economics major, he expected a clear lead among the many candidates applying for the same jobs. But he was never successful. One time, he decided to do what so many Ugandans were doing: solicit the help of a Godfather— a powerful person to intervene during the application process.

His Godfather was a government minister from his hometown. The minister's younger brother, Father Bonaventure, was friends with Kagaba's father, and their mother friends with Ssenga Jovia. Father Bonaventure wrote a "Please Assist" note for Kagaba to take to the minister. But it had all come to nothing. The minister's PA had promised to pass on the note to her boss, and would call him for an appointment with the minister. But she never did.

In desperation, and after the break-up with Ajuna, when she tried to boss him around, he had returned to the village to live with his father and stepmother, taking on a teaching post at a bogus commercial college where he taught accounting to A-level dropouts.

Had it not been for Ama's insistence that Kagaba return to the city, work on his relationship with Ajuna, and begin looking for job prospects in the UK, he would have fallen into total despair.

5

Toward the end of November, Musana had to return home unexpectedly. He was in a state of panic. He discarded his blue uniform and changed into civilian clothes.

He said he had to go underground for some time. His Rwandan colleague had stolen two sets of drapes from a hostel they were guarding and sold them to a woman residing nearby. The woman turned up later to claim them.

"I told her I did not know what she was talking about. At first, she had mistaken me for the guard with whom she had sealed the deal, 'because all of you Africans look the same, anyway.'

"When I asked the Rwandan, he confirmed that he had dealt with the woman, but that the drapes had gone missing. Someone must have seen him hiding them. The woman threatened to call the police, but I pointed out that she would be implicating herself for dealing in stolen goods. She seemed convinced and walked away grumbling that all Africans are thieves, and they should be removed from the UK.

"I hate it when white people talk like that," Musana shook his head. He stood up and walked to the window, looking down at the quiet street.

"What happened?" Kagaba asked.

"If we all were to leave, who would do their dirty jobs?" He spoke facing the window. "Who would clean their streets, wipe their grandmother's poo in care homes? Who would drive their buses, work on their farms and whatnot?" He chewed at his lower lip.

"Did she inform the police?" Kagaba prompted.

"Yes. They arrived soon after she left. We don't know what she told them, but there were about ten of them in five cars, sirens blaring. I escaped by the breadth of my hair. I was lucky to be at the back of the building and sprinted to the bus station. The Rwandan was arrested, and by now he must be on his way to a detention center, from where he will be deported. In this country, the moment the police arrest you, the first thing they ask is your papers. Always remember that."

Kagaba told Musana about the job advert at KFC. "What?! You want to get yourself arrested? Such jobs are only for people with papers. Be patient, we'll find you something soon."

"But what about a work permit?"

"A work permit? Ha! Who is filling your head with such ideas? Those things are for professional people, not our category. We get our jobs through other ways."

"But I am a professional. I have two—"

"I told you I will sort this out—I am still busy right now. You haven't even been in this country for three months. These things take time."

Musana spent several days hiding from the police, but Kagaba hardly ever saw him. He was working as a volunteer at Pastor Moses' New Revival Church in Deptford, and only returned to the house late in the night smelling of cigarettes and booze.

Pastor Moses was believed to have powers to reverse deportation orders from the Home Office through prayer. He had given Musana anointing oil, which he smeared on his face and hands every time he left the house to prevent any further misfortunes with the police or potential arrest. Musana wanted to introduce Kagaba to Pastor Moses, which would mean attending church service every Sunday, but Kagaba declined. He stopped going to church when he was at university, as soon as he knew he wasn't under the watchful eyes of his father and Ssenga Jovia anymore.

6

Musana was in a cleaning mood. He was busy tidying up their room, something Kagaba had never seen him do. He dusted the windowsill, sprayed generous amounts of Mr. Sheen on the wooden table, and vacuumed the worn-out carpet until it was spotless.

He was exuberant. "This afternoon," he said to Kagaba, "we shall go out to celebrate a landmark achievement of someone very special to me. Her name is Sharon, and she got her papers last week, but we wanted to keep that a secret. People are evil and you can't tell who wishes you well and who doesn't."

Kagaba didn't know Musana had a lover. He seemed too busy and cynical to engage in such pleasures. In any case, he did not feel like going out at all. What was the point of celebrating Musana's girlfriend's success?

He also suspected Ajuna was beginning to think he was not disclosing the whole truth. He did not want to lie to her, but at the same time, he wasn't sure what to tell her. That he did not even have money to feed himself? If it wasn't for Sean lending him some money, he would have starved. Musana never bothered to find out how he was managing.

But on second thoughts, he decided to go. He might meet some other Ugandans he could talk to about his job problems.

Musana went for a haircut, and when he returned, his hair groomed to an immaculate trim, he fished out a silky, floral tie from one of the half-open suitcases on top of the closet, a white shirt, and shiny black trousers. He urged Kagaba to dress equally smartly, because the function was very important. So, he dressed in the brown three-piece suit he had bought from Primark on sale at half-price.

They left at lunchtime, by which time a thick sheet of cloud had gathered and was looming over the sky. Piles of yellow-brown leaves had collected on sidewalks and verandas, as if brought there by an invisible hand overnight. Temperatures had continued to drop since the beginning of the month; and it rained every day. Musana said this was typical of November weather; that Kagaba should expect the weather to take a turn for the worse as they approached December.

On their way, Kagaba asked Musana how Sharon had managed to obtain her right to stay in the UK while Musana had failed.

"A dog's luck is not the same as the leopard's. I came to the UK three or four years earlier than Sharon. My first attempt was to claim I was a brother to Herbert Itongwa, the infamous rebel group leader of the National Democratic Alliance back in Uganda. My Nigerian lawyer argued that even when the rebel group had been defeated way back in the late nineties, the current government still hunted down anyone associated or related with their leader. To prove the point, I had my picture posted in a Ugandan newspaper."

"What for?" Kagaba interjected.

"'Wanted!' the caption screamed. 'Believed to be in the areas near Mityana or Luwero. If you see him, don't approach him. Call the police.'"

"My God! But suppose someone recognized you from the picture!"

"It did not work. Home Office saw through the lie."

"Another time, my lawyer advised me to claim I had been tortured by government operatives in Uganda because I was gay. I was at risk of being killed if deported to my home country. You've seen my missing toe," Musana continued. "I used it to my advantage. I claimed it had been plucked off with pliers."

"Jesus!"

"I had to take a picture kissing a fellow man."

"Did they believe you?"

"Nope. My friend, when luck is not on your side you can claim anything and no one will believe you. After that, they started sending me letters telling me to leave their country. Those letters!" Musana chuckled, "they talk like a human being. If you are not strong, you can pack your bags the next day. But you have to be patient. You need the patience of a hyena to survive in this country." He fell silent, his focus on the road ahead.

"How *did* you lose your toe?" Kagaba nudged.

"That's a story for another day."

Musana had booked the Crested Crane Bar & Restaurant in Forest Gate for the party. The owner of the place was called Joyce, a Ugandan businesswoman who owned a few Ugandan restaurants in East London. Musana demanded to see the food and drinks, to make sure there would be enough for all his invited guests. He also inspected the chairs and tables, and asked Joyce to change the tablecloths and replace them with white ones. The DJ hadn't arrived and Musana was beginning to fret. He called the man's number several times, but he didn't answer.

Joyce tried to reassure him. "He's a responsible man. He's not like some of these Ugandans who are not serious. The last one we hired disappointed us. We paid him half the money in advance, but he never showed up. Sometimes I wonder if such people came to this country to work."

She was about to call the DJ herself when the man arrived, his arms loaded with two loudspeakers, several cables and wires.

"I'm so sorry, Ssebo, sorry, Nnyabo," he apologized, addressing Musana and Joyce. "I passed by Mulongo's place and got delayed."

"Who's Mulongo?" Musana puffed.

"The video man, Ssebo. I provide videoing as an extra service to all my clients. It's a bonus, Ssebo, you don't have to pay for it."

"I told you he's good at his work," Joyce beamed.

Musana relaxed. "Thanks. I had forgotten about that. There was too much to do in such a short time."

"Webale, Ssebo." The man bowed with gratitude. He started setting up his equipment, and soon music was booming. The DJ played familiar Ugandan numbers by the Afrigo band, which carried Kagaba's mind back home; he briefly wondered how Ajuna was. He hadn't called her in more than a week because he couldn't afford it.

People were streaming in, smartly dressed, as if they were going to a wedding. He did not know any of them, but most spoke Luganda and greeted him like a long-lost friend—gyebale ko, Ssebo.

The party got underway. People were drinking and talking boisterously. But the guest of honor hadn't arrived yet, and Musana instructed Joyce not to serve food until she came. He ordered more beers, and the guests were served with Bell, Nile Special, Pilsner, and other Ugandan brands. He constantly checked his watch and phone.

Finally, two women strolled into the restaurant. An indiscernible magnetism catapulted Musana toward the smaller of the two ladies. He intercepted her halfway, grabbed her hand, and began leading her to the high table. The video man jumped into action and started filming the "procession" into the party area. Everyone stood up. The DJ played a number, and the gathering clapped in rhythm, shrieking with happiness for several minutes … "Wow! Otyo! Abo! Bebo! Ogwo!" Musana's smile reached his ears. After everyone had sat down, Musana asked Joyce to start serving food.

Kagaba ate with gusto. This was the first real Ugandan food he had tasted since arriving in the UK. He piled his plate with his favorite cuisine: matooke and smoked fish in groundnut sauce, adding barbequed goat ribs, generous servings of nakati, chapatti, and sweet potatoes, all freshly cooked. He ate with his fingers, savoring the delicious, subtle flavors oozing from the banana leaves in which most of the food was cooked.

So, this was Sharon! He observed her from the corner of his eye. She was beautiful, with strong, angular cheekbones and short, trimmed hair. Her presence emitted an aura of confidence, the kind that is meant to intimidate. She wasn't eating much. Instead, she was engaged in conversation with the other women at her table.

"Congratulations," the women said to her.

"Thank you," she mouthed back with a cheerful face.

The woman who had arrived with Sharon sat next to Kagaba and, after a while, she said to him, "Are you Musana's roommate? The one looking for a job."

He nodded. She had small, searching eyes and they shone when she spoke, like sunshine. She smiled guardedly at him and continued speaking in Luganda. "So, how are you finding London? Are you still homesick?" She had such an ethereal voice, childlike almost, which did not match her big, tall frame. But it was difficult to carry on the conversation amid the flurry of activity around the table, and Kagaba turned his attention to the other guests.

There were about thirty people. They all looked to be Ugandans. Did they have the right papers to live and work in the UK? Or were they all illegals? They appeared to be happy and carefree and, judging from their clothes and smartphones, not short of money.

His own visa would expire in five months' time. He would soon have to decide if he would go the Musana route to find a job—which scared him—or choose to return to Uganda empty-handed.

He focused his attention on the group again. The women wore wigs or long extensions, and they swung their heads this way and that as they spoke, pushing away strands of the fake hair falling in their faces. Most were busy capturing the proceedings on their smartphones.

The woman with the delicate voice tried to engage him in conversation once again, asking him his name, how long he had been in the UK, how he was related to Musana, and what kind of job he was looking for. After he had divulged the requested information, she, in turn, informed him that her name was Julia, and that Musana's lady, Sharon, was her best friend. They had shared a room once when Julia first arrived in London, eight years ago.

She went on to tell him that Sharon had three children and a husband, whom she had left in Uganda. Her husband was not really her husband anymore; after waiting for Sharon to return or to send for him and the kids, he had declared that he was now separated from her and had taken another wife.

"People back home don't understand how long it takes to sort out papers," she said, switching to English, her voice a pitch higher, her tiny eyes beginning to dilate. Kagaba felt her hot breath on his ear. She smelt fresh—like a flower. He could sense Julia was getting flirtatious. He shifted his body away from hers, toward the edge of his chair.

"I can help you get a job," she whispered, reaching for his hand, but he quickly snapped it back.

"Don't you want to find a job?" Julia moved her body, drawing closer to him again. He stood up just as Musana called for everyone's attention. He sat down again.

"I want to thank everyone for coming," Musana began. "Thank you for your prayers as well; especially Pastor Moses'. He, unfortunately, couldn't make it here today. Let's dance. DJ, give us a good number!"

Ululations and clapping followed Musana's announcement. Everyone stood up and began clearing chairs and tables to create room for dancing. The guests poured onto the floor, stamping their feet, throwing their hands in the air. Kagaba remained sitting. He had never liked or learned how to dance. He blamed it on the strict upbringing from his father, and the Catholic schools he had attended. But Julia came and grabbed his hand. "Come and dance." He declined and stuck to his seat. He did not want to embarrass himself. When Julia realized she could not persuade him, she moved on and started dancing with a group of men.

Kagaba observed her as she danced. She looked to be about twenty-eight years old; younger than Ajuna, but because she was big and tall, and Ajuna small and short, their ages could easily be switched.

Only one other guest remained in his seat. His cheekbones were chiseled with tribal marks like tattoos, his black complexion glistening against the blue light. Kagaba did not remember seeing him arrive or serve himself; perhaps he had just joined the party. The man grinned at Kagaba when he caught him staring and walked over to his table.

"My name is Ochola," he extended his hand. Kagaba stood up and took his hand. The loud music made it difficult to make conversation and they both sat down again.

The DJ was playing Kipepeo. The dancers went wild, bawling and hugging one another as they did paka chini strokes, rotating their buttocks until they touched the floor. Julia spun her big body without much effort. When she did the paka chini, her G-string showed and her trousers looked like they were going to fall off. Ochola looked Kagaba's way, and they grinned together.

Most women wore knee-high boots and some tripped and fell, but they didn't seem to care. They rolled on the floor, not minding their exotic hair and good clothes. The video man never stopped filming.

"I like Chameleon," Ochola yelled above the music. "He's my favorite Ugandan singer."

"Then you should be on the dance floor," Kagaba shouted back.

He shook his head. He went to the bar and returned with two Nile Specials and handed Kagaba one.

Toward 2 am the party finally broke up. Musana pulled out a wad of cash from his wallet and paid the bill. "A man deserves some happiness once in a while," he boasted, justifying his extravagance. The buffet cost ten pounds a plate, and the beers were not cheap either.

Musana staggered out of the restaurant hanging on Sharon's arm like a leech, and they disappeared into the cold night toward where he had parked his car.

"The trains have stopped running," Julia said to Kagaba. "If you wish, you can ride with me in my car, and I will drop you somewhere you can catch a bus."

Kagaba hesitated, not wanting to abandon Ochola, who had offered him good company even though he seemed to be a reserved person. Besides, he was apprehensive about being in the same space as Julia.

"Come on, let's go." Julia urged, slipping her hand into his. "Don't worry about him," she continued, referring to Ochola. "He'll find his way."

"You know him?"

"Ochola? He's my brother! He'll find his way; he's been in this country nearly three years now."

"I will come with you," Ochola said. "I didn't bring my car and I will need a lift to the station." He spoke while looking at Kagaba.

7

At the beginning of December, two months after arriving in the UK, Kagaba got his first job. Julia had kept her promise and connected him with a charity to deliver leaflets requesting homeowners to donate unwanted clothing, drapes, handbags, shoes, belts, underwear, blankets and towels to be sent to Third-World countries to help clothe the poor.

What he liked about the leafleting job was that he did not have to talk to anyone. The van driver said nothing when he picked him up; he did not have to see or speak to the homeowners when he delivered the leaflets—he slotted the leaflets through the letterboxes—and there was no chance in a million that he would encounter anyone from Uganda who knew him who could potentially tell Ajuna. She believed he was helping one of Musana's student friends with his research paper on data analysis, and that he was being paid for it, as he waited for the big job Musana had promised before he left Uganda.

"This is how it works," Julia had explained when she called him two days after they had met at Sharon's party. On the phone, she wasn't flirtatious. Her manner was that of a professional broker. "You have no right to work in the UK," she stated. You came on a visitor's visa, which does not permit you to work. Your pay will be deposited in my friend's bank account. She will take off a commission, and pass the rest on to me, which I will be giving you in cash."

After the commission for Julia and her friend, he would earn between £140 and £180 a week, depending on how hard he was willing to push himself. Not too bad, Kagaba reckoned; it was still more than an average monthly salary for a young professional in Uganda. He would be frugal so he could save at least half to remit to Ajuna. He would deliver all the one hundred flyers contained in the bag. He would not be deterred by the freezing temperatures that had ushered in December.

But could he trust Julia to deliver the money to him? He did not know much about her. He did not know where she lived or worked, or anything about her family back in Uganda.

He called Musana for advice. Musana had not returned to the house since the party to celebrate his girlfriend's citizenship, but he continued to pay rent, which was a great relief for Kagaba. "You're asking too many questions, my friend," Musana warned when Kagaba asked about Julia. "You need a job. Julia has got you one. Work. Things will get better with time."

The accident happened about two weeks into his leafleting job. On the day, the van picked Kagaba up in front of his house at five as always and dropped him off at the top of Abbey Road with his day's leaflets in a plastic bag. It was deceptively bright and sunny, but being December, it was bound to be chilly. Already, the deep cold made his bones chatter and hot vapor was blowing out of his mouth like a steam train.

It was about eleven in the morning when he pushed his right hand through a letterbox to deposit a flyer. He heard a fierce bark, before excruciating pain consumed his whole arm. What happened next seemed to do so in slow, coordinated motions. His fingers were gripped and held captive by powerful jaws. He gave a sharp yelp and attempted to wrestle his hand out of death's clutches; when he pulled, it felt as if his fingers were being ripped off his hand.

But he continued desperately pulling away his hand, and when that failed, he tugged at it with his good hand. Pulling, tugging, pulling, tugging, yelling, yelping for help. Finally, he secured his hand. There was an incredible amount of blood everywhere. He pulled off his wool scarf and bandaged his mangled hand with it.

The street was empty; nobody had witnessed the terrible attack. It was terrifying to think that the dog had been waiting for his hand to come through the letterbox so it could tear it to pieces. Perhaps the owner was in the house when it happened, listening to his agony in silence—a cruel way of saying he did not want any more junk mail delivered to the house.

The first person he called was Julia. "You cannot go to hospital. You can't trust those doctors. They might ask for your papers." Julia was adamant.

"But this is an emergency! My hand is bleeding; I'm losing blood!"

"Don't panic. I have some antibiotics and a first-aid kit. I'll come over and look at your hand."

"But ... are you ..."

"I used to work as a nurse in a children's home. I'm sure I can handle your injuries. Lewisham is close to where I live. I'll come right away."

Julia arrived within an hour. She had instructed him to sit on the bench at the Lewisham Centre bus stop. He should not talk to anyone. He kept his head down. Passers-by and people waiting to board the bus were staring at his bleeding, bandaged hand. No one offered to call an ambulance. Strangely, he felt no pain, only numbness and shock.

"Get in," Julia commanded as she reached for the handle to open the passenger door. They drove along Bankside Avenue for a short distance, until she found a parking space. She had brought the first-aid kit and an assortment of liquids and ointments. She removed the improvised bandage expertly. The pain kicked in the moment Julia took off the bandage. Kagaba bawled, but Julia put her forefinger on her mouth, urging him to remain silent. "You'll attract the attention of the police."

She fished through her bag for a spray that she applied, saying it would dull the pain. After about twenty minutes, she had washed and sanitized the injuries. She sprinkled on a powder that smelled like medicine. Lastly, she dressed the wounds with fresh bandages.

"I will need to change the dressing every two days," she said, as she closed her medicine kit.

The pain had subsided. All his fingers were intact. "Thank you so much."

"No worries. I have to rush back now, otherwise I'll be late for my shift." She gave him the antibiotics and something for pain; assured him that the wounds were not deep.

8

Evening came and went. Kagaba hadn't left the bed. He hadn't eaten but he wasn't hungry. The pills had dampened the pain, but he was beginning to feel feverish. He contemplated what had happened. This could be the end of his job. His hand may never heal. He might get an infection. He could not tell Ajuna because she would get worried and stressed. Not a good idea in her current state. He called Musana, but his phone was switched off.

Maybe he should call his father and Ssenga Jovia. They would regret having allowed him—as if they had a choice in the matter—to travel to the UK. An untreated infection could cost him his hand; might even kill him. His greatest regret would be dying without seeing his yet-to-be-born child.

He was six or seven years old when he asked his father to show him his biological mother. At the time, it was only him, his father, and Ssenga Jovia living in the symmetrical house his family had since occupied. In those days, the walls were painted with white chalk, and the flowers now bounding the small patio at the front were not there.

His father had not yet married Ama's mother, Amooti. Ssenga Jovia said he was reluctant to wed Amooti, even after she gave him a daughter—Ama. Ama and her mother lived separately, and his father supported them from their own home. When they finally joined the family, Ama was thirteen or fourteen.

In those days, Ssenga Jovia was still a young, unmarried

woman with broad hips, long, shapely legs, and skin as smooth as a baby's, which she constantly smeared with shea butter. For most of the year, she kept her hair plaited, and only undid the braids on special occasions, like Christmas. Kagaba wished she could do away with the artificial hair altogether, because her own hair was long and silky. She had not yet developed high blood pressure, and she was half her current size.

His father was the head teacher at the mission school Kagaba attended, and everyone, including himself and Ssenga Jovia, called him Mr. Nathan. Mr. Nathan observed a strict household routine, waking Kagaba up at five each morning to brush his shoes and draw his bath, while Ssenga Jovia prepared their breakfast. At seven they would ride on his father's bicycle to school; himself perched on the crossbar, clutching his cloth schoolbag because his father's briefcase had to be strapped to the carrier.

When he returned home in the afternoon, Ssenga Jovia would have already prepared lunch. After washing the dishes, he would go out to play with Tomas, whose family lived nearby.

His father arrived home at 5.30 pm. He would run to welcome him, and he would envelope him in an embrace. His father smothered him in his muscular, strong arms—Kagaba didn't regard his father as a small man in those days. He would inhale the freshness of his smell, amazed by how neat and clean his father always looked, even after he had been riding his bicycle in the evening heat.

At supper time, Ssenga Jovia would narrate what had transpired in the day: how the plants were doing, who had visited, whom she had seen at the stream; and his father would listen attentively, not interrupting her even once. He never ever spoke while eating. Later, he would respond to all her queries and comments with an astuteness that astonished Kagaba, like he had kept a mental note of all that Ssenga Jovia had said throughout dinner. By 9 pm, they would all be in bed.

It was a Friday when Kagaba asked his father to tell him what happened to his mother. His father said nothing, and that night, as they ate supper, Ssenga Jovia was uncharacteristically quiet.

His father normally spent Saturday mornings on the farm with Ssenga Jovia, inspecting what the workers had done during the week, and listening to Ssenga Jovia's complaints about the unrewarding harvests and the lazy farm workers. In the afternoons, neighbors came to the house to talk to him about their children's misbehavior or to ask for a favor to keep them in school because the harvest had been poor that season and they could not afford to pay school fees until the end of the month.

"Mr. Nasanairi," the older men and women would address his father like that, unable to pronounce the foreign-sounding syllables properly. "My child does not listen to me anymore. She does not want to come to school to learn. She wants to get married instead. I'm going to send her to you so you can tell her the importance of education."

His father would listen to the elderly men and women most of the afternoon, and thank them for the food, chickens and fruit they brought as gifts.

That Saturday, however, by the time Kagaba woke up, his father was already dressed.

"Get ready now, we're going somewhere," he told him.

Was his father taking him to meet his mother? If so, where, and what did she look like? Did she have other children? Why did she not live with them? They rode on the bicycle for about three miles without saying much. The sun was already high up in the wide, open, blue sky—hot and sharp.

They arrived at a big compound with several grass-thatched houses and one big iron-roofed house. Children were romping about in the yard, skipping rope and riding old car tires, making sounds like car engines. They were expected, Kagaba could tell, judging from the way they were welcomed.

A smiling young man ushered them into the iron-roofed house. The moment they sat down, a young girl entered with a tray covered with a white cloth, with two glasses and two bottles of Mirinda fruit. She fidgeted with the opener until she gave up and left the room giggling.

His father opened the two bottles and handed one to Kagaba. The soda was warm, but he was thirsty and drank it in a few gulps. Soon, people started coming in to greet them: two elderly men, children, and about three or four young women.

About an hour after they had arrived, a woman carrying a very small baby appeared in the living room. She was big and tall, with a kind smile and big eyes that made her look friendly and warm. She simply appeared in the room and, for a moment, Kagaba could not figure out which entrance she had used to come in. Instead of walking, she seemed to be sailing. She was so composed, so confident, so ladylike. She sat in the chair facing his father's and appeared to take forever to arrange and adjust her flowing, brightly colored gomesi. The baby was wrapped in a white shawl that hid its face. The shawl also covered the whole upper part of the woman's body.

The woman was cradling her baby in the crook of her left shoulder, instead of holding it against her shoulder, or on her lap, as Kagaba had seen many women do with small babies.

His father sat up and pulled his legs together, chin leaning forward, like he was about to say something. But he said nothing. Kagaba could not take his eyes off the woman. A magnetic device seemed to be pulling him to her. He wanted to cross the short space between them and sit on her lap and be swathed in her gomesi, cuddled, loved. This is my mother! He thought. She is so beautiful and kind. Why doesn't she live with us?

"Kagaba, this is your *new* mother," his father said, aglow with happiness. "And that's your little sister." He made like he was going to lift Kagaba out of the chair. "Go on, say hello to your new mother. Go!"

Kagaba did not move. He shifted his gaze from the woman

to his father, then back to the woman. She shifted the bundle in the white shawl from the crook of her arm and extended it to his father. His father sprung to his feet and took the baby in his arms, holding it delicately. "Go!" he whispered hoarsely into Kagaba's ear when he returned to his seat.

Kagaba was watching the woman sideways. She extended her right hand to him, inviting him to come to her. He recoiled. She was not his mother.

"Kagaba looks like his sister," she remarked, like it was the most natural thing to say under the circumstances. "And he's going to be so tall and handsome," she added.

"Would you like to hold your sister? Daddy, pass on the baby to him. Let him hold his sister," the woman addressed his father, the only person he had ever heard refer to his father as Daddy and not Mr. Nathan.

"Alright then, would you like to go and play with your friends? Go on. Jimmy, Frank, Simon, come," she called out. "Come and play with Kagaba. He's bored with our adult talk, and he's afraid to hold his little sister," she gave a short laugh. When she raised her voice like that, a sharpness crept into her tone, like she was always commanding people to follow her wishes.

The boys assembled in the doorway. Their clothes were soiled with dirt, emitting a foul smell, their faces unfriendly. He glanced at his father for approval, and he nodded. Kagaba did not go immediately. He tipped the Mirinda bottle into his mouth, draining the dregs of the purple liquid slowly. After, he left the room with the fierce-looking boys.

His father kept talking with *her* for a very long time, long after the football game with the three boys had ended, a trip to the mango tree accomplished, and another to check if the trap to catch porcupines had been successful. And long after the moon had risen, draping the big compound with her silvery rays.

As they rode back home, his father picking his way through

the small footpath with the aid of the bicycle's head lamp, he wondered, once again, what had happened to his *real* mother.

Later, perhaps one or two months after they had visited, he overheard Ssenga Jovia and his father discussing Nyanjura—that was her name. Her baby had died. She had buried her at her home and only informed his father afterwards. Ssenga Jovia was upset. The matter was never discussed again in the house.

A year or two later, Ama and Amooti moved in. "This is your sister," his father said.

"My real sister?" Kagaba queried.

"Yes. Your real sister," his father confirmed.

Kagaba's happiness knew no bounds. He questioned why Ama had not lived with them until now. Ama pampered him to no end. She acted as though she was protecting him from some imminent harm. Their bond grew and strengthened fast. To this day, Ama behaved like his guardian.

Kagaba dialed her number; when she answered, an over-whelming sense of relief filled his heart.

"You don't sound well, kid brother," she said. Her spirits were high, as always, but there was worry in her tone.

"It's the cold. We've been suffering sub-zero temperatures the whole week."

He could tell she wasn't convinced, but if he told her about the accident, she might tell Ajuna, which would stress her. She might end up in hospital again. So far, the pregnancy was going well, for which he was grateful.

9

Julia continued coming to the house to dress his wounds. She was a good nurse. She said if Kagaba had gone to the hospital he would have got a few sutures; but the daily cleaning and dressing would let the skin heal with time, and the antibiotics would prevent infection.

He had not gone out of the house for days because of the horrendous weather—blizzards of snow and wind would only exacerbate his fever, though Julia had tried to convince him that the rise in his temperature was not an indicator of a serious infection, insisting the fever would abate as his injuries got better. Sometimes she would bring him a Chinese takeaway. He would eat the food sparingly to last him until her next visit.

Julia told him a whole lot of things about herself during the time she spent at his house. She used to work as a nurse in a home for disabled children—that's where she had stolen some of the strong antibiotics and painkillers. Like many other illegals who could not access medical services on the NHS, Julia also kept a stock of medicines, usually sent over from Uganda.

She had quit her job at the disabled children's home a little over a month ago, because cleaning the children's poo was depressing her. She had come to the UK about nine years ago on a student visa that had long since expired. Since then, she had been engaged in full-time illegal employment, working under a false identity.

Julia was sending money home to support her aging mother, pay school fees for her brothers and sisters, and maintain her ten-year-old daughter. She was waiting to benefit from a blanket amnesty, which she claimed the British government offer people who had overstayed their visas for more than ten years. One more year to go, and then she would be granted permanent residence. She would then go back to Uganda and bring over her daughter.

She had last seen her when she was just a year old and missed her terribly. In fact, the longing to be with her was part of the reason she had stopped caring for other children, who reminded her of her own daughter.

Kagaba could not resist asking about the whereabouts of her daughter's father. They had met at university in Uganda, Julia revealed, but after the baby was born, they had found it difficult to make ends meet because both were unemployed. He had come to the UK first, worked for a year, saved up enough money, and financed her trip to join him. The baby would come later, they had agreed, and Julia had taken the child to live with her mother in the village.

But that's not how it happened. Charles, her daughter's father, was idling about in Hyde Park on his day off one Saturday when he heard a commotion behind him. When he turned around, two black youths were running in the opposite direction. Before he could figure out what was happening, three policemen were on him, asking him if he knew the two men who had just run off. He said he did not know them. But the policemen were not convinced. The two young men were suspected of dealing in drugs.

Charles insisted that he did not know what the policemen were talking about. Then they asked him to go with them to the police station to record a statement as a witness. At the station, they asked for his identification papers, immigration status and so on and so forth. The only document he had on him was a debit card belonging to his friend. Since Charles was not eligible to hold or open a bank account, his friend had allowed him to use one of his bank accounts. The police said they were going to hold him on suspicion of theft of the debit card, because when they traced its owner and called him, he denied knowing Charles.

Charles ended up in a detention center and was later deported. That was five years ago, and Julia had since lost contact with him.

"What about Ochola?" Kagaba asked her one day. Sometimes he's the one who picked her up in the night when she came to the house a bit late in the evening. At times he would sit in the car and wait for her.

"What about him? I told you he is my brother."

"I find that hard to believe—I mean—your surname shows you're from central Uganda, and Ochola, well, he's from the north, isn't he? The tribal marks, the name ..."

"He's my brother," Julia said with finality, and he let the matter rest.

Kagaba had to admit that he was physically attracted to Julia. He shared his anguishes with her: the loans he had accumulated back home; how much it pained him not to be present for his baby's birth. He told her bits of his family history: his missing mother; his bond with Ssenga Jovia. Some of this information he had never shared with Ajuna.

Christmas was approaching. Kagaba's neighbors had decked their houses with colorful, dazzling decorations, which shone in their windows and doors. In the evenings, people sang Christmas carols in the street. He did not come out to offer them money, as he would have done in Uganda.

Shopping malls and streets shimmered with Christmas garlands. The mood was jubilant, reminding Kagaba of the shopping craze that engulfed Ugandans just before Christmas.

Julia had recently got another job in a retirement home, which meant she could not invite him to her house for Christmas as she had earlier promised. She would be working that day. "We make more money when we work on big days, like

Christmas. There's no rest from this job," she complained when she came to check on his bandages. "I've not seen daylight since I started working. When I leave the house, it's still dark and, when I return, it's already dark."

Her car wouldn't start. Kagaba fidgeted with the engine for about half an hour, but when he tried starting it again, it continued making sad noises. "Stay the night," he suggested jokingly, not expecting her to say yes, but she agreed.

He regretted the invitation as soon as he had offered it. Where would Julia sleep? The house had no living room where he could have thrown a mattress for her to crash on. They could not share the only bed in the tiny room. He could not disinvite her. She had accepted his invitation so easily!

Since making a pass at him at Sharon's citizenship party, Julia had maintained a professional, if friendly relationship with him. He vacated his bed and slept on the spare mattress Musana used to sleep on. He did not sleep much, wondering about Julia, listening to her gentle breathing as she snoozed. He dozed off toward morning. When he opened his eyes, Julia was gone.

Kagaba had resigned himself to spending Christmas on his own. Sean had gone to his parents' home. Musana was still living at Sharon's house; in any case, he said he would be working on that day. On Christmas Day, however, Ochola surprised him with a call, and picked him up to spend the day at his flat in South London.

This was Kagaba's first Christmas away from home, away from his family. As a child, Christmas was the most wonderful time of the year. Ssenga Jovia would come over three or four days before Christmas, bringing food and fruit and a chicken or two, and, always, a new shirt for Kagaba. Everyone wore something new on Christmas Day. His father would buy a new gomesi for Amooti, and she would ask the tailor to make a dress for Ama out of the piece that remained after making her gomesi.

His father would make them go to church early enough so they would get the front seats. He wanted Father Bonaventure to see them and register their participation in the choir and during offertory. Afterwards, Ama and Kagaba would run outside to ogle the city children who would have come with their parents to the village for the Christmas holidays, speaking English, dressed in expensive, fancy clothes.

Tomas's father and his whole family would join them on Boxing Day, when neighbors and friends would also be invited to eat the goat that his father had reserved for that day. Over the years, not much had changed, except Ama now traveled to her husband's village, and Kagaba would sometimes remain in the city, preferring to spend the holidays with Ajuna.

Ochola's one-bedroom abode was clean, tidy and warm; stacks of books reached up to the ceiling. He was an organized person, Kagaba could tell, admiring the orderly manner of his lifestyle. Was he really Julia's boyfriend? Kagaba tried to find traces of Julia's presence in his flat—a picture, a forgotten scarf, the smell of her signature flowery perfume. Julia's name did not come up the whole time he was there.

Ochola was not the chatty type and, after eating, they mostly drank beer and watched a game of football on the telly.

"When do you plan to return to Uganda?" he asked Ochola.

"I would leave tomorrow if I could, but I was assigned the laziest supervisor in the whole world. I wonder sometimes how he ever became a professor. Three months now, and he's still looking at the last chapter I submitted. My stipend is running out and I want to return so I can get a job. I've been living on a shoe-string budget for three years."

"There are no jobs in Uganda," Kagaba warned.

In the quietness of the empty house after Ochola had dropped him off, thoughts of returning to Uganda penniless filled his head.

PART TWO
2008

Kampala

1

Ajuna experienced her first complication at six months. It started with her feet swelling with edema. At first, she put it down to the intensity of the January heat. But soon, the high appetite she had experienced at the beginning of the pregnancy flew away and was replaced by regular bouts of dizziness and exhaustion. At the insistence of Ama, she had visited a doctor to have her blood pressure measured. It had turned out to be higher than normal, and the doctor had prescribed complete bed rest for at least four weeks.

After the initial shock of getting pregnant while on the pill, the panic had worn off. She was beginning to feel the first tremors of excitement at the thought of becoming a mother, but she was terrified of going through childbirth—alone. She had not counted on being a single mother. She had always envisaged a supportive, caring husband holding her hand when the pain became unbearable, and later, sharing the burdens of looking after a baby.

Kagaba still hadn't secured a proper job. He had mentioned an injury to his hand; then his visa not permitting him to work professionally in the UK. Ajuna sensed he wasn't telling her the whole truth. The previous month, he had sent a parcel containing baby clothes, two feeding bras, and some money through Sharon, whom he said was Musana's girlfriend.

Bed rest made her restless. She longed for activity, however trivial; anything to take her mind away from her current worries. She called Kalayi for some ideas.

"I will come on Friday and stay until Monday morning. You need some company," Kalayi promised. But she didn't come, citing an impromptu outing with her friends. Always unreliable, Ajuna grumbled inwardly, her mind straying to the time just after she had told Kalayi to leave her flat. That's when Kalayi dropped the bomb. She was pregnant. The news hit Ajuna like a tidal wave.

Confused and alarmed, she had turned to Jane for advice. Jane suggested an abortion, illegal in the country. She would help to find a good doctor, who could do the procedure safely, though expensively. But Ajuna dismissed the idea.

"It's too dangerous. My parents would kill me if they got to know that I colluded with their daughter. They are staunch Catholics."

"So, what do you suggest? Kalayi has no job, no money, no husband; tell me, who's going to support her and her child, if not you? I think you need to think more prudently."

"She can go back to the village and live with her parents. She's not an orphan. Let them take care of her and her baby." Ajuna was angry.

"That's not how things work in this country, Ajuna. You know that very well. You are already taking care of your two nephews. Do you want to add extra burden?

"You will still be expected to look after Kalayi and her child. You can't send her back to the village. You will be creating a bigger problem for yourself. You need to sort her out—push her to get an education and a job so she can take care of herself in future. I'll help with the expenses," Jane was calm, "and I've talked with Kalayi. She's ready to do it."

"Thank you, Jane. I hope Kalayi appreciates the sacrifices we are both making; especially you."

The rest happened fast. The doctor said she would attend to Kalayi from her private clinic in Entebbe, an hour's drive from the city. It would have to be at night, when there was likely to

94

be little activity at the clinic. The next day, Jane drove them there and entered the treatment room with Kalayi. Ajuna sat in the waiting area, not knowing what to think, fearing for the worst.

Minutes ticked by. It could have been an hour, or thirty minutes, or three hours, but the waiting seemed to last an eternity.

The hollering that suddenly erupted from behind the closed door jolted Ajuna from her daze. The doctor had assured them there would be minimal pain. She was going to perform a surgical abortion. It would involve the use of a gentle suction to remove the pregnancy tissue. She would give Kalayi an injection to numb the cervix before performing the vacuum aspiration. The procedure would take about fifteen minutes.

Ajuna wanted to put sticks in her ears. She could not feel her hands. A cold shiver dashed through her spine. After what seemed to be hours, the doctor came out, pulling off blood-stained surgical gloves which she dumped in the bin near the door. She stood in front of Ajuna, not saying anything. Ajuna opened her mouth, her heart thumping.

"It's done," the doctor said in the end, not sounding pleased.

"Is something wrong?" Ajuna was whispering.

"No, not in the way you mean. But I was led to believe it was eight weeks."

"And?"

"At least twelve weeks."

"Does that mean ... will that result in a complication?"

"It was risky. I wouldn't have agreed to do it if I had been told the truth."

She walked back to the room, and Ajuna could hear a muted argument with Jane. Finally, Jane came out. She was composed, and Ajuna could not tell what had transpired. Soon, they were joined by a man dressed like a night watchman. He exchanged words with Jane. She gave him some money. The man scurried away.

Ajuna stood up. Her legs were shaky. She entered the room.

Kalayi's face was turned to the ceiling, her cheeks tear-stained and pale. She had pulled her legs up. There was blood on the white sheets, and many reddened blobs of cottonwool in a small bin in the corner. Ajuna gingerly touched Kalayi's face. She grabbed Ajuna's hand and brushed it against her cheek, her tears. Ajuna rested her head on Kalayi's chest. They held each other until Jane called to Ajuna to come out.

They got into the car after the doctor had given them medication to control the bleeding, to prevent infections. She did not offer to see Kalayi again in case something went wrong later. The night watchman joined them and got into the back next to Kalayi, who was whimpering. About ten minutes later, Jane stopped the car, and the man got out. He was carrying a small plastic bucket, and he walked up to a heap of rubbish by the roadside, looked up and down the road, and emptied the contents of the bucket into the garbage.

He heaped more rubbish on top of what he had just deposited there, inspected his handiwork and, satisfied, walked back to the car. Jane switched off the headlights, which she had left on so the man could see what he was doing. She dropped her hand in her handbag, fished for more money, and handed it to the man. He grinned and said, "Thank you very much, madam. May God bless you."

Afterwards, Jane told Ajuna that the doctor had insisted they take the fetus and bury it. The clinic could not dispose of it for ethical reasons.

"How much did you pay the watchman?" Ajuna was horrified.

"Enough to buy a meal for two at the Sheraton."

After the abortion, countless questions raced through Ajuna's mind. Kalayi must have already been pregnant when she came to live with her. She must have known how far gone she was, but had chosen to lie to the doctor. Why?

Jane said the fetus was already formed and looked like a lizard, with identifiable little fingers and toes. There was a man, somewhere out there, responsible for Kalayi's pregnancy. Who was he? Kalayi had refused to discuss the matter.

Kalayi was only nineteen. Would she still be able to have children in future? She would have to ask the doctor. If their parents ever got to know, they would kill Ajuna. As the big sister, she was supposed to guide Kalayi.

How did Kalayi feel afterwards?

"Ask her," Jane advised. "Sit her down and have this conversation, however difficult. Abortion is a big deal."

And so Ajuna did.

"How do you feel, Kalayi? I mean after the … the … procedure?" Ajuna started.

No answer.

It was two weeks after the abortion. Kalayi had continued to experience pelvic pain and cramping. Jane had called the doctor who performed the procedure, and she had advised them to use a hot water bottle, which did the trick. For the other symptoms, dizziness and bleeding, the doctor assured them the symptoms would clear within weeks.

"Kalayi, would you like to speak with someone, a professional, a therapist?"

Ajuna was met with more silence.

"Still early days," Jane concluded. "Give her time."

After two months, still Kalayi remained completely mute on the subject. Ajuna decided to let the matter rest.

2

Ajuna was beginning to enjoy her bed rest. She had established a routine, which kept away her restlessness. In the mornings, she read the "mother-to-be" magazines Kagaba had sent her through the mail. In the afternoons, she napped, and at night, she exchanged text messages with Kagaba. He missed her insanely, he would tell her. She missed him more, she would insist. They would discuss the approaching birth. *Three more months to go,* Kagaba would remind her; *a little less, I think,* Ajuna would correct him. *I have started on my seventh month now, but either way, it still feels like an eternity. I can't wait!*

Focus on the prize, darling, Kagaba would text, *our baby!*

She had opted for a caesarean, hoping it would be less traumatic and safer. Ama sniggered when she told her.

"How can you invite a knife to yourself? Do you know the risks involved in surgery? Besides, a C-section denies you the chance of being a *real* mother."

Ajuna should have known better than to ask Ama's opinion—her and her archaic views. She turned to Kalayi, knowing she would bolster her confidence.

"A caesarean birth is neater. You won't get messed up down there. Go for it," Kalayi encouraged her.

Kalayi could be unreasonable in many aspects, but Ajuna admired her straightforwardness, her confidence, and the fact that she never let anything or anyone put her down. Ajuna reflected on the abortion episode, wondering if Kalayi had recovered. It was nearly four years ago. They never discussed the incident, despite Ajuna's efforts to get Kalayi to open up.

Kalayi was currently jobless, having lost her bookshop job when she took two days off without permission to attend to Ajuna in hospital. She was using the free time not to look for another job, but to get settled in with a new boyfriend in his rented house. She planned to set up a business so she could become her own boss. She said her new boyfriend would sponsor the initial capital.

"Tal is serious," she confided. "We want to sort out a few things before getting married."

"What things?" Initially, Ajuna had been weary of Tal. Talemwa was his full name, though Kalayi chose to abbreviate it to Tal, because, according to her, that sounded more romantic.

"Tal has a baby already with another woman," Kalayi revealed.

"And?"

"This woman dumped Tal soon after the baby was born."

"And?"

"She wants to come back, because Tal has a lot of money now. He is not interested, of course. But she says if he doesn't take her back, she will abandon the baby to him."

"And what will you do if she carries out her threat?"

"I'll tell Tal to take the child to his mother, or sister, or aunt. He has a big family. I'm not ready to raise anybody's child."

"You sound so naïve, little sis. Why do you want to get yourself into a relationship that's already crowded?"

Kalayi was unyielding. "I love Tal."

"And he loves you?"

"Of course! Or what did you think?" She sounded like she was going to explode in Ajuna's face, and Ajuna knew she had crossed the line.

"Just asking, that's all. I don't want to see you hurt."

The first time Ajuna met Tal, she remembered wondering

how a person could be so imperfect. His pyramid-shaped nose appeared to have been appended to his square face as an afterthought; the small, black eyes were widely spaced on his broad face. Still, the man was pompous and looked twice Kalayi's age.

The more she got to know him, however, the more she realized how wrong she had been to judge him at face value. He had many virtues. His love for Kalayi was sincere. He was generous and warmhearted; and the only person Ajuna knew who successfully accommodated Kalayi's fluctuating temperament.

Ajuna was not sure what Tal did for a living, although Kalayi believed, and informed anyone who asked, that Tal was an engineer working with Uganda Railways. But how could someone who did not even complete his secondary schooling be an engineer?

Ajuna never ceased to be amazed at how fast Kalayi changed boyfriends. She had long ago dumped Samuel, who had lent them the money for Kagaba's trip, saying he behaved like a communist; that he never even bought her a necklace in all the three months they dated.

There were times when Ajuna wished she had some of Kalayi's care-free nature, so she wouldn't always look at the serious side of life; so she wouldn't be too critical, even of herself.

When their mother arrived unannounced, Ajuna knew she was going to kiss her sedentary lifestyle goodbye. Mayi was a talker and liked to probe. She treated all her children as if they were still infants whom she had an obligation to keep safe and happy.

Knowing she would not cope with their chatty mother on her own, Ajuna phoned Kalayi to come over and keep her company. Mayi seemed overexcited about the coming baby, and Kalayi could not hide her irritation.

"Mayi, you already have six grandchildren, what's so special about Ajuna's baby?" Kalayi asked her.

"I'm happy for Ajuna," Mayi defended herself. "I was worried that while other women of Ajuna's age held babies in their arms, Ajuna would be holding her books. All that education is not good for a woman."

"That's not the reason you're here, Mayi," Kalayi continued to taunt her. "It's an open secret that Ajuna is your favorite child. You're scared that something might happen to her. It's only February, and Ajuna isn't due until April."

They were in the living room. Mayi was sipping tea from a plastic mug, seated on the colorful mat she had given Ajuna as a present when she first moved into the flat. She looked puzzled by Kalayi's statement, yet she was not hearing it for the first time.

"Don't speak like that, Kalayi," she sounded tired.

"Don't deny it, Mayi! It's true."

"Kalayi, you're the Umutuwa uwa Mayi," Ajuna hazarded, trying to make light of her sister's accusations.

"Still, being the lastborn doesn't make me her favorite. Mayi says she was happy when you finally arrived. That after four boys, it was so wonderful to hold a baby girl in her arms, knowing she would always have a confidant and a friend."

Mayi sighed and pursed her lips tightly, as if she worried that another word might escape that would cause Kalayi to torment her more.

"And it has always been Ajuna with the big brain, the good grades, the reasonable one. Even this mishap has completely been overlooked by everyone. Father had sworn never to tolerate any of his daughters getting pregnant before marriage. Has he become mellow in his old age, or what? Can you imagine if it were me?" Kalayi charged.

"Stop bullshitting, Kalayi!" Ajuna had not meant to swear. The effort made her breathless, and she dragged her heavy legs from the sofa and placed them on the mat next to Mayi's. She dropped her throbbing head into her palms, and gently massaged her temples with her fingertips.

"Jesus, Kalayi, you can really be annoying. You know that every single word you've uttered today is not true. Just don't say anymore, please. You seem to forget that I'm a full-grown woman of thirty-one, with a job, a house, and a solid qualification under my belt. I can afford to look after this baby no matter—" This came out more arrogantly than Ajuna had intended.

"Are you jealous of your sister?" Mayi asked Kalayi.

"Me? Never. I am just stating facts."

Ajuna eyed her sister. There was no indication on her face how she felt over Ajuna's pregnancy—if it reminded her of her own—or how the abortion had impacted her.

Kalayi started to cry. Mayi looked at her with something akin to pity, but she made no move to comfort her. She pretended to be sipping her tea still, but Ajuna knew she was distressed by Kalayi's outburst. Kalayi covered her face with a handkerchief and sobbed sorrowfully.

A weighty silence followed. Ajuna wanted to say that Kalayi still had the chance to earn herself a better qualification, as long as she became more focused. She also wanted to add that the achievement gap between them was because of Ajuna being nine years Kalayi's senior. When Mayi finally got a girl, she had decided not to have more children. Kalayi wasn't planned. But referring to Kalayi as a mistake might anger her more.

Instead, Ajuna turned her attention to Mayi, noting, once again, how she just seemed to grow younger with the passing years. How did she manage it? Six children had come out of her womb; four boys and two girls. She had lost two in their infancy and the third boy, Jimmy's follower, had died in a car crash a few years back, leaving behind a widow and two sons, whom Ajuna took care of.

But the only indicator that Mayi had produced six children appeared to be the stretch marks etched on her belly. She had never had a house help throughout her married and child-bearing life. She cooked, washed, ironed, raised the babies, and looked after their demanding father. Looking at her now, Ajuna observed that her skin was suppler, her hair still the tangle of beautiful black as she remembered it as a child, when Mayi would ask her to oil it with coconut oil. Later, Ajuna would pretend to twist it into cornrows.

It's only her nails that were chipped, her hands calloused; but the big, luminous eyes told a story of a happy, contented, middle-aged woman. Perhaps her pregnancies had been easier. She was young when she married and conceived her firstborn, seventeen at most, and she must have had more energy than Ajuna felt now.

It was Kalayi who had taken after Mayi: the babyish, smooth face and the glowing eyes, which seemed to hold bottomless peals of laughter, were Mayi's. Ajuna had only gotten the gap between her upper front teeth, and her shapely hips and legs. Kalayi's only complaint was her broad, flat feet, the only feature she had inherited from their father.

Ajuna often wondered why she was so short. Their parents were tall, her brothers soaringly tall, and Kalayi tall enough. She glanced at Mayi once again, resplendent in a colorful cotton gomesi, the square neckline giving away just the slightest hint of cleavage. The gomesi's shoulder blades stood high and sharp. She must have spent up to an hour ironing it.

Ajuna broke the silence, saying she was going to her bedroom to call Ama so they could fix the following day's appointment with the doctor at the National Hospital. Kalayi had stopped crying, and Mayi was speaking to her like she used to do when Kalayi was a little girl and she had thrown or was about to throw one of her infamous tantrums.

A few moments later, Ajuna could hear Kalayi's elevated voice without any trace of sadness in it.

"Ajuna," she shouted across the confined passage leading from the living room to the bedroom, "I was telling Mayi about Tal. He's an engineer and works with Uganda Railways."

"Yeah, you told me already," she shouted back.

Ajuna dialed Ama's number. It rang for a few moments and the connection went dead. She tried several times, until she decided to wait till nightfall, when the networks had better signals.

She closed the drapes and lay on the bed, feeling more tired than she had in the past weeks. Her mind lingered on the coming birth, but she willed herself not to brood. Mayi and Kalayi were chattering. She envied their close relationship.

Kalayi had cooked dinner, rice, beans, and vegetables, but Ajuna was not hungry. Kalayi ate with Mayi in the living room as they watched TV. She knew Kalayi planned to spend the night. And they would continue talking late into the night with Mayi. They would share the same mattress she had prepared for Mayi on the floor in the living room.

Ajuna could not remember when last she had shared the same bed with Mayi. They were not that close. She believed she was closer to her father, because she had spent a year with him when he worked as a junior manager at the tea plantation in Fort Portal. She was about eight and, being the only girl in the family at the time, she was the one to accompany her father to help him to cook and clean the house.

During school holidays, they would return to the family home in Mbale. Her father would stay a short time, a week at most, but Ajuna would stay the whole vacation. She would enjoy special treatment from Mayi and her older siblings because everyone had missed her.

One holiday, when she was about nine, she came home to find a baby girl. Her sister. That changed her relationship with Mayi permanently. She felt betrayed; she felt displaced by the newcomer. Mayi and the other siblings gave more attention to the baby than to her. She withdrew into herself, seeking love and attention, and acceptance, from her father.

When she found out she was pregnant, it was her father she told first; and then Kalayi broke the news to Mayi. When she was going to introduce Kagaba to her parents as their prospective son-in law, she had planned to tell both her parents at the same time, but Kalayi had beaten her to it, telling Mayi first.

When they were young, Mayi would fondly refer to Kalayi as "the beautiful one—just like the meaning of her name." Kalayi was a child with a beautiful heart, that's what Mayi meant, not necessarily physically beautiful. It was her kindness toward strangers, her willingness to give and share, and her generosity toward her siblings that made her beautiful and endeared her to everyone.

3

The next morning, Ajuna came from the bathroom to find a missed call from Ama. Worried that Ama was calling to cancel the appointment with the doctor for the following day, she called her back straight away. But Ama wanted to tell her something else.

"Ssenga Jovia is coming on Friday."

"Oh. Is it her health again?"

"No, it's not her health. She wants to come and nurse you back to health. I think I'll bring her straight to your house."

"You can't do that, Ama! I have no space. My mother's already here. And I am not sick. I am just under bed rest."

"You think I don't know that? But how can I stop Ssenga Jovia?"

"You have to explain my situation to her. You know the size of my flat, Ama. There's literally no space. When the baby is born, we'll go and visit her in the village."

"I think her mind is already made up. I don't see how I can stop her."

"Then you will have to take her to your own house!"

"Hey, listen. It's you she wants to be with. Not me. Why don't you call her and tell her you have no space? You don't seem to understand the close relationship she has with your husband. She wants to look after you, and make sure you're okay before the baby arrives. She says she owes it to Kagaba."

"Ama, I'm not in the mood to pick a fight with you."

"Neither am I. I just don't understand why you're so against

Ssenga Jovia paying you a visit, that's all. If you have room in your heart, you'll find room in your house."

"Interpret it the way you wish, then. Just tell her that I'm not ready to receive her, period."

The phone went dead in Ajuna's hand. Her credit had run out and she hadn't even confirmed the appointment with the doctor. God! Ama was so old-fashioned. How could she not see the situation Ajuna was in, and explain it to Ssenga Jovia?

The following morning, however, there was a text message from Ama: *will pick u up @ 10.meeting doc@ 12.* Ama had booked Ajuna into the National Hospital for the delivery. As the country's referral hospital, it was equipped with all the specialized doctors and facilities.

Ama had been working at the hospital for eight years, and she knew how to go about everything. She would book her a good room with her own toilet and bathroom, and an extra bed for her attendant. She would make sure Ajuna was given all her drugs on time, that the drip was replaced when it emptied, that the dressings were changed, and that she got an extra painkiller if the pain became unbearable.

When Ama arrived to pick her up, she had another passenger in the car: a middle-aged woman who had painted her lips and nails bright red. She was wearing a colorful kitenge, with a large, embroidered wrapper running up from her ankles. Ama introduced her as Kate, her husband's sister who had arrived from the village two weeks earlier.

"My house is now full," Ama added in English, not wanting the woman to understand what she was saying. "This woman had a thriving business. Kato gave her seed money to start it up, but she squandered all her profits on make-up and clothes. Now she expects her brother to give her more money to start a new business." Ama shook her head in dismay. Ajuna expected her to bring up the subject of Ssenga Jovia again, but she did not.

She parked in the bay reserved for staff at the south end of the six-floor building. The doctor's office was in the opposite direction, near the main foyer, and they had to walk fast to catch him before he went on his rounds.

"Let me carry your handbag," Kate offered. Ajuna gratefully handed it to her. She wondered how much longer they had to walk. Ama kept turning corners, disappearing into spacious, endless passageways, making it impossible for Ajuna to keep pace with her.

By the time they reached the doors to the elevator, she was feeling woozy. Ama was way ahead, and she ran to hold the doors. Ajuna lumbered on, Kate bringing up the rear.

There were already about ten or fifteen people in the elevator. A patient was lying on a thin stretcher, her blank eyes staring at the ceiling. Tubes ran from underneath her body, a blood drip attached to her hand.

"They even transport dead bodies in these lifts," Ama whispered in Ajuna's ear. "Would you rather we took the stairs? It's only one floor up."

"Let's use the stairs." Ajuna was already feeling weak in the legs.

"That's the Maternity Ward for kayoola," Ama continued talking as they made their way up the stairs, pointing to a group of women writhing and screaming in pain on the hard, cold floor. "We receive between eighty to a hundred women a day on this ward. Yesterday alone, we lost five women because there are only three operating tables and the same number of surgeons. We need more referral hospitals, surely. I wonder why the government can't see that."

"Why are the women outside?" Ajuna was panting from the effort of climbing the stairs.

"There are only a few labor suites, and the women are only allowed inside when the baby is ready to come out. But don't worry. The private wing where you're booked is not like that—since you're a paying patient."

The doctor hadn't arrived, and they waited for him on the

bench outside his office. Ama had to rush to the ward, and Ajuna was left alone with Kate. It was Kate's first time to visit the hospital. She marveled at its size, at the high floors that "reached up to the sky."

Ajuna was still breathing heavily, her hands placed on her looming stomach. She was in no mood for conversation, but Kate seemed like a nice person and, in any case, talking to her kept away the shrieks from the floor below. The women on the kayoola ward were hollering like animals. She threw her companion a weak smile. Encouraged, Kate asked, "Would you like some water?"

Ajuna shook her head.

"You are so big, is it twins?"

Ajuna laughed and shook her head again. But Kate was right; she was much bigger than what she had imagined she would be at seven months.

"Ama told me you teach at the university."

"Yes, I do."

"I am a businesswoman. Well, used to be, until the government collapsed my business. I used to sell mivumba. I had many customers, including powerful working women. I would take the stuff to their offices because they did not want to be seen in the market haggling over second-hand bras. Then the government banned second-hand underwear, with no consideration at all for people in the business or those who cannot afford new clothing.

"They claimed mivumba carry diseases. Which diseases? Do you really think that the Bazungu who donate these clothes to Africa have skin diseases? Do they even know how ringworm looks like? Those people live in heaven! There are no bacteria there, no dust or mud in those outside countries."

Ajuna laughed.

"Mivumba are oligino. One hundred percent cotton," Kate continued. "They are not fakes. Nowadays the government only allows new underwear imported from China. But these are nylon and too hot for our weather. That's what will bring us diseases."

The doctor came after an hour. When Ajuna entered, he offered her a seat. The office was littered with papers, and the windowpanes and floor were covered in dust. A stethoscope lay on the dirty desk. He scribbled in a notebook as if he was unaware of her presence.

She busied herself by looking at his fingers as they moved back and forth on the notepad. They were thick, the nails delicate and neatly trimmed, like a woman's. He wore a glittery gold wedding band, which seemed too small for it. Perhaps the finger had grown big after he got married. She imagined him probing with his fat fingers into a woman's womanhood during an examination. She wondered if he first removed the wedding ring or wore the gloves with it still on the finger.

At last, without raising his head from the desk, he asked, "So, you want a caesarean?"

"Yes." They had already been through this on the phone, when Ama first introduced them.

"It will cost you." He was still engrossed in his writing.

"You told me a million shillings."

"That's my fee. The hospital will charge you as well. There are theater fees, medicines, nursing care fees ..."

"How much does all of it come to?"

"About three million."

"What?"

"I told you it would cost you." He spoke softly, never raising his head from his writing desk. "I'm only doing this as a favor. Ask people who go to South Africa or even to Nairobi; do you know how much they pay for such a service? Three thousand dollars—and I'm not even asking a quarter of that." He held Ajuna in an unsmiling, uncompromising gaze.

She felt blood pumping into her ears. She was both angry and panicky. Her eyes filled with tears. She wished Kagaba hadn't gone away or had managed to fly back for the birth as she had begged him to. She did not want to go through this alone. She let the tears drop on her cheeks without bothering to hold them back.

"Do you have a particular date for your baby's birthday? How does 26 April sound?"

She recollected herself and looked up to meet his gaze.

"It sounds fine." Her tone was more confident than she felt. "I'll have your money ready by then." She was determined not to be bullied by this patronizing man. The payment for the operation would wipe out her savings. It was more than two months' salary. Perhaps Kagaba would have gotten a job by then.

She stood up.

"Good day, doctor," she said, proud of the sound of her voice and professional manner. She took a taxi back to the university. Kate said she would wait for Ama to finish her shift.

Jane called her that night wanting to know how the meeting with the gynecologist had gone.

"He's a merchant, not a doctor." She still felt angry at the way she had been treated. At least he had taken her off her bed rest after examining her feet and measuring her pressure.

She later agreed to Jane's suggestion for a Sunday outing to the beach. She had promised to take Mayi to visit Ama and her family, but the idea wasn't appealing anymore. She expected Ama would only talk about the constant squabbles with her husband over money issues, the bigheadedness of Musana's children, and how she was determined to send off the eldest girl, Eva, to boarding school at the beginning of the new term. She would go on about her father's pension money not coming through and having to fill in the financial gaps, Kagaba not sending them any money, Ssenga Jovia's illness and how much it cost Ama to treat her. What Ajuna needed was cheering up, not distressing family problems.

4

They had only covered a few miles on their way to Entebbe Beach when Ajuna's phone rang. She fished it out of her messy handbag, wondering who it was. The day was sunny and hot, but Jane had on the air-con, and Ajuna was enjoying the leisurely ride. Sunday traffic was light. Jane was a careful driver, and her car was cozy and powerful—a Toyota 4WD Prado.

"It's Dr. Tindi," she cupped the phone's mouthpiece. "He's actually here in Entebbe as well."

"Ask him to join us. What's he doing here?" Jane asked.

"He was seeing off a friend at the airport."

"Tell him to meet us at the beach."

Ajuna spoke into the phone again.

"I'll call him when we arrive at the beach. He says he doesn't want to hang out there on his own."

She reclined her seat and threw her head back in relaxation, feeling fortunate to have Jane and Dr. Tindi as her friends. The fact that they both got on very well was a bonus.

Even though Jane came from a wealthy, influential family, it did not affect the way she related with people from a less advantaged background. Jane's expensive car had belonged to one of her brothers, who had meant it to be a gift, knowing how miserable their pay at university was. But Jane had insisted on paying for it in installments, however long that took.

Whereas Jane's three brothers were all family men, Jane, at thirty-two, did not even have a boyfriend—at least not to Ajuna's knowledge.

"Men in this country have eyes but they cannot see," Ajuna would tease her.

"They can see alright, but they've all refused to abide by my simple rules."

"Which are?"

"Be my husband but live next door."

"Seriously, Jane, we need to find you someone."

"Forget it, dear friend. I have four nephews and three nieces, and being an aunt is much less stressful. After living on my own all these years, I suppose it makes one a bit selfish. I don't think I can cope with sharing my resources and space with anyone."

Entebbe Beach, on a small island on Lake Victoria, was ringed by scenic hills over the horizon. It was close to Entebbe town, a favored residential area for well-to-do families due to its greenery, serene lifestyle and cool temperatures.

When Ajuna and Jane got there, the beach was already crowded. Excited children played on swings; others threw pebbles at each other. Overdressed women milled about, their high heels digging holes into the sand. The men strolled along the shoreline with swagger; laughing and thumping one another on the back. Some were dressed in three-piece suits and kept wiping water from their sweaty brows. Few revelers were dressed in beachwear.

The blue-white water extended miles and miles toward the skyline and the waves made slapping sounds on their infinite voyage. Ajuna and Jane drew closer to where the currents chased water from the lake, driving it in a mad rush to the shores. Ajuna placed both her feet in the sprinting water, up to her shins, its calming effect spreading through her whole body.

"I wish I could swim, but I'm sure if I tried, I'd simply sink."

"Stop putting yourself down. You're pregnant, not an invalid," Jane reminded her. "Come on. Let's walk for a few minutes. Did you let Dr. Tindi know we are here?"

"Yes. He's finishing up some emails at an internet café and will join us later."

Rickety canoes, the only means of transport to the other islands further out, made their journeys across the lake, overloaded with passengers and merchandise.

"They're so vulnerable. Even a light wind can blow them away. Why doesn't someone think of putting a ferry in place?" Jane said.

Before Ajuna could answer, a white couple approached them. The man was smiling at them and asked Jane to take their picture. The woman was dressed in skimpy beachwear, her sagging stomach gushing out of the swimsuit, as if in protest. The man was shirtless and had on a pair of Bermuda shorts.

After Jane had taken their picture, they lingered.

"Lake Victoria is pretty massive, isn't it?" the man commented in a lazy tone, like he wasn't really expecting an answer.

"Yes, it is," Jane replied.

Ajuna started walking away but Jane held her hand, urging her to stay put.

"We call it Lake Nalubaale," Jane added.

The man cupped his ear to catch the word.

"Do you know how big it is?" the woman asked. "Do you come here often?"

"It's the largest in Africa. It covers three countries including Tanzania and Kenya, and it's the world's second largest freshwater body. The first is Lake Superior in North America, by surface though, and not by volume. By volume, it's Lake Baikal in Siberia."

They thanked her before moving away. Ajuna followed them with her eyes. They had stopped walking and were admiring the snapshot on their digital camera. They seemed to have lost interest in the lake altogether, and she wondered if they had grasped any of the information Jane had provided.

She turned to Jane. "What got into you? One would imagine they were paying you for a geography lesson."

"They come to Africa to learn. They even had the cheek to ask if we come here often. We *live* here. This is our country. This is *our* lake."

"I remember when we were in primary school and our geography teacher telling us, 'Lake Victoria is the size of the Republic of Ireland.' As if any of us knew, or even cared, where or how big Ireland was." Ajuna was still fuming.

"Enough. Call Dr. Tindi and ask him what's taking him so long."

"Talk of the devil. I can see an SMS from him. He's not coming after all. He says an emergency has come up at home."

"Oh." Jane sounded disappointed. "Did he say what the problem was?"

"No." Ajuna, too, was saddened that Dr. Tindi wouldn't be joining them. She enjoyed his good humor, and they never got much time to talk at university because of the heavy workload.

"Most probably it has to do with his wife. Do they have kids, by the way? I have never heard him mention children," Jane asked.

"I don't know. He never talks about his family. We should ask him sometime."

Ajuna was tired and wanted to rest her feet. They walked in the green grass looking for a spot to sit. Coconut trees threw wide shadows that formed wonderful shade, and they chose one tucked away in the corner where they spread their mats.

Ajuna propped herself up with two pillows and a cushion, leaning her back against the tree trunk. As she moved her bulky body to find a comfortable position, bile rose to her throat. She was getting indigestion even before eating anything.

"You look like an Amazon, dear girl," Jane teased.

"Believe me, I don't feel like one." She was wearing a cotton maternity dress with sleeves falling off her shoulders. It was comfortable, but made her bump more pronounced.

"You'll be alright," Jane said.

"I hope so. I feel like my whole life has gone awry. I can't even sit straight."

Jane went to fetch a foldaway chair she kept in the car. It was what Ajuna needed. She felt more comfortable sitting up and stretching her legs on a couple of pillows piled in a heap.

"Has Dr. Tindi's relationship with your Head of Department improved by now, or are the gender wars still raging?"

"Eh?"

"She strikes me as territorial."

"My boss?"

"Yes."

"A bit, I guess. Some staff think she's malicious, but I get on well with her. Her problem with Dr. Tindi is really small. I'm sure they'll sort it out. In the meantime, I'm happy to share my small space with him until he gets his office. He's good company. He makes me laugh all the time."

Jane turned to look at Ajuna. "How's Kagaba fairing? Has he found another job yet?"

"No. Not since he hurt his hand."

Ajuna told Jane about Sharon, who had brought the gifts from Kagaba, showing off the sandals he sent. She also showed Jane the pictures Sharon had brought, which Ajuna had in her handbag.

"He's put on some weight. He looks happy," Jane commented as she flipped through the photographs. "It can't be easy, though, breaking into that kind of job market, especially if one is coming from a small country like Uganda," she chuckled. "I'm sure some of those employers have never heard of Uganda, let alone our National University. But he'll sort it out," she added.

"My whole life suddenly feels too complicated," Ajuna said, standing up to belch.

"It's Kagaba's absence?"

"No, it's not that. Well, not that alone. I guess it's also his family. Kagaba's family setup is complex, Jane; I doubt I was prepared to deal with it. I don't know if it's because I come from a nuclear family myself. Or because Kagaba did not explain things to me from the very beginning."

"Men never warn us, do they?"

"No! So, there's this so-called Ssenga Jovia, whom everyone seems to revere … the one with a special bond with Kagaba."

"The one who made Kagaba miss his flight?"

"Yes. She wants to come to my place."

"What for?"

"Mbu, to look after me as we wait for the baby. I still have at least six weeks to go."

"Oh, Lord. And she will stay for that long?"

"I can't allow that, Jane. I don't even know her that well. I spoke to Kagaba about it."

"And?"

"Well, I could tell he was conflicted about the whole thing. I told you already how close he and Ama are—it's hard to imagine they are step siblings—I can sense Kagaba is worried about upsetting Ama. It's Ama who is insisting on bringing her.

"And then there's my mother. We don't exactly get on like a house on fire, as you know. I think she shouldn't have come this early. She's very headstrong; I don't want to be in her company constantly. She makes one feel like a failure."

"I am so sorry, Ajuna. Don't let all this stuff get to you. They say stress affects the baby as well. Try to keep calm. And, hey, I am here. Let me know if there is anything else I can do."

They were silent as they trained their eyes on the lake, observing more tourists who were busy fishing with trolling rods and a variety of lures. Presently, a group of about five or six came out of the water, hauling an enormous fish, shouting victoriously. It was a gigantic Nile perch, which can grow to more than six feet and weigh an astonishing 400 pounds.

"I wish I had brought my camera." Jane stood up to catch a better view of the huge fish.

"I've never seen one that big! My appetite is whetted, where are these waiters?" Ajuna clapped to catch the attention of a waiter strolling about idly. Smoke from the barbequing sigiris swirled in the air, filling it with the aroma of cooked fish. "Bad service is what greets you everywhere you go in this country. We've been ignored for the past half an hour since we sat here."

The waiter hurried to them. He was dressed in a drab black-and-white uniform. "Can we have two of those?" Jane pointed at the Nile perch that the tourists were holding up for a photo shoot.

The waiter grinned, wondering whether to take Jane seriously or not.

"My friend is now eating for two, as you might have noticed," Jane feigned seriousness. "Okay, if you can't catch the Nile perch, give us two large tilapias. What do you serve it with?"

The waiter relaxed and answered, "Cassava, plantain, tomatoes, avocado ..."

"Bring everything; we're starving," Jane glanced at her watch. "It's three.

"Hey," she called after the waiter, "what about drinks? Can we get one cold beer and a soft drink, please?"

"Yes, madam."

"Yes, madam," Jane mimicked. "He didn't even ask which brands."

Their meal arrived sooner than they had expected. The waiter brought a Bell for Jane and a Fanta for Ajuna. "No serviettes," Ajuna grumbled as she dived in, starting with the salads. They ate with their fingers; not bothering to change their drinks order, knowing it might take forever to arrive.

The fish was grilled to an opaque brown and tasted delicious, with the right amount of spices, salt, and fresh rosemary. Afterwards, Ajuna sat back. She breathed in a waft of the refreshing breeze, feeling her frayed nerves begin to settle, her domestic and pregnancy woes forgotten.

Twilight was beginning to approach when they set off for Kampala. Ajuna threw a last glance at the islands forested with thick, tropical trees, grateful, once again, for the wonderful friend she had in Jane.

When she arrived home, Mayi informed her that Ama had come by. She had persuaded Ssenga Jovia to cancel her trip. Ajuna was glad she had taken a firm stand on the issue.

5

They had been engaged for two or three months when Kagaba said to her: "I must now take you to Hoima to meet my people." By his people, Kagaba meant his father and stepmother, Amooti, Ssenga Jovia, his uncle and his two wives and eighteen children ... Ajuna had already met a few of them when they came to her father's homestead to ask for her hand in marriage. But Kagaba wanted her to visit his home officially.

She arrived late, about midday. People were already gathered. Kagaba had traveled ahead two days earlier. She suspected he wanted to make sure everything was in place. Ajuna walked with care as she approached the big compound, stopping frequently to pull her high heels out of the soft, wet grass. She could hear the murmurs and feel the hundreds of pairs of eyes glaring at her from the crowd under the two tarpaulins erected on either side of the house. In the center, on a small patio, was the Holy Table, its surface laid out with church paraphernalia: a chalice to hold the wine, paten to hold the bread, white linen cloth, candles, and the Sacramentary. Kagaba had not mentioned Mass. What was it for?

It was lucky she had chosen an outfit that would not draw too much attention: a paneled fish-skirt in African print, and a single-colored top. She wore no jewelry, only the engagement ring: a simple, pear-shaped platinum with a natural white sheen. The heels were a mistake. She wanted to enhance her diminutive height. If Kalayi had kept her promise, Ajuna would now be wearing her flamboyant headgear, which would have added a whole inch.

Kalayi was supposed to have picked up the thing from the Congolese tailor the previous evening and helped her fix it early in the morning. Kalayi was even supposed to have accompanied Ajuna, for moral support, so she wouldn't be facing this curious crowd alone. But Kalayi never showed up. She should have asked Jane—the dependable one.

The mud sucked in her stiletto again. As she struggled to raise her foot, she lost her balance and tipped to one side, her left leg suspended in mid-air. She smelled the grass and raw earth rising to her nostrils. Someone was walking, half running toward her. He extended a hand. She clutched on to it and dug her fingers into his flesh to maintain her balance.

"Mr. Kagaba asked me to take you straight to the Holy Table," the young man said to her, keeping her hand in a firm grip. He was wearing a smart blue pin-striped suit with a red tie. "There's a chair already for you, madam," he added with a sunny smile.

The priest was sitting in an armchair flanked by two altar boys, Kagaba on a plastic chair to the right of the Table. Kagaba's father and Amooti occupied the chairs on the left. The vacant chair next to Kagaba was presumably for her. It looked wobbly, and Kagaba bent to check its legs, pushing them firmly into the ground.

"Sit here," he said. "What happened? I thought you were not coming. The priest couldn't wait; he has another Mass elsewhere."

"The road … it was very slippery… and narrow. I had no idea it would be like that, otherwise I'd have left enough time for the journey. I had to tell the driver to go real slow." Her voice trembled. She was still shaken from her near fall.

She recognized Father Bonaventure, the priest who had accompanied Kagaba when he came for the kwanjula ceremony. He looked bulkier, the green-and-yellow chasuble he wore swallowing up his tall stature. She would choose him to wed them, she thought to herself. He had a strong altar presence.

"I rang your phone many times, but it was off. I was sick with worry. I thought that maybe the car had broken down, or worse still, you'd had an accident." She could feel Kagaba's hot breath on her crown. He was still so much taller than her, even in her high heels.

"The network was off most of the time. These rural areas have no signals," she whispered, afraid to attract the attention of the priest. He had paused with his sermon when she walked in. He was talking again, his deep voice making an echo in the vast compound.

"I thought that perhaps your phone's battery was down because of the power cuts," Kagaba continued, like he had not heard her response. She moved slightly away from him and tried to focus her attention on the sermon.

She stole a glance at Kagaba's father. His eyes were fixed on the priest, his face wearing a small smile. She remembered meeting him for the first time during the kwanjula ceremony and thinking how unlike Kagaba he looked. He was short and small; his tiny eyes hidden behind a broad forehead. He looked away when he caught her staring at him.

Amooti had her full attention on the sermon. She was adorned in a shiny dress with matching headgear, which was perched on her head like it was about to fly off. She turned to stare at Ajuna, and the metal earrings that had formed loops around her ears clinked noisily, like charms.

People were bringing their offertory of chickens, sugar cane and fruit to the front, where the two catechists were standing, each holding out a large papyrus basket to receive the gifts. Ama was among them. She placed an envelope into the basket. It must contain some money.

"You look very beautiful, by the way," Kagaba turned to Ajuna, "but why aren't you wearing the headgear? And I thought you were coming with Kalayi?"

"It's a long story. You too look stunning in your suit. The colors suit you, but aren't you burning in this heat?"

"They say smartness knows no weather," Kagaba grinned, and Ajuna laughed with him.

There were about thirty or forty people seated in the bigger of the two tents. Kagaba had not mentioned that there would be so many people! This was supposed to be a family event. The men were smartly dressed in long, white tunics and dark-colored jackets. The women were clad in three-piece traditional outfits with binding scarfs draped over their shoulders. Town people, judging from their demeanor and good clothes.

The occupants of the second tent were largely men and were shabbily dressed, bare-footed, with overgrown beards, their faces partially covered by battered straw hats. The poorer locals. Children carrying other children stood at the edges.

Two women were sitting on the grass behind a clump of banana trees. Ajuna could observe them without their seeing her. They were garbed in bright, mismatched tropical colors. One of them had a baby on her lap and thrust a flabby breast, stretched to the limit from continuous years of breastfeeding, into the baby's mouth. Wasn't the baby going to choke on it? Ajuna wondered.

The second woman was enormously fat. Her black-dyed hair was set in curls and coiled on her head like large caterpillars. She had wound a large, red scarf round her neck in a tight noose and raised her head when speaking, as if she was struggling for air. When she caught Ajuna's eye, she waved, her big face cheery. There was something vaguely familiar about her. Ssenga Jovia! Kagaba had many pictures of her, all of which he treasured. She had brought him up. But why hadn't she attended their kwanjula ceremony? She was tall and dark, like Kagaba, the curve of her full lips like his.

Ajuna's shoes were beginning to pinch. She shifted her weight to one side and leaned on Kagaba's shoulder. The whole thing was taking forever. Her watch showed it was 3 pm.

And then, when she thought it had ended, the young man, Tomas, who had saved her from falling flat on her face, stepped forward, a microphone in his hands. He tapped on its head: "Testing, testing, testing ..." The microphone made a loud echo, and he grimaced. He waited a few seconds and said loudly, "Ladies and gentlemen, on behalf of Mr. Nathan's family, and on my own behalf, I would like to welcome you to this function and to thank you for coming to celebrate with us this very important day ..."

Ajuna's mind switched off. She wanted to eat. She had missed breakfast in haste to arrive on time. She hardly ate her supper. The anxiety to meet her in-laws was palpable.

She turned her attention to the house. Compared to the other houses she saw on her way, this one was bigger. It would require refurbishment to restore it to its former glory, she noted. The corrugated roofing was rusty, the wooden front door had lost its color, and the window frames needed fresh paint.

Mr. Nathan had taken over the microphone and he had a written speech. "We are here to celebrate our son's achievements," he started, then stopped and looked directly at the crowd, as if to make sure he had their absolute attention. Ajuna loved the way he said "our" instead of "my" son.

"Just the other day, Kagaba started school," he proceeded, speaking in a low voice, "and I used to walk him there, fearing the dogs might eat him because he was so small. Just the other day, he completed school. Not only that, but he went up to the highest ladder of education in this country and acquired a degree. Not one, but two degrees." He stopped again and peered at his papers, then continued: "And then, the other day, Kagaba came to tell me he had found a wife and asked me to accompany him to the woman's home to pay the bride price and bring our mugole home. We traveled all the way to the place of the mountains, which is a long way from here. Today, we officially welcome her in our home, in her new home. I have slaughtered a bull and invited you, my friends, my relatives, and my neighbors, to come and eat with us. Welcome!"

As soon as Mr. Nathan ended his speech, Ajuna was swamped with women wanting to embrace her. Children also come to peep at her. The men approached more cautiously, hugging Kagaba first before taking a step back to scrutinize her.

"So, this is our mugole! Thanks for bringing us a woman, Kagaba," they chorused.

Father Bonaventure tried to catch Ajuna's attention, but the mob wouldn't let go of her. "I'll not stay for lunch," he shouted. "I have another engagement. I have to leave now."

Ajuna searched for Kagaba. Where had he disappeared to? It was Ama who rescued her. "Come with me," she said, leading her inside the house. The small living room was teeming with people jostling for space. Young children, their big stomachs visible from their ill-fitting T-shirts, scurried to the wooden table in the center of the room, where saniyas laden with steaming piles of pilau rice, matooke, and meat were placed.

"I'll take you to Kagaba's old bedroom," Ama raised her voice above the hive of activity.

The bedroom was already crammed with people, mostly women. When they saw Ajuna, they started chanting, "Mugole, mugole, mugole. Sit here," they spoke together, making space on the bed.

Ajuna was sandwiched between two women.

"She has ekyasi," one screeched.

"A gap in the front teeth is a good sign," another added.

"It means she smiles a lot and is not quarrelsome."

"No, it means she has strong teeth, strong bones."

"Broad hips; sturdy thighs for childbearing."

"She is fertile. She will give us many sons."

Ajuna frantically looked around for Ama.

"Welcome, my daughter," Amooti appeared in the bedroom, parting the flimsy drapes shielding the room from the narrow, dimly lit passage.

The other women had fallen silent at Amooti's appearance. Then Ssenga Jovia stood up and left the room.

Animosity hung thick in the air, like a rain cloud about to explode.

"Mother!" Ama appeared. "What are you saying to Ajuna, now? Can't you leave her to rest? She's been traveling the whole morning."

"Have I said anything?" she turned on her daughter. "Now that you accuse me falsely, I will say what's on my mind. Ajuna should have—"

"Don't start with her!" the woman who had been breast-feeding her child cried, pointing a finger at Amooti.

Amooti took a few steps toward the woman. "Don't speak to me like that. And who even invited you to our ceremony? You—"

"Mother! Will you please stop it. Come with me," Ama pulled Ajuna to her feet, "I'll take you somewhere else."

"Ajuna should have come with someone else. There, I have said it," Amooti uttered. "That's how things are done in our culture. How can a new bride go to her man's people alone? Doesn't Ajuna have sisters? Or aunties? It's not right. I cannot keep quiet about it."

"Now hear this one," the woman with the breastfeeding baby drew closer. Amooti took a step toward her.

"She is right," another woman spoke in defense of Amooti.

"Let's go." Ama led Ajuna out of the room. She was feeling dizzy and the beginnings of a headache. Outside, she was grateful for the gush of fresh air fanned by the pinnate leaves of the towering mahogany. It stood in the middle of the compound, spreading its massive roots to all corners.

She followed Ama to the back of the house, which was shaded by a short, sagging timber fence. The enclosure was covered in climbing plants, like loofas. Ama removed a key from her purse and opened one of the rooms. It was sparsely furnished with a bed, table, and three plastic chairs.

"This is the boys' quarters. Sit here," Ama pointed to one of the chairs. "I'll go and get you some food. You and Kagaba will sleep here." Ama had gone to a lot of trouble to ensure they would be comfortable. It was amazing how much she looked out for Kagaba's well-being, even at the expense of annoying her mother. "Your bags are over there. And here comes Tomas. He'll keep you company. Tomas is our cousin."

Tomas had removed the sweltering suit and was now dressed in a pair of black jeans and a green shirt, freshly ironed, redolent of Lifebuoy soap.

"Why are you hiding in here?" he asked, "everybody wants to see you." Before Ajuna could respond, the woman who had been breastfeeding her baby entered and sat on the bed. She didn't have her child with her. Tomas eyed her but said nothing.

"Wama for us we love you. We welcome you to our home," she said to Ajuna with a smile. "Just ignore that evil woman. She—"

"Will you stop!" Tomas's tone was threatening. "Just leave her alone, okay?"

The woman didn't take much notice of Tomas. She reached for the sisal bag strapped on her shoulder, and brought out a plastic bag, which she handed to Ajuna. "It's for you, our daughter." She was still smiling as she strode out of the room.

"Who is she?" Ajuna asked, peeping at the fruit in the plastic bag.

"She's our aunt. A cousin to Ssenga Jovia, my father, and Mr. Nathan. She's very close to Ssenga Jovia, though. They are like sisters. She is—"

Before Tomas could continue, Kagaba came through the door. Tomas retreated.

"Are you alright?" Kagaba asked.

She shouldn't have come alone. Amooti was right. "I think we should leave tomorrow."

"Why?" Kagaba sounded perplexed. They had planned

to spend three days. After the welcoming party, they would spend the next two days visiting close family members, neighbors, and friends of the family.

"Don't you like my family? Has anyone mistreated you? Or spoken badly to you?"

"No."

"But what shall we tell my father, and Ssenga Jovia? They had already made plans."

"I can't do this, Kagaba." Ajuna was on the verge of tears. He should have warned her that there would be so many people.

"Why are you being like this? Can I ask Ama to help?"

"No, I just want us to leave."

In the morning, before anyone woke up, Kagaba tapped on his father's bedroom window.

"Are you two leaving?" he sounded shocked.

"Something has come up."

His father said nothing for a while. He was standing on the terrace, where the Holy Table had been the previous day. Presently, he went back inside the house and returned with a chicken.

"Take this chicken then, which your stepmother was planning to cook for you for lunch." He handed Ajuna the rooster. It flapped its wings furiously, like it didn't want to be given away, but its legs were firmly tied with sisal rope. Ajuna held on to it tightly.

"Come and visit us often, Ajuna. This is now your new home. Don't forget about us," Kagaba's father continued.

"She has a busy job, Father. It's not easy for her to get away that often," Kagaba's tone was calm, like he had already explained this fact to his father many times.

The old man's hand jutted out unexpectedly. It was marked with freckles, and it shook in the early morning chill. Tradition did not allow Ajuna to shake hands with her father-in-law, but it would look rude if she ignored him. She started to go down on her knees to take his hand, but he abruptly withdrew it. She stood there, not knowing what to do or say. After a moment, Kagaba took her hand, and they started moving to the car.

"Wait." His father disappeared into the house again and returned with Ssenga Jovia in tow. She was wearing a long, free dress over her nightdress. Kagaba walked back to the patio, took her hands in his, and whispered something in her ear. She started to protest, but Kagaba hushed her up with a hug. She whispered a few more words to Kagaba, before disappearing back into the house. She returned with a parcel wrapped in an old newspaper which she held out to Ajuna. Ajuna walked back to the patio and knelt to receive it. She could tell it was a basket.

"It's endiiro. I weaved it myself. Use it to serve your husband akaro," Ssenga Jovia said, her eyes wet. Ajuna didn't know what to say. She was overwhelmed with gratitude. And guilt. Endiiro seemed like a special gift she didn't deserve after she had pushed Kagaba for them to leave earlier. She thought of Ama and the trouble she had gone through to organize everything. Maybe she should let her know they were leaving. But that would mean waking up the whole household and having to explain.

She put the chicken in the boot, and they got into the car, the basket on her lap. It would be several years before she returned to this home, under very different circumstances.

London

1

The first time they made love took him by surprise. It shouldn't have. Julia returned his call. Kagaba had been pestering her to connect him to another job. After his hand had healed, in February, Julia had found him a job as an on-board train cleaner.

His duties entailed cleaning passenger seats, scrubbing toilets and replenishing toilet paper, picking up litter, and removing graffiti and unauthorized stickers. He worked two shifts, 7 am to 2 pm and 4 pm to 11 pm.

The pay was higher than what he had been earning delivering leaflets, but he hated the train-cleaning job. It was demeaning. It was killing his spirit. He recalled the so-called job interview he had endured. Skills required: Good time management, problem solving, attentiveness, friendliness. *Really?* To clean trains? The company had given him a bonus, free train travel, but he rarely went anywhere. The company had added that they would help further his career in "train-cleaning."

He abhorred the uniform he had to wear while on duty. Someone could easily recognize him and report back to Ajuna. He had told her he was working for a railway company as a sales manager, analyzing sales statistics, developing new sales strategies, and creating budgets.

Had Musana helped him to get the job? Ajuna wanted to know. Yes, in a way, Kagaba disclosed, through his—Musana's—friend. Kagaba prayed Julia would soon connect him to another, decent job.

Julia had called back to say they should meet at her house. She wanted to introduce him to her contact who worked at a hotel in Central London. The contact would fix Kagaba with a job at the same hotel, where he had been working for ages. But they needed to discuss passport renting and commissions.

Kagaba hesitated. Since the night Julia stayed at his house, he had been wary of being alone with her in the same space. Couldn't they meet at a central place, like a café? No, Julia insisted. They were going to discuss private business. Who knows who might be listening to or watching them in a café?

Kagaba needed another job. Julia said that the hotel job would pay better than cleaning trains. April was around the corner; Ajuna's due date was looming.

He had given up on Musana, who was now busy planning his wedding to Sharon. Musana had called to say he could only help find Kagaba a job after the wedding, which was about a month away. He had kept paying rent, even though he now lived with Sharon at her apartment.

Julia said she would make them lunch. It was a Sunday afternoon. Kagaba had a few days off work. So, he went.

The contact never turned up. It started raining. Kagaba drank more wine than he should have.

Sex with Julia was explosive and left him breathless and exhausted. With Ajuna, it had been slow and sweet, yearning for more afterwards. In the morning, when he woke up, Julia had already left for work. There was a note with a picture of Julia, and the number of her contact at the hotel. Kagaba called the man, who said Julia had already finalized the deal with him: Kagaba was expected to start work within two days.

As Kagaba ate the breakfast Julia had left on the dining table, he avoided thinking about what had happened the previous night and, instead, focused on the food in front of him. Julia had prepared African tea—milk, tea leaves, honey, fresh ginger and budalasini—just like the way Ssenga Jovia made it. Julia had added cinnamon, which enhanced the taste. She had also made katogo of matooke, goat's offal, and garden eggs. Kagaba had not eaten such a delicious Ugandan breakfast since coming to the UK.

On the train as he returned to his house, Kagaba finally allowed himself to focus on what had transpired. Did Julia not have a boyfriend already? What about Ochola? Would Ajuna ever get to know? Would there be a repeat?

When he got home, he took out Julia's picture. It was a version of her as a young girl, her face glossy, her small eyes looking away from the camera. She was dressed in a seductive red miniskirt and a low-cut purple blouse.

He found a photo of Ajuna in the drawer next to his bed. He scrutinized the faces of the two women. Julia's had a childish quality around her plump mouth. Ajuna's aura exhibited a sense of maturity and stability, but her smile was tender and unassuming.

He put Julia's picture on top of the drawer and Ajuna's inside but pulled it out again and placed it on the table, next to Julia's. *Stop it, you fool!* he thought.

2

The new job required him to arrive at work before 6 am. The shifts were long and draining, ending at 6 pm, with an hour's lunch break. But the money was good. After the passport owner had taken his cut, what remained was enough to live on, and send some to Ajuna. Musana continued paying rent.

Kagaba told Ajuna he worked in the hotel's marketing department. He was on probation for two months, by which time Ajuna would have delivered and settled in with the baby. He was going to tell her the truth when his probation was over. No more lies.

His relationship with Julia was a puzzle. That he was smitten by her beauty and charm was no secret. Sex aside, their love life didn't feel like that of *real* lovers. They were more like friends. Sometimes, Julia even reminded him of Ssenga Jovia: motherly, caring—scolding.

Was it providence that had brought Julia into his life? She was his hope. His faith. She made him believe that everything was fine just the way it was. In her company, he could assume that being in a foreign country and doing kyeyo jobs was alright. He could pretend that it was fine for expectant Ajuna to be on her own at this critical time, and that his baby would be born in his absence. With Julia, he did not have to lie about anything.

Julia never seemed to mind about his going on about Ajuna and the coming baby. She wasn't jealous. She constantly asked how Ajuna was fairing.

Saturdays were both his and Julia's day off, and they normally went to the Crested Crane, the restaurant where they had first met while celebrating Sharon's citizenship. They would feast on mouth-watering Ugandan cuisine, while the resident DJ played Ugandan music in the background. Julia would pick a random reveler, and together they would pull off provocative strokes on the dance floor, making Kagaba envious.

On other Saturdays, he would accompany Julia to Tottenham to buy matooke and posho and tilapia fish and goat's offal and vegetables from the Ugandan grocery shop. She bought more food than they would need in a month. She was an extravagant cook, and no amount of protestation would change her opinion on food. "We've got to eat properly," she would assert. "Me, I don't eat muzungu food. These guys live on sandwiches—that's a snack, not food. That's why they have weak bones, and that's why they will always need us to do the hard jobs."

She would tell him that, when she first arrived in the UK, she struggled to find her dress size. She was a size eighteen then, but most shops were stocked only up to size fourteen, at most, sixteen.

"My workmates wanted me to lose weight. Me? Why? I was happy with my size. I am now size twenty; shops can stock up to twenty-eight sizes."

After a late night out at the Crested Crane, Kagaba would spend Sundays at Julia's. It was a tiny but neat, and beautifully decorated two-bed council flat in Camden. She had recently moved there from Lewisham. She had painted it herself—in bright, sunrise colors that chased away the gloom of the drab building. She was subletting from the real owner, who occupied the second room. Julia paid only a fraction of the rent.

It was like she reserved Sundays for just the two of them. Kagaba had never encountered visitors, or friends, or the flat mate. As the day drew to a close, Kagaba would struggle to pull himself away. The idea of returning to his hovel after a feast of Ugandan food washed down by red wine wasn't appealing, not to mention an erotic episode as the crowning glory.

Julia always packed for him several wraps of chapatti and beef, or chapatti and chicken, to carry to work in the week. "Add some tomatoes and onions, and mayonnaise in the mornings; keep it in the fridge until lunchtime. What? Ask for a microwave at the hotel, no, they won't mind, I've worked in a hotel before," Julia would instruct him like a mother commanding her child.

This has got to stop, Kagaba would tell himself while on the train back to his squalid quarters. *It is not right. I am engaged to Ajuna. She is carrying my child. What if she finds out? If I leave Julia now, will she take revenge, leaving me jobless again?*

3

It's a girl. The news of his baby's birth came in the form of a text message from Ama. It was about 10 am, and he was at work. He already knew they were having a daughter, because Ajuna had an ultrasound. He dashed to the toilet and called Ajuna's number.

"Hello, Daddy," Ama answered. She was beaming and in high spirits. "Ajuna is still under anesthesia. But both your girls are well. I will call as soon as she's awake."

He wanted to dance or sing or jump. He started calling Kato, but figured he must already know; maybe he should call his father or Ssenga Jovia, but everyone must have heard already. He wanted to break the good news! *God blessed us with a baby girl this morning*—he composed a text message, and scrolled through his phone address—Musana, Sharon, Sean, they would all be at work—and in any case, he hadn't spoken with Musana for ages now. Would he be interested in the news? He sent the text anyway, to everyone. Ochola and Julia were the only ones who called to congratulate him.

By midday, Ama hadn't called back, and he began to get worried. At lunch break, he called Ajuna's number again. She was still asleep, Kalayi informed him, and told him to stop fretting. Everything was fine. He decided to call his father. Yes, of course, they had already heard the good news from Ama. Kagaba asked him to go to the city the following day to see the baby on his behalf. He could even take along Ssenga Jovia. Kagaba would send the transport money through Ama.

"Ajuna will bring the baby to us," his father said. "That's what she promised when Ssenga Jovia wanted to go and nurse her. And that's how it should be."

"Then send Tomas! That's my baby we are talking about; someone else in my family ought to be excited. Tell Tomas to go and see my baby at once. What will Ajuna and her people think? That we are not interested in our own baby?"

His father was adamant. "She will bring the baby to us."

When he finally got to speak to Ajuna, she was still groggy, and they only spoke briefly. "Who does she look like? Ama said she's very beautiful," he asked her.

"I haven't seen her; she's still in nursery," is all he got from her.

On the train back home that evening, he closed his eyes and let the warm, affectionate sensation still gushing through his body since learning of his daughter's birth transport him to the same room at the National Hospital where Ajuna was lying. He smoothed out the hair on his little princess's forehead. He uncurled her tiny fingers; placed her pink cheek against his. Her skin was tender, though still creased. He patted the dimples on her head into shape. Her eyes were tightly closed, sealed with rheum.

This baby was his own blood! If they were to test her DNA, it would match his. He had *created* something. He had added to humanity. Did she cry when the surgeon lifted her out of Ajuna's womb? Did she notice that her daddy was not there to cut the cord and name her?

He contemplated adding a superlative to the message he had composed earlier, something like "prettiest," or "most beautiful" baby girl. Maybe he should append a name, which would distinguish her from the many born in Uganda that day. DAISY, yes, that's what he had decided to call her, like the little daisy flowers born during spring in the UK.

Five days later, he finally received a picture from Ajuna by courier, with an inscription: *AMALA. Born Saturday, 26th April, 2008, at 8.55 am, weighing 3.01 kilograms, measuring 51 centimetres.*

"What kind of a name is that?" Ssenga Jovia fumed when Kagaba called to tell her.

"It's Ajuna's idea; I named her Daisy."

"What does that even mean?"

"It's an English name for a flower."

"No, I mean, 'Amala'?"

"I don't like it myself, Ssenga Jovia, it sounds like a man's."

"My point is, it means 'Enough.' Is that what you want? Just one child? That's a name reserved for lastborns."

At first, Ssenga Jovia was happy that Ajuna had a girl, which surprised Kagaba. He would have expected her to prefer a baby boy, because boys prove a woman's worth and expand the clan and bring home brides to till the land and build houses for their mothers, but a girl?

But Ssenga Jovia reasoned that Ajuna would now be forced to have a second child and, if that turned out to be a girl as well, she might try again, and again, in search of a baby boy.

"I will talk to Ajuna, Ssenga Jovia, and—"

"That's *your* baby ... *our* baby, and we must give her a proper name."

It would have been great to name her after his *real* mother, as Ajuna had suggested when they found out it was going to be a girl. Ajuna said she didn't want to name her after hers, because there were already two nieces named after her mother. But Kagaba didn't want to tell Ssenga Jovia that.

Daisy was growing fast. At just four weeks, Ajuna said she had outgrown the clothes Kagaba had sent. Julia offered to accompany him to the shopping mall to buy more clothes for Daisy. She recommended an outlet near Oxford, where they sold factory rejects at eighty percent off. The journey would take two to three hours by train, but it would be worth it.

They went on a Saturday and were among the first customers to arrive. "If you get there late, the nice things will be gone," Julia had warned.

She was a seasoned shopper, Kagaba saw, as they moved around the vast store. "Don't buy the small ones only," Julia would advise. "The baby will outgrow them quickly; here, let's take these for six months, no, they're not too big, they grow quite fast in the first months."

Julia also insisted that they buy "something nice" for Ajuna. "Look at this handbag. It's a Saint Laurent. These normally go for over a thousand pounds. See," she flipped the label to see the price, "just over thirty pounds with the discounts. Buy it for her."

Next, they relaxed at a MacDonald's for lunch.

"I've never bought anything at full price in this country," Julia chuckled as they ate ice cream. "I just wait it out. For sure, prices are eventually discounted to make room for fresh designs for the new season."

She loved clothes, Kagaba concluded.

Another money-saving trick for special occasions was to pay for an outfit, wear it for the event, then return it to the shop a few days later, saying it was the wrong size or color. She would get a full refund. "See how nice this country is?" she chortled.

It *was* a nice country. But his visa would expire in less than two weeks. Whenever he raised the issue with Musana or Julia, they dismissed his anxiety. What mattered was that he had a job. To sort out papers, he would need lots of money. He had to save first. That's what everybody did. Once he had made enough money, they would help him find an immigration lawyer. Musana would continue paying rent so Kagaba could save for the lawyer.

One Wednesday morning, after negotiating with a Congolese co-worker to switch shifts, Kagaba set off to the University of Greenwich. He wanted to explore his options to study in the

UK. If he secured a place at the university, then he wouldn't have to think of life as an illegal.

He marveled at the sight of the buildings and endless glass-covered walkways. What a wonderful place to study. Compared to the National University in Uganda, Greenwich looked like a mini city, sitting on the banks of Thames. He remembered his claim for obtaining a visa. He was supposed to attend the graduation of his "brother," who had studied at the University of Greenwich. He wondered what had happened to his travel companions, if they had settled in the UK by now.

"Will you be applying as an international student?" The young man at Reception asked to see his passport.

"This is a visitor's visa," the receptionist explained, smiling like he was delivering good news. You'll need a student visa."

Kagaba was encouraged by the man's amiable manner. "How do I get one?"

"You have to return to your country and apply from there," the man said simply. He handed Kagaba a few flyers and brochures with information on how to apply as an international student, courses offered, tuition, and housing and accommodation.

But he could not return to Uganda. Not yet. In two to three months, he would have paid off most of the pressing loans he had accumulated back home; he would have saved enough money to engage an immigration lawyer; he would continue remitting money to support Ajuna and his daughter.

4

It was the last Friday of June. Kagaba woke up feeling lethargic, but managed to make it to work before 6 am, as usual. By lunchtime, however, it was like two logs had been tied to his feet; he was shuffling in the corridors as he moved from one floor to the other cleaning. His head ached, his joints creaked, and his eyes were watering. At about 5 pm, he removed his uniform and told his supervisor he had malaria, just as Julia had once advised him. "If you ever want to pull a sickie, just mention that you have malaria. These guys fear it like it's the plague; they believe it's contagious."

She had also told him what to do when his feet became sore: pretend to have a running stomach. "Sit on the toilet and rest for at least 20 minutes; you are not a machine to be on your feet for over ten hours."

He called Julia, knowing she would be at work at the old people's home. He just wanted to see her, though he wasn't sure what that would achieve.

She met him at the train station and gave him the key to her apartment. "I will try to leave early, and there's some food in the oven."

After he ate the barbequed pork ribs and potato wedges, he lay on her spongy, cozy bed, and wrapped his weary body in the voluminous white duvet. His headache disappeared the moment he placed his head on the feathery pink pillows smelling of lavender. Where did Julia find the time to clean and cook so perfectly? She worked two jobs, Monday to Friday, including most nights. He remembered Ajuna's struggles with the cleaning woman, she herself unable to find the time to do the cleaning.

He did not hear Julia come in. He was in deep slumber when he registered a warm caressing on his still-aching feet. She had wrapped one foot in a hot hand towel, massaging it with her delicate fingers, one toe at a time. "This is the same massage oil I use on my patients," she said, as she pressed each toe. The feeling was heavenly. He fell asleep again, and, in the morning, when he opened his eyes, Julia was still asleep beside him, her head resting next to his on the soft pillow. Sharing the same pillow—something he hadn't noticed before—created an intimacy, a unique connection between them, and the tantalizing sensation of her presence. He pulled her in his arms and fell asleep again.

"Let's get married."

The statement seemed to drop from the sky. He turned to face Julia, to make sure he'd heard properly. They were still in bed. She had brought him breakfast, millet porridge with milk, a Spanish omelet, fresh juice, and fruit. She argued that he had missed supper, hence the big breakfast.

"What did you say?"

"You can move in with me permanently. You don't have to depend on Musana paying your rent. You will save more money for the immigration lawyer. We've been together more than three months now."

"What about Ajuna? And the baby?"

"What about her? As for the baby, didn't I leave my own child in Uganda? The baby will join you once you sort your papers." Her tone was serious, her tiny eyes hard.

"I don't want to get into this conversation now."

She made no comment.

"I think I should leave."

She made no effort to stop him.

5

A man must be prepared for all scenarios, especially when in a foreign country. A man must be ready for all eventualities. If a man falls, he must rise again, learn how to rise.

Kagaba's Saturdays and Sundays began to feel like an ordeal to get through. He had nothing to look forward to. His calls to Julia remained unanswered, unreturned. Ajuna's calls came often, as if on instinct, as if to seal his misery.

"Kagaba," she started one Saturday, and he immediately knew he was in trouble. She never addressed him by name. "Are you cheating on me?"

"Honey, where is this coming from?" His heart was thumping; he feared she might hear it through the telephone line.

"Don't 'honey' me! Do you think I'm stupid? Or a child born yesterday? Who is she?"

"Ajuna, please."

"Shut your mouth, Kagaba." She'd never raised her voice like that, except that time when she had reminded him about living in her apartment and driving her car. They had ended up separating.

"I'm not a fool. There's another woman in your life. You think I don't notice your silences on weekends, lying that you work throughout; or the presents you send me and Daisy. There's a woman helping you with all that!"

"But, Ajuna, that is not true," his voice was hollow, he noticed, shaky with fear.

"I will not tolerate infidelity, Kagaba." There was finality in her tone before she hung up.

That night, sleep eluded him, even after emptying a bottle of wine. Frustrated, perhaps in an attempt to convince himself that Ajuna was still in his life, he yanked out the picture album of their kwanjula ceremony Ajuna had sent him through the mail when he first arrived in the UK.

He had traveled with his father, stepmother, Ama, Kato, Tomas, and Father Bonaventure. The whole delegation comprised twenty-one people. For some reason, Ssenga Jovia did not come with them, which greatly surprised and disappointed Kagaba. He wanted her to be proud of him. He did not want his stepmother to take Ssenga Jovia's place. Throughout the ceremony, he felt disappointed in Ssenga Jovia for choosing not to accompany him to Ajuna's home for the most important event in his life.

The first photos in the album showed the women in his entourage in single file, carrying basketfuls of fruits, food, and meat. The baskets were decorated with pink ribbons that formed beautiful spirals. The men carried crates of beer and sodas, and, right behind them, two young men were pulling a cow and three goats by ropes.

Another picture showed the spokesperson handing over a rooster to Ajuna's brother Jimmy, who was attired, like them, in a white tunic and navy-blue coat.

Jimmy had been appointed the official muko; his role was to introduce Kagaba's group to Ajuna's parents and family. His payment for the service was the cockerel. He was already stationed at the enclosure when they arrived. After leading them to the compound where the ceremony was to be held, he said to his father, "Father and all the elders here present, these are my visitors. Please welcome them. I beg you to listen to what they have to say."

"Do you know them well, then?" the spokesperson for Ajuna's family asked.

"Yes, sir. I know them very well. They are good people, and they come with good intentions." He held up the cockerel for everyone to see.

"Let them be seated and we shall listen to what they have to say."

The presents for Ajuna's family were all symbolic tokens, because her father had refused a formal bride price. It would have entailed too much haggling over how much to pay him in exchange for his daughter's hand in marriage. The goats would go to the women in the family—one to Ajuna's grandmother; another to her mother; the third to her paternal aunt—for the role the three women had played in Ajuna's upbringing. The cow was for her father and other male relatives.

The next set of photographs showed Ajuna walking into the compound in the company of her bridesmaids, who included Kalayi, Jane, and three of her cousins. They were dressed in soft-pink gomeses, and Ajuna's face was veiled with a white shawl, to distinguish her from her escorts.

Kagaba managed a smile as he flipped through the pictures that had captured that scene, remembering the Kadodi playing in the background. Kalayi and her three cousins danced to its frenzied tune, as they escorted Ajuna into the compound, throwing their hips and buttocks in the air, thrusting their breasts forward.

Afterwards Ajuna and her bridesmaids sat on the mat facing Kagaba, his father, and Kato, who was acting as his best man. Ajuna kept her eyes lowered. She should not look directly in the eyes of her husband-to-be—lest the gesture suggest she was an over-confident woman who would not bend to her husband's will.

Ajuna was asked to confirm that Kagaba was her chosen husband and, without lifting her head, she answered in the affirmative in a muted voice—the only words she would be uttering during the whole ceremony.

The next few photos showed Kalayi and Jane helping Ajuna

to her feet. They walked up to Kagaba, and Ajuna garlanded him. The crowd had burst into thunderous applause. He was also asked if Ajuna was the woman he had come to take as his bride. In answer, he unveiled her. There had been more clapping and ululation.

More pictures showed Ama handing Ajuna a bouquet of flowers: a symbol of friendship to a prospective sister-in-law. He handed Ajuna a suitcase containing dresses, shoes, perfumes, and lingerie—to prove his ability to dress his bride.

At last, the formalities were done with, and they became husband and wife in the eyes of the family and community, and under the Ugandan traditional marriage law. Many pictures captured the moment. The bright skyline, suffused with blue and silver, lent a beautiful background to the images: Ajuna, beaming with joy at the camera, her eyes luminous, her hair in a tall pile, adding about an inch to her diminutive stature. Kagaba's right hand on her shoulder, cheek to cheek, grinning with contentment.

This form of traditional marriage, however, allowed for a second wife, even a third. That's why Ajuna's father had asked Kagaba to commit to a Christian wedding, which would prevent him from marrying another woman. Their spokesperson gave the date. At the time, Kagaba was certain he would honor his promise. His dreams of finding a remunerative job had still been intact, his faith uncorrupted by disappointments and skepticism, his commitment to Ajuna as his only woman unquestionable.

And now? There were no more certainties.

6

Musana surprised him with a call to invite him to his wedding preparatory meeting to Sharon.

Sharon's apartment was in Hackney. Kagaba got there late, having boarded the wrong bus. He should have taken the 277. When he finally got on the right one, they were held up in the evening rush-hour traffic and he arrived toward seven. At the elevators of the highrise, he halted, waiting for a group of menacing-looking, hooded teenagers to go up first.

When the elevator returned, he identified himself on the buzzer and entered. The elevator was wide and filthy and stank of urine; the floor strewn with empty beer cans, paper bags, even a used condom.

He entered through the back door and found himself standing in a tiny kitchen. He was immediately engulfed in strong whiffs of roasting, frying, and steaming flavors. Julia sprang out of nowhere. A cheery smile spreading from her eyes to her mouth and his legs went weak. He took a deep, slow breath, letting out air through his nostrils. After a few seconds, he stabilized and returned her smile.

"Hello," she said. "Come in, you're late, the meeting started already." She threw him a playful glance. He tried to read the expression in her eyes. Did she want him back?

He followed her as she led him through the kitchen door to the small reception room, already crammed with people. Some were squeezed in on a big leather couch. Others perched on its armrests or sat on the carpet; a few on dining chairs wedged between the TV and hi-fi. A tower fan in the center cooled the crowded room.

Musana acknowledged his arrival with a brief nod and continued addressing the gathering. Kagaba took the only chair that was unoccupied, next to Musana.

Julia left the room but soon returned to ask if he needed anything to drink. Her flowery perfume hit Kagaba in the face and he almost put out his hand to embrace it; to hold it in his hands and store it in the pores of his skin so he could smell it whenever he wished to. She came back with a can of Stella beer and handed it to him. She left the room again, swinging her hips flamboyantly.

"The most important expense has been taken care of," Musana said, glancing at Kagaba to include him in the discussion, but also to give him an eye to say he had caught him staring at Julia's buttocks.

"The money was delivered to Pastor Moses two days ago—all of it—one thousand pounds."

"Excuse me, what was the money for?" a woman who was sprawled on the carpet asked.

"Pastor Moses asked for a fee to wed us," Musana explained. "Standard procedure for people who don't have the right papers. It's like he's doing us a favor, really. The mainstream churches would never marry us without asking to see our passports first."

"But all that money!"

"This fellow is taking a big risk. If the authorities found him out, he could be deported back to Kenya," Musana explained.

That seemed to silence the querying woman and, after a while, Musana continued to give the report on the progress of the wedding plans. Invitation cards: done and ready for distribution. People at this meeting will be given five each to invite their friends and families. In total, two hundred guests will be invited. Catering: deal finalized with Nalongo's Catering Services in Edmonton. This is where the wedding reception will take place. Ugandan food and beer will be served. Entertainment: a troupe has been hired to perform traditional Ugandan music at the reception. Pledges: He started reading a long list of people who had pledged to make a financial contribution and how much had so far been collected. More money had been raised through fundraising activities, such as barbeques and raffle tickets. The total budget for the wedding came to six thousand pounds.

"It's too much money," a man to Kagaba's right grumbled.

"Summer is a peak period for weddings when service providers hike their fees." This explanation came from Sharon.

Kagaba dipped his hand in his pocket and brought out his wallet to honor the pledge he had made to Musana on the phone.

The meeting ended, and food was being served. A plate cost ten pounds; the proceeds would go toward the wedding budget. Drinks were on the house, and someone had brought waragi, which was given out generously.

"How's the job at the hotel?" Musana asked. They had moved to the balcony and placed their steaming plates on the wooden terrace rail. They ate while standing. Some people were seated on plastic chairs that had been brought over to the balcony, their plates on their laps. A few had remained in the reception room, while others could be heard chatting in the kitchen. Sharon was moving about, making sure everyone was comfortable and served.

Before Kagaba could answer, two women, one dressed in a kitenge with vibrant colors and heavy jewelry, walked up to them. "Is this Julia's new man?" the colorfully adorned one asked in Luganda.

"Yes," Musana answered. The response amused the two women, and they began giggling. The one who had not spoken moved on, but the other lingered. Musana sensed she had more to say and excused himself, saying he was going to grab a drink.

"How long have you and Julia been an item?" she grinned at Kagaba encouragingly. "How long have you been in London?" she continued, the smile never leaving her face.

"About nine months."

"Oh, you're still a novice. I've been here thirteen years. I've never been back to Uganda since." She had switched to English, but her brazen manner made Kagaba uncomfortable. "I know Julia quite well. We shared a room when she first came."

"I thought it was with Sharon."

"That was after living with *me*."

Kagaba regretted having encouraged the conversation. She seemed not to like Julia very much.

"Well, I wish Julia all the best," she pronounced with a smile that did not reach her eyes. "I might be going to Uganda this summer, in case you have anything to send back home."

"We'll see," Kagaba said cautiously. He hoped she would leave him alone. He looked around for a familiar face, for Julia. Where had she disappeared to?

"I understand."

"Eh?"

"I said I understand if you have no money to send back home. It's not easy to save. In this country, we spend money faster than we make it. People back home don't understand that. If I told you my own story, you'd be shocked. I used to send money to my sister. First, to buy me a plot of land and, when she said she had bought it, I started sending money to build a house, but it all ended up in her stomach. Now that she knows I've sorted my papers and will be coming home soon, she's taken cover. She hopes I will not find her."

Musana returned with two small bottles of waragi. He handed one to Kagaba, ignoring the talkative woman. She got the cue and shuffled away without saying another word.

"What was she saying to you?" Musana asked. "She's a dangerous woman. Talks like a parrot, which means if she has nothing to say, she makes it up. Be wary of her."

"Who's she?"

"Her name is Nambozo. Actually, she's from your wife's hometown. She's been here a long time, but she has no friends. People say she's a police informer. She tells on people who don't have papers, and the police pay her for it. She has much more money than anyone else I know, and she's bought lots of property back home. I don't know who invited her. I don't like her. As I said, steer clear of her."

Kagaba was panicking. Nambozo might know Ajuna! They could have gone to the same primary school, or they could even be relatives. Did she tell Ajuna about Julia?

"I'm only doing this wedding for the papers," Musana stated. "Once everything is sorted, I'll bring over my children—and their mother. Sharon and I ... well ... I'm not really into her."

Kagaba wondered if it was the booze talking. They had moved to the furthest corner of the balcony, but he still worried that someone might listen in on their conversation and tell Sharon.

"She's never remarried; I mean the mother of my kids. Our problems began after I lost my job. She didn't have the patience to stand by me during the hard times. But I truly loved her, and I still do."

"I thought she had returned to Rwanda?" Kagaba lowered his voice.

"She did, but only for a short while. Things did not work out as she had planned, and she recently returned to Uganda. I've been in touch with her already, and she's willing to join me—if I can arrange for her to come over.

"Don't breathe a word of this to anyone. I don't want Sharon getting suspicious. I'll bring the kids first. But Home Office keeps introducing more stupid new regulations. Now they insist that any child coming into this country from overseas must have their DNA tested first, to prove the relationship between the inviting parent and the child."

"But DNA tests can be done in Uganda?"

"Yes. Except at the moment, they have run out of testing materials and the samples have to be sent to South Africa, which doubles the cost."

Kagaba was still thinking about Nambozo and how she had come to know about Julia and himself. He thought Julia had kept it a secret.

He was getting bored. He didn't know any of the faces. He approached a cluster of four people and joined in their conversation. They were making plans to attend the kasiki party, which had been arranged for Thursday night, two days before the wedding. The more they discussed the kasiki, the more he grew angry for having contributed fifty pounds to a bogus wedding.

He was ready to leave. He called Julia's number but, as usual, it went straight to voicemail.

"Hello, again," Ochola said as he walked toward him.

"Hello," Kagaba was happy to see him. "I haven't seen you in a while."

"Studies," he laughed. "This is my final semester, and my supervisor has turned from being lazy to being impatient. I've been working flat out to submit the last chapters within the impossible prescribed deadlines. But we should meet again before I return to Uganda. Let me know when you're free and I'll pick you up."

"I will, thank you."

"Well, I should be on my way now. I only dropped by to pay my pledge. Julia pestered and pestered, saying Sharon was her best friend and we should all support her. Are you still around?"

"Yes." He had already decided. He would not leave without seeing Julia.

He went back inside, walked through the reception room and stood by the banisters, listening to the loud female cackles coming from the bedroom above. He continued up the stairs. When he reached the landing, he pressed his ear to the bedroom door and singled out Julia's silky voice. The booze he had swallowed all evening lent him confidence and spurred him into action. Without bothering to knock, he swung the door open.

Julia was sandwiched between two other women on the large bed. They were sipping beers and eating goat muchomo.

Julia beamed when she saw him. "Look who's here!" She slurred. Her eyes flashed mischievously in the dim glow of the orange bulb. "Come and sit next to me."

The other two women moved to create space on the bouncy mattress, but Julia elbowed them further away, urging them to leave the bed altogether. After they moved out of the room, Julia stood up and moved to where Kagaba was standing. She smelled of booze and perfume. She led him to the bed. She sat down and straddled her right leg across his thigh, resting her head on his shoulder. Her body exuded a sexiness.

She turned his face to hers and kissed him fervently on the mouth, sucking out his breath. Her mouth tasted delicious, and he wanted more, even when it felt like she was suffocating him. She pressed her full breasts against his chest.

Within moments, they were tumbling about in the sheets, flinging off their clothes, tossing them on the carpet. When their naked bodies touched, it ignited a fire that had lain dormant for months. He was on top of her, sliding in and out of her wetness, gently at first, but the fire inside him pushed him to aggression, matching Julia's crazy gyrations.

Afterwards, he lay still, listening to her gentle breathing.

It had all happened so fast and so blissfully. Like they had never been apart. He peeped at her sleeping face and wondered what had caused her to snub him. Was it because he refused to marry her?

He should leave. He got out of bed and dressed, then let himself out of the room. The house was quiet; only a few people were still on the balcony. Musana and Sharon were sitting on the couch side by side, drinking more waragi. He ducked behind the door when he thought he saw Sharon turn to look in his direction, but she shifted her attention back to Musana and started kissing him frantically. In a minute, Kagaba was out into the dark night.

A kaleidoscope of thoughts whirled through his mind as he sat on the bus. Ajuna. They had not spoken since the phone call, more than a week ago. He feared calling her, imagining she would detect the lies in his voice. And she had not called him again.

Julia. Suppose he had made her pregnant? She had insisted on protection since they started dating, but he wasn't too sure about this last episode. She must be on the pill, surely.

A sense of revulsion over his affair with Julia consumed him. What had possessed him? How could he betray Ajuna again, after the silent promise he had made to himself? He shut his eyes and breathed out to expunge all thoughts of Julia.

By the time he reached his house, it was after midnight. He crawled into bed, not bothering to undress. As he lay down, his phone pressed on his hipbone. Before placing it on the small table by his bed, he glanced at it, hoping for a missed call. There was a message from Julia. *Where did u run off 2? p'se kol me ASAP*. He toyed with the phone, weighed down by indecision. Finally, he put it away.

The week that followed, he resisted calling Julia, despite several messages from her. After the encounter at Sharon's apartment, the hot desire to have sex with her had ebbed. What he felt now was deep regret.

The day before the kasiki party, Musana called to say that the party had been canceled. Rumors had started spreading that immigration officers had been tipped off by an informer and that they planned to raid the wedding venue to arrest those without papers. Fingers pointed at Nambozo.

Musana was furious. He said he would make Nambozo pay for ruining his party.

"What about your other friends?" Kagaba asked.

"Which ones?"

"Like the ones who were at Sharon's flat? Were they all illegals?"

"Not all of them. But you will get to understand these things, my friend. The ones who are okay keep away from us. They don't want to get involved with our baggage."

"What baggage?"

Musana grunted but did not speak.

"What about the troupe? I thought you had already paid them," Kagaba pressed on.

"They have papers, yes, but no license. They need a work permit to perform officially."

The wedding almost didn't happen. Many of the invitees absented themselves, including Julia. The reception venue was changed; Pastor Moses offered his church hall but forbade them to serve any alcohol. The venue was small and crammed with plastic chairs and tables. The decorations were hastily done and looked out of place on the plastic furniture. The Ugandan troupe hired to perform also kept away. Instead, a DJ played some bad music, a mixture of Congolese and Ugandan songs.

Kagaba felt an obligation to attend. Musana still paid his rent. He prayed that the police would not turn up.

Musana looked dapper in a tuxedo, and Sharon wore a long, cream skirt and a see-through top, like a fish net. Her make-up was so heavy that it made her look like a different person.

The food was plenty, though not well cooked, because the hired catering service didn't come either. The matooke looked lumpy on the plate, and the soupy, plain meat, cooked by Sharon's friends, was tasteless. But Kagaba pretended to eat with zest not to offend his hosts.

Later, they all joined in performing the conga dance, in which dancers in snake formation placed their hands on the waist of the dancer in front of them. The dancers slithered about the room in a zigzag single line, following the DJ, who was leading them as he beat the drum strapped across his chest. The frenzied dance excited everyone, but with no alcohol to sustain the excitement, people left early.

As Kagaba walked to the train station, his phone gave a lyrical beep, announcing the arrival of a message. He waited until he got home before reading the text. It was from Julia, asking him to call her. He should delete her number.

7

It being August, when summer is at its peak, meant that London was swarming with tourists. Every day the hotel registered full capacity. Nowadays, Kagaba took painkillers to get through the day; his back was constantly sore.

The passport owner had also become greedy and demanded a higher commission. Kagaba would have gone back to Julia, so she could talk to the man, but he wanted to cut her out of his life entirely.

His fortnightly remittance to Ajuna had decreased. And so had the baby toys he sent along for Daisy. Ajuna's terse responses to his messages showed that she still had no desire to talk to him, and he only did it for the sake of Daisy. Ajuna might have found out more about him and Julia—probably from that woman Nambozo, who must have traveled to Uganda by now.

He was struggling to get by. He had gotten used to Julia's food and other comforts. If Musana wasn't still paying his rent, he would have been thrown out by now. He needed to find another job.

He approached Sean, though their friendship had remained lukewarm in the past months. "I can ask my sister Emily; she might be able to help. Like I said, she runs a company that supports African issues," Sean offered.

Emily invited them for lunch the following Sunday—she still lived with their parents.

Kagaba selected his clothes with care, opting for a dark-red shirt, black trousers and wine-red tie. He hesitated over the black jumper. It would not go down well with his smart attire, but it might get cold. He settled for a maroon jacket with a red carnation on the left lapel, hoping it would not make him look overdressed.

When Sean saw him, he suppressed a giggle. "You're not going for lunch with the Pope. It's only my family. And it's summer, for Lord's sake! Why the jacket?"

Kagaba tried to make light of his joke, but he was nervous. His biggest fear was that Emily would want to see his passport—and then see his expired visa.

"Don't worry about my sister one bit," Sean eased his anxiety. "She's an easy girl. My dad's a sweetheart, and my mum is okay. It's my mother's sister you should worry about. She came to live with us a few years ago, after her husband passed away. She's the eldest of our mother's siblings but looks the youngest. She can be a bit annoying. She gets on well with Emily, though."

The house was a detached brown-brick bungalow. The garden was neatly kept, sprouting beds of marigolds, their golden petals swaying in the soft breeze. Sean glided to a stop at the head of the driveway, designed with natural stone.

The front door was not locked, so Sean let them in. It felt hot inside. Two sets of leather couches, set in a semi-circle, and two glass coffee tables, spotless, as if they were brand new, took up most of the spacious living room. In one corner, pillar candles created pools of light and emitted a delicate, sweet fragrance.

Kagaba stood in the center of the open, wide space, at least ten times the size of the crumpled quarters he called home, wondering where everybody was. Sean had gone straight upstairs. After some minutes, he sat down on one of the couches.

"Ah, there you are."

Kagaba turned to see a plump woman wearing a gray skirt with large box pleats and a transparent nylon blouse with tiny embroidered red flowers on one side of the breast. He stood up and the woman grinned at him, exposing nuggets of golden fillings in her front teeth.

"We're used to Emily bringing home friends, but not Sean. He doesn't have many friends. He's reserved and a bit, well, a bit weird," she dropped her voice conspiratorially. "He told us you're housemates?"

"That's right," Kagaba answered, taking his seat again. His hostess remained standing.

"And you are from Africa?"

"Uganda."

"Is that in Africa?

"That's correct."

"Would you like some tea?"

"Yes, please." He did not want to drink anything hot. He wished he was dressed in a T-shirt and jeans.

"Milk?"

"Yes."

"Sugar?"

"Yes."

"How many sugars?"

"Ah ... two."

"Two?" she frowned.

"I mean one, just one, please."

"But you're sweating, would you like to start with water?"

"Yes. A glass of water would be okay." He was beginning to feel awkward. He could hear someone speaking on the phone, perhaps Emily. But where was Sean?

"Sparkling or still?"

"Still."

"Would you like it cold or room temperature?"

"Cold, please."

The woman returned with a glass of water and placed it on the coffee table.

"So, what's Africa like? I'd love to visit someday. Perhaps Emily will take me along on one of her trips."

He sipped at the water; it was tepid, and he could tell it was from the tap. Since coming to the UK, he had never drunk tap water. He always bought it bottled or boiled it first and kept it in a jug in the fridge. Before he could reply, Emily walked into the living room.

"Hello there, you must be Kagaba," she said brightly. "Come, let's sit outside. It's nice and breezy, and we shouldn't be cooped up in the house."

He followed her outside, abandoning the glass of water.

"My aunt can be effusive; don't mind her. She always means well but she doesn't know how to show it. Her name is Abby, by the way. She doesn't like being called aunt. She says it makes her feel anonymous. Sean can't stand her. I'm sure he's hiding somewhere in his old bedroom. My parents have gone to church. Can I offer you a drink?"

Kagaba laughed.

"What's so funny?"

"A fruit juice please, and I …" He was uncertain how to put it, but Emily made him feel comfortable and he was beginning to relax. "I hope you won't take me through a litany of all sorts of brands on offer."

"Oh, you mean Abby did that? I'm so sorry."

"Don't be sorry. It's just a different culture here. Back home, it is taboo to ask a visitor what they want to eat or drink. You just offer what you have, and it's impolite for the visitor to decline. In any case, there isn't as much choice. I mean … tea is tea and water is water."

Emily laughed with him, nodding. She wore her black hair in a crisp bob, which covered her nape and ears. They sat on the garden chairs, and he poured a cranberry juice from the selection of packs on the table. It was cooler outside, contradicting the weather forecast for the day which had predicted a maximum of twenty-four degrees Celsius.

"My parents will be here soon and then we'll have lunch," she explained. She was wearing a flowing, wide-sleeved dress, like a caftan, with little elephants and zebras printed in jade. When she caught him admiring it, she said she had bought it in Tanzania on one of her working trips with her company, Africa Beyond.

"How many countries do you operate in?" Kagaba seized the opportunity to bring up the subject of his visit.

Emily's face lit up. She began reeling off facts and figures. The company had charitable status; its goal was to temper constant images of famine, disease, and war with the more beautiful side of Africa. She shared an office in Central London with another charity, three years after starting up, and was planning to open an office in Botswana.

"I'm not really an academic; maybe I shouldn't even have bothered with a PhD. I love working with people, not theories, and Africa has always inspired me. So, I set up AB. I wanted to tell Africa's other story—what is usually left unsaid by the media."

She wanted to know more about Kagaba's life in London. He told her about Julia helping him to find odd jobs. Emily reckoned Julia must be a kind person. Kagaba agreed. Their fling aside, Julia had acted with kindness toward him, and helped him settle in a new place, which is what he had expected from Musana. A bit of him would always remain indebted to Julia.

Emily's eyes became teary listening to his hardships since arriving in the UK. "And you've not even met your daughter; you must miss her, and your fiancée, and all your family." He showed her Daisy's picture that he kept in his wallet, and she said his daughter resembled him.

Her parents came through the back door into the garden. The mother was tall and skinny, her pointy nose cut in two by a deep groove in the middle, making it look like she had two noses. She smiled at Kagaba reservedly and took the chair next to her daughter.

Their father was a big man, but frail with age. His hair had gone completely white, but the eyebrows had retained their blackness and looked misplaced, like they were younger than his other features. "You alright?" he murmured, before excusing himself to go inside. He came back moments later with Sean trailing behind him.

Sean remained standing when his mother indicated the vacant chair next to Kagaba with her bony forefinger. No one else had ginger hair like Sean's, and, after they had all sat down at the big dining table for the Sunday roast, Kagaba couldn't help thinking that, somehow, Sean did not fit in with the rest of his family.

Their talkative, spritely aunt occupied everyone with conversational chatter, and Emily tried to draw Kagaba in.

"Which other parts of Africa have you been to?" she asked.

"I'm afraid none."

"What a shame!" Abby interjected. "From what Emily tells us, and from the pictures I've seen, Africa is a truly awesome place. The landscape and wildlife are breathtaking." She opened her blue-green eyes wide.

The mother looked impressed; the father raised his dark, bushy eyebrows. "You're not interested in a little tourism in your own continent then?" he asked.

"It's very expensive to travel within Africa, Dad," Emily said.

"But there are many Ugandans who travel to come here," chirped Abby. "Look at those poor fellows who attempt to cross the Mediterranean in makeshift rafts. Emily, do you remember that documentary we watched on Channel 4? About those hapless families trying to cross borders hiding inside freezer trucks."

"Abby, the things you mention—that's what AB wants to change. Nearly a quarter of the grapes we consume in this country come from South Africa. And we get most of our cocoa products from Ghana; Kenya supplies us with tea; Morocco, tomatoes; bananas and coffee come from Uganda." Emily was ticking off the items on her fingers. "But the mainstream media is not interested in reporting on that."

"Maybe that documentary was shot somewhere else,"

Kagaba interjected. "Uganda is a landlocked country; the closest sea, the Indian ocean, is …well … thousands of miles away."

"But Uganda is in Africa, no?" the mother asked.

"There are more than fifty countries in Africa. You make it sound like, like …" Emily was getting agitated. Sean stood up and asked if anyone cared for dessert.

After the meal, Abby cleared the dishes. She packed them in the dishwasher, refusing any offers of help from Emily and her mother. The parents said they were going to take their afternoon nap; Abby wanted to continue with her knitting.

It had turned chilly. Emily went upstairs to fetch her shawl. When she returned to the living room, she offered him a cup of coffee, which he declined.

She looked tired and kept raising her thick eyebrows—the only feature she seemed to have inherited from her father—like she was trying to shake off sleep. She still had to prepare for an early-morning meeting. And there was an upcoming trip to Botswana in a week's time. She curled up on the sofa like a cat and, before long, she was snoring.

Not knowing what else to do with himself, Kagaba observed her sleeping form for a while. Sprawled out on the sofa like that, she looked like a little girl. He wondered how old she was.

Sean came into the living room and took the seat next to his sleeping sister. "Perhaps we should just leave," he said. "Emily's likely to sleep the whole evening, and I have to prepare for work tomorrow."

"What about your parents and Abby? Shouldn't we say goodbye?"

Sean was dismissive. "I'll call them later. Let's go."

They left without taking leave of anyone, which Kagaba thought odd.

Also without discussing job prospects with Emily.

8

Had the Jubilee Line trains not been canceled, and had it not rained the whole night into the early hours, Kagaba would not have witnessed what happened to Julia that Monday morning at Stratford train station. Having taken the overground from Deptford to London Bridge, he planned to board the Jubilee Line, which, ordinarily, would have taken him straight to Bond Street, near where Emily's office was located.

He was due to meet Emily at 10 am. She had called him following their visit with Sean the previous week, and apologized for having fallen asleep before they could conclude. "Sean should have woken me up," she complained.

Emily wanted to introduce him to the chair of the Africa Beyond board, a Mr. Joseph Masego from Botswana. Mr. Masego was the founding director of Archway Talent, a recruitment agency. Mr. Masego's core focus lay in Africa. He traveled around the continent looking for young, talented graduates.

"I've told him about you, and he is keen to meet and interview you. Who knows? You're young and qualified. And he is a nice man," Emily assured Kagaba.

"I was lucky he agreed to chair my board. He brings loads of experience and insight to Africa Beyond. He is in London for just a brief period. He is heading back to Botswana the next day."

On reaching London Bridge, Kagaba learned that the Jubilee Line was suspended due to a signal failure. His first reaction was that of alarm. He had timed his journey to precision. The ride from London Bridge to Bond Street would take him just under ten minutes—five stops. He would then walk five blocks east of the traffic lights, do a right, and there, facing him, would be Millennium House, where Africa Beyond had its offices. He had rehearsed the journey a week ago, the day after Emily had confirmed the meeting.

Think, think. He approached the uniformed man directing stranded passengers to alternative routes and asked him how to get to Bond Street.

"You can take the replacement bus," the man began to say, but Kagaba dismissed his suggestion.

"I need to take a train. They are faster and I already bought my one-day travel card, here," he pulled it out of his jacket and flashed it in the man's face.

The man smiled and said, "You can use the same ticket on a bus, and—"

"You don't understand," he cut him off midsentence. "I'm going for a job interview. It's very important to me."

"I'm sure it is, but—"

"I know how to get there by train, not by bus." He was speaking in a rush, encouraged by the man's attentiveness.

"Then you need to go to Stratford and change to the Central Line. It will carry you to Bond Street." The man handed him an underground map.

He still had plenty of time, so the disruption wouldn't cost him. He had woken up at five and the interview wasn't until ten. He felt vindicated for having acted with prudence.

Fifteen minutes later, he was at Stratford station. It was big and confusing. Tens of arrows pointed everywhere. To Platforms 1 and 2, then to 5, 8, and 10, to the Jubilee Line, to the National Rail. Announcements buzzed repetitively in his ears: *Please do not leave items of luggage on the train or at the train station. Please note that for security reasons this train station is monitored twenty-four hours by CCTV cameras. Please mind the gap between the platform and the train.*

Finally, he saw the arrow pointing to the Central Line and

followed it, but after a wrong turn, he found himself outside in a wide yard, facing the main entrance to the train station.

It was pouring with rain. He ducked for the bus terminal, which was protected from the showers with elegant, inverted cone canopies. He stood under the beautiful awnings and thanked whoever it was that had designed it to protect bus commuters and stranded passengers like himself from the erratic British weather.

The sign reading *Stratford Station*, originally emblazoned in silver, had paled to almost gray due to pollution. Multidirectional finger signposts pointed travelers to various destinations: to Stansted Airport, to Newham, to the University of East London. Red double-decker buses in their tens arrived and departed from the bus terminal, ferrying people to their places of work.

Throngs of human traffic buzzed by. Arab women draped in burqas, some Africans in African garb. A few white women dashed by, slicing the tarred yard with their impossibly highheeled shoes.

He glanced at his watch. Twenty minutes past eight. Still plenty of time to kill. He was beginning to feel groggy from lack of sleep, yet he had to remain focused and alert for the interview. Wind blew water into his face—the rain was not letting up. He took note of his surroundings: a fruit stall to the left; across the road a Burger King, Subway, and other eateries. Stratford Centre.

A man walked up to him. "Good morning, sir, can you spare me some change?"

"Change?"

"Yes, for a pint." His skin was white like ash, his clothes ragged and dirty, his long hair tangled in knots.

A preacher came next, shouting out the name of Jesus, his woman companion handing out leaflets. She thrust one into his hands. *Jesus Is Real*, it read. Rainwater fell on the leaflet and washed away its color.

More people continued to pour into the station. They marched zealously, their heads raised, their eyes focused, their faces stiff, like masks. Men blurred into women, young into old. No one recognized one another.

Back home, it was different. If you walked on Kampala Road at a busy hour, a familiar voice of a friend of a friend, or a relative of a workmate, or a sister of a neighbor, will shout a greeting. "Ki kati?" The man behind the newspaper stall might engage you in conversation as you wait to cross the street; a hawker will grin in a friendly manner and ask about your family while trying to sell you a pair of second-hand shoes. Or you might bump into a former classmate, who will ask, "Obulamu?" How's life treating you?

Nostalgia filled his head. Time to move. He would have to brave the downpour. Suddenly, a loud cry pierced the air: "Mama nze nfudde!"

Was it still homesickness playing havoc in his head? The scream was followed by another, "Munyambe!" Help. "Banange munyambe!" Please help. "Bambi munsonyiwe!" came the supplication for mercy.

The words echoed across the yard in flowing Luganda. He had last seen Julia at Sharon's apartment, but there was no mistaking who had spoken the words.

He immediately picked her out of the crowd. She had broken into a run after realizing that she was being chased. She was throwing furtive glances over her shoulder, her stilettos making it impossible to make any progress, and her screams of munyambe were growing fainter.

People scattered, trying to avoid a head-on collision. She had started negotiating the stairs leading up to the station when her heel got stuck; as Kagaba was about to reach her, she came cascading down in a heap, hitting her head on the sharp edge of a step. She wasn't moving.

He fell on his knees, called her name, and framed her bleeding head with his hands. A chunk of her flesh protruded through the gauzy, lilac blouse she was wearing.

"Don't interfere, please keep away, this is an immigration case, we're immigration officers." A female officer flashed the ID card connected to her belt.

"She's my friend. I know her. Her name is Julia. She's from Uganda. Please don't let her die!" Kagaba yelled. The female officer pressed closer. "Did you say you know her?"

"Get lost, brother," a second officer said, close to his ear. "This is an immigration offense. She was trying to run away. We followed her from Forest Gate." Kagaba looked into the black man's eyes. "Do you want to get mixed up in this mess? If you're wise, you'll leave now," he hissed, brandishing handcuffs.

Everything became blurry. Kagaba thought he heard the siren of an ambulance approaching. He imagined the black officer was trying to handcuff him. Then he believed he saw Julia's handbag fly out of her wobbly hands and land on his feet, and before he could reach for it, the female officer dashed for it and secured it tightly under her arm.

People were not milling around her or trying to offer help like they would do back home. They walked by purposefully, skirting the scene of the accident and avoiding looking at the spot where Julia lay, comatose.

The paramedics placed her on a stretcher and whisked her into the waiting ambulance. Before they drove off, the black officer made impatient signs for Kagaba to leave, but he sat on the sidewalk instead, numb, his white shirt stained with Julia's blood.

His phone rang. He ignored it. It rang a second and third time. He wrenched it out of his jacket and stared at it. It was Emily. He placed it next to his ear but did not speak.

"Where are you; did you get lost? Why didn't you call me?" she sounded angry.

"It's my friend, Julia. She's dead."

"What! What happened? Where are you now?"

He told her.

"I'll come straight away."

After those terrible words had come out of his mouth, his head began to clear. Sharon! He must call Sharon. And who will break the dreadful news to Julia's family in Uganda?

"She's not dead." Sharon was emphatic. "She was with two other Ugandan women on the bus. When they reached Forest Gate, they spotted the immigration officers in the back seats. They got off and split up at Stratford. But the immigration people followed them. Julia panicked and started running. The officers went after her."

"You mean she's alright?" he found his voice.

"Yes."

"Are you sure?"

"The two ladies recognized the one officer. He's Sierra Leonean, but he's married to a Ugandan. He gave us information about Julia. They treated her at King George Hospital."

Emily arrived about two hours later. Kagaba had already told her about Julia not being dead, but she still insisted on coming.

"You're drenched," Emily said to him.

"I guess I'll go back home now. I'm sorry about all this ... the interview and ..."

"Are you sure you'll be alright on your own?" Emily gathered her short hair in a ponytail but it fell back on her face. She shook her head, like she was unsure of what to say or do next.

"I'll be fine." He was positive.

"Okay, then. I'll go back to my office." But she did not move. "Perhaps I can buy you lunch. It's already one o'clock, anyway."

He started to shake his head, but then realized how hungry he was. After they had eaten, Emily did not seem in a hurry to leave. "Listen. About the interview, I'll try to reschedule, but it won't be easy. He's leaving tomorrow for Botswana."

Kagaba didn't know what to say so he remained mute.

"Call me when you have some news about Julia."

Emily collected her bag and coat and Kagaba followed her outside. It was almost 3 pm when he stepped on the train to take him back home. Around 6 pm, he called Sharon and she spoke to him briefly before passing the phone to Musana. Musana wanted to know what he was doing in Stratford that morning and why he wanted to get involved in Julia's affairs.

"It's dangerous. From now on, keep away from her. She's been in this country nine years. One would expect her to know what to do under the circumstances. She should never have run."

"Do you know where she's been taken?" Kagaba asked, ignoring Musana's tirade.

"Most certainly to the Women's Removal Centre. That's where immigration offenders are kept before being deported. But don't try to get involved; I'm warning you."

That evening, as he was about to call Emily to give her the news about Julia, Ajuna called.

"I've been waiting to hear from you."

Kagaba had sent her a text about the job interview. It had been weeks since they had last communicated, but he thought news of a job would break the ice and ease the tension between them. And then he would come clean about Julia; after all, she was already out of his life.

"How did the interview go?"

"Ah ... it was ... postponed. Mr. Masego changed his flight. He's coming back next week; I mean ... next month. Emily will try and reschedule."

"That's disappointing! I was crossing my fingers. But are you alright? You don't sound well."

"I'm fine. It's the disappointment, I guess." Another lie. But she did not push him further. She had probably detected that he wasn't telling the truth.

He dozed off toward daybreak. When Emily called to inquire if he had gathered more information about Julia, he must have sounded incoherent.

Apart from the sandwich Emily had bought him the previous day, he had not eaten anything solid since. He was ambling around the house like a zombie, wondering what to do next, worried about his job at the hotel because he had only asked for one day off. Worried about Ajuna not having bought his lie.

"I might drop by tomorrow to see how you're doing," Emily said. But she came that evening, just after six.

"I thought you said tomorrow." Kagaba was alarmed. He had not tidied up the place. The kitchen had not been cleaned for weeks. Sean left before 5 am these days; and by the time he returned in the night, he was too tired to do any cleaning. He had left laundry in the washing machine for days and it stank.

If Emily noticed the untidy state in which the house was, she did not voice her concerns. She accepted the can of Coke he offered her, the only thing in the fridge he could give her. She was more concerned about his physical state.

"You might be catching a cold," she began tentatively, like she was clearing the air for some more important discussion to follow. "Perhaps you should come back with me to my house."

"To your parents' house?"

"Yes. You could stay a few days until—"

"But ... it's not ... it's not proper."

"You can use Sean's old room. I'll ask Abby to prepare it."

"I don't think so. I'll be fine here."

Emily looked disappointed. "That's alright," she managed to say with some cheeriness. They agreed that she would drive him the next day to the center where Julia was being held.

"Let me know if you need anything. And don't forget about your mail," she pointed at the letter that she had picked up outside the front door when she arrived. She said it had fallen out of the letterbox. "It has a Ugandan stamp, perhaps it's from your family."

He took the letter and opened it, read through it briefly, and threw it back on the table. Emily was watching him with a puzzled expression.

"Ah, it's not important," he shrugged.

The moment Emily was out of the door, he picked up the letter and read it again. It was from Tomas.

Dear brother,
I salute you in the name of our Lord Jesus Christ. I wish to thank you very much for the phone. But, brother, the thing is as big as a pistol! I prefer a Samsung, the latest version please, with a 5.2 megapixel autofocus camera, internet, apps, radio, earphones and Bluetooth. I'm sure it's very cheap those ends. God bless you. NB: And my pocket is completely dry, brother, if you could please send me a little something. God bless you again.

He crumpled the letter and flung it on the floor. He stamped on it, grinding with his heel until the paper disintegrated into tiny bits. He wanted to reach out and grab Tomas by the head; bang it against the wall. Bash sense into his stupid head so that he could stop bothering him with requests for money and phones.

9

The windscreen caught the light; bounced it off again. Kagaba pulled down the visor and tilted back his head to avoid the sun's reflection on the sleek tarmac. Through the egg-shaped side mirror, he observed monster trucks as they powered past their minute Mini Cooper: *Sainsbury's, Argos, Kuehne + Nagel,* all heading north to deliver goods, their double exhaust pipes spitting out plumes of thick smoke.

Emily kept her foot on the accelerator, refusing to let the trucks intimidate her. He was enjoying the silence. It was fresh and comfortable, occasionally punctuated by the Sat-Nav's announcements issued in a silky, bossy female voice: *Follow the road for nine miles; at the roundabout, take the second exit*; or, *Prepare to make a U-turn* when Emily disobeyed the voice's instructions and veered off at the wrong turn. *Beware!* The voice shrieked when she exceeded the speed limit.

His thoughts were on Ajuna, still wondering if she had been sold to the job interview lie. What if she had found out about Julia being the cause of his missing the interview? He had called her again the following morning, when he thought he would sound more coherent, but she wasn't picking up. When he called again, she was stressed because she was having problems with babysitting arrangements. Daisy had missed her vaccination jab because she had no one to accompany her to the clinic. Kalayi, who had promised to come and help her out, had not turned up. Their mother had come at the wrong time—a whole two months before the baby's arrival—which meant she could not stay long after the birth. He waited for her to bring up the job interview again, but she did not. Her concern was more on how to get help with Daisy. He should be there with her, Kagaba chastised himself.

What Ajuna needed was a baby car seat, like the ones women in the UK used. They did not have to depend on anyone. The baby would safely be buckled in the back seat as their mother drove to wherever they wanted to go, with colorful notices announcing the presence of the baby in the car: *Very Important Princess (VIP) on board.* That's the one he would affix to Ajuna's screen: *Princess Daisy on board.* Ajuna had had to reschedule and had asked her colleague and friend at the university to carry Daisy. A Dr. Tindi. She should have asked Jane, instead. He'd have to find the money to buy a car seat and ship it to Uganda.

Julia. He was sinking deeper into her affairs, against Musana's advice. He was taking himself to a place where he could be arrested; risking his job at the hotel by taking off an extra day.

The Women's Removal Centre was a symmetrical gray-brick building with a high wall. It looked intimidating, sitting on a large expanse of land, bound with razor-wire fencing. The driveway was shiny and smooth, the parking lot spacious, but it was virtually empty as Emily pulled into a free bay, close to the entrance.

The reception area was small compared to the size of the rest of the building.

"Your name, please," the woman at Reception asked Emily. There was a short queue of about five or six people who had arrived before them. As the receptionist scanned through her computer, a woman in the queue whispered to Emily. "Are you a lawyer?" Emily shook her head, before turning her attention back to the receptionist.

"Did you make an appointment?" the receptionist asked.

"No."

"You needed to have done so. You can secure an appointment within twenty-four hours."

"Sorry, I didn't know that." Emily spoke in a low tone. "We've come a long way. We've done almost eighty miles, and we can't simply go back without seeing Julia. We had to take time off from work."

The woman behind the desk remained impassive, her face like stone. "If you don't mind, I'd like to serve the next person, please." Her tone was crisp.

Emily moved aside to make room to the man who was next. After everyone had been served, she went back to the reception desk to plead with the woman again. The receptionist kept shaking her head vigorously, a frosty smile playing at the corners of her mouth. After a while, Emily slumped into one of the blue chairs. Kagaba went and sat next to her. He wanted to take her hand and comfort her. She looked deflated and confused.

Minutes later, another woman joined her colleague at the desk and asked if she could help. Emily sprang to her feet. "Please," she entreated the newcomer. "I can't possibly take off another day, and I'm traveling abroad next week."

"I can book you in for tomorrow at nine," the new receptionist said with an easy smile. "Can you make it? This is what you need to bring with you," she jotted down information on a piece of paper and handed it to Emily. There was already another queue forming behind them.

The fog hung low and dense as they drove back. Emily was once again taciturn, but this time Kagaba felt the heaviness of the silence hanging in the air like a bad smell.

After about an hour of driving, Emily finally said, "Why did the receptionist insist on referring to the women as 'residents' and not inmates? The former connotes choice. They are prisoners, for Christ's sake!"

Kagaba was thinking of the center himself. It was a top-security prison, no doubt. Julia did not belong there. She was not a hardcore criminal. He did not want to remember the scene at Stratford station. How had the immigration police found her? How had they known which bus she was on that Monday morning? Was it true that by visiting her he was endangering his own safety? Would that lead the immigration officers to him? Were Sharon and all her other friends wise to keep away? Just the thought of ending up in such a place gave him the shivers. He had left a message on Ochola's phone but got no response. What was his excuse for keeping away since he had the right papers?

The return journey was slowed down by roadworks. As they neared the Dartford crossing, Emily said, "I can't afford to take off another full day tomorrow." Kagaba waited, not knowing what was coming. He wasn't sure if accepting Emily's offer to drive him all the way to the center had been a good idea, after all. He could take a train and return to the center on his own the next day. He had already called the hotel to ask for another day off.

But then, Emily said, "Would you mind if I asked you to spend tonight at my house, so we can start on the journey early and be back by lunchtime? I know you're not that keen but ..."

"I have no problem with ... with ... staying at your house."

"Good," she sounded relieved. "You'll stay in Sean's old bedroom."

That's not what he had intended to say. He wanted to explain how in his culture, it would be regarded disrespectful to the parents for a daughter to invite a male friend to their house—maybe if it was Sean inviting him. But he did not want to antagonize Emily and not show his gratitude for her kindness.

Abby was in the living room watching television when they got to the house at about three in the afternoon. When she saw Kagaba, her face brightened and she said, "Will you be staying the night?"

"Only tonight, Abby." It was Emily who replied.

"I will prepare some food then."

Emily led Kagaba to Sean's room and showed him the shower room and toilet, before handing him some fresh towels and an old robe. She must have sensed his discomfort, because she put her hand lightly on his shoulder and said, "You'll be fine, trust me."

Kagaba sat on the bed, unsure of what to do. He could hear Abby in the kitchen, but there was no sign of the parents, and Emily had gone straight to her bedroom. The house felt empty and cold. He went downstairs and into the kitchen. Abby was preparing a salad, cutting seeds out of green peppers and tomatoes, and, as he had expected, she launched into conversation.

"How do you like London?" she started. "Have you visited any museums yet?"

"No."

"Shame! Not even Madame Tussauds?"

"No."

"It's a wax museum."

He shook his head.

"What about the Imperial War Museum?"

"No."

"It was founded during the First World War as a record of the war effort and sacrifice of Britain. You should go. It's free admission and you'll see a lot of interesting war equipment and films."

"I see. I'll try to go."

She eyed him with doubt, shaking her head in disappointment.

She would faint if Kagaba told her he'd never been to a museum in his life. Back home, that sort of thing was considered muzungu culture. She asked if he was hungry. He was. She handed him a wedge of cheese, but he declined. He had never learned to eat cheese except when used as a topping, like on pizza. Prior to coming to the UK, he had never tasted cheese.

Dinner was served at 7 pm and the parents and Abby were already seated at the dining table when he walked in. Emily's father led a short prayer before everyone got engrossed in their eating, like they were holding a private conversation with the salad. Abby said Emily wouldn't be joining them as she was finishing up some urgent work.

Abby was in her usual jocular mood, asking if anyone needed more salad dressing, coffee, but the parents remained uncommunicative. He noticed something about the father he hadn't seen before. His hands shook when holding a glass or fork. Back home, people with the shaking disease were said to be suffering from a curse brought on by touching a son or daughter-in-law.

The salad was too cold, and he ate only the two baked potatoes Abby offered him.

"You seem to like potatoes; do you grow them in Uganda?"

"Yes, but back home we call them Irish potatoes."

"Is that so?" The wife spoke softly, like she was afraid of opening her mouth.

"Why is that?" Abby leaned forward.

"It's because Irish potatoes were imported from Ireland many years back," Kagaba explained.

"That must have been before the potato famine," Abby said. "The Great Famine. Have you heard about it?"

"No."

"It killed one million people."

"In Ireland?"

"Yes. It went on for a long time. Many people emigrated from Ireland and came to England; others fled to America."

"What killed the potatoes?"

"A strange disease."

"In Uganda, there's a strange disease killing our bananas. It's called the banana wilt, and many families are short of food. My father is worried that soon, people won't have any food to eat anymore."

"Is that why you people are migrating to England? Because of this banana disease?"

"No."

They finished eating, but he was still feeling hungry. The parents excused themselves and Abby went to watch TV. He returned to his bedroom and dropped on the bed. He could not sleep. Fireworks went off, like bullets. It was Guy Fawkes Night.

The previous weekend, he had witnessed Halloween for the first time. Adults and children dressed up in spooky outfits and carried lanterns made of pumpkins with a candle inside. Would he ever get used to the strange British customs?

By midnight he was ravenous. The pediatric dinner portions had long since evaporated. He tiptoed downstairs to the kitchen and got some biscuits. If anyone caught him, he would claim he had gone to use the toilet downstairs. He did not sleep much after that. He was thinking of Julia, and what state she was in; about his job at the hotel, and how he was losing money every time he took a day off. This is what Musana meant when he talked about the illegal's baggage. Now he understood. He was taking on Julia's baggage.

To pass the time, he opened a drawer by his bedside. He went through it and found a framed picture of Sean and Emily beneath a stack of papers. Sean, the only ginger-haired member of the family, had inherited his father's wide, thick shoulders and hard smile; Emily looked a bit like their mother; black-haired and skinny.

They could have been about six and five when the photo was taken, or slightly younger. Emily looked cheeky and lively; Sean, sulky and grumpy, even at that young age. They were playing in the sand on a beach, but there was no date or place on the back of the frame, only an inscription of their names: Sean and Emily MacArthur. The family name had been rubbed off and only a faint trace of the letters remained.

10

"What's the name of the person you'd wish to see?" This time, it was a youngish man behind the glass desk.

"Julia," Emily said.

"I'm sorry; I'll need a surname."

Emily turned to Kagaba. He supplied it and edged closer, knowing he'd be asked to spell it.

"Oh, it's one of those long Nigerian names?"

"No, it's actually Ugandan," he replied.

The man scanned the computer in front of him, but did not find what he was looking for. "Are you sure she's at this center?"

"Yes," he answered firmly. "Positive." Sharon had confirmed it.

The man shook his head. "I'm afraid we don't have such a person here. When was she brought in?"

"A few days ago," Emily answered, turning to Kagaba, bewildered.

"I'll call Sharon," he whispered.

Sharon answered on the first ring.

"Don't tell me you went asking for 'Julia,'" she said.

"What do you mean?"

"They wouldn't have that name on record. That's her working name. Did you not know that?"

Sharon made him look like an imbecile, but nonetheless gave him another set of names: Kabatongole Harriet. Too perplexed to argue, he thanked her and returned to the desk.

"Your passports, please? Or any other photo ID?" the receptionist asked.

Emily handed over her driving license. For a split second, Kagaba thought of bolting. Musana's stern voice rang in his ear, cautioning him several times never to carry his passport with him, arguing that, if arrested, immigration wouldn't know where to deport him to and might just let him stay. He said most illegals had thrown their passports into the River Thames.

But he always tucked his passport in the rucksack that never left his back. If he collapsed dead, someone might contact his family back home. Living in a vast city like London made him feel like an insignificant dot on Earth; his passport was the only proof that he was a living organism with the right to occupy space on this limitless globe.

Seeing how Julia's other friends had distanced themselves, he would run the risk. He held eyes with the receptionist and, with shaky hands, slipped him the passport. The man glanced at it flippantly before dropping it in a drawer below the desk.

The rest followed quickly. They were fingerprinted, scanned through the metal detector, searched, photographed, then led into the waiting room. The chairs were painted in bright colors. The floor was surgically clean, the aura serene and tranquil. Four guards manned the room, two women and two men.

The waiting room was half full of guests and inmates. Kagaba and Emily were pointed to a table marked 3 and told to wait. At the next table, an elderly Indian woman was whispering to her visitors, two teenage boys, probably her grandsons. At table 6, a middle-aged Chinese man was talking in hushed tones to someone who looked like his wife. There was a group of Arab-looking men crowded at table 8, comforting one another, their olive skins shimmering against the unblinking light. It was difficult to tell the visitors from the "residents."

When Julia was finally escorted into the room, Kagaba was caught off guard. She was dressed in a pair of faded jeans and an oversized emerald shirt, her feet in socks, no shoes. He did not know whether to smile, look sad, embrace her, or simply extend his hand. The rules engraved on the tables were clear:

You are allowed to hug or kiss only at the beginning and end of your visit.
Don't talk to people at other tables.
Don't raise your voice.
Don't—

Emily knew what to do: she stood up and opened her arms. Julia collapsed into them, almost crushing Emily's thin shoulders. They began to sob. The two women had never met in person, but the prevailing circumstances dictated that they embrace like old friends. After Julia had composed herself, she sat down next to Kagaba.

"Hello," Julia said, touching Kagaba's arm lightly. He took both her hands in his and squeezed them, noting how cold and shriveled they felt. He wanted to kiss her. A chiseled line ran the length of her eyebrow above her right eye where she had been injured; it was almost healed. She noticed him staring. "It was nothing," she said. "I got a few stitches and now they've dissolved into the skin."

"How are you?" Emily asked, looking anxiously into Julia's eyes. "How are they treating you here?" Julia shrugged off the questions, but a shiver passed through her body. Emily removed her red coat and draped it around Julia's quivering shoulders.

"I'm fine," Julia's voice cracked. She blew her nose into a napkin. When talking, she twitched her fingers. She had lost weight. The slim size did not suit her. Kagaba was used to her voluptuous body. She started to hiccup, and Emily crossed the room to a vending machine and returned with a can of 7Up. Julia began to sip at it slowly, as if she was afraid to finish it.

There were many questions hanging on Kagaba's lips. Had she been charged? Could she apply for bail like other, normal prisoners? What would happen to her daughter and mother and all her siblings whom she had been supporting? And why had she not told him her real name?

"What do they feed you here?" he asked instead.

"Chips and chicken, sometimes rice."

"Is it any good?" Emily interjected.

"It's—" A twinkle spread across her face. She stood up and beckoned to a woman being escorted into the room. She had a child of about two hanging onto her skirt. "Over here," she called out. The woman hesitated, but Julia smiled encouragingly.

"This is my friend, Yolanda," Julia said when the woman joined them. "She's from Cameroon. And this is her lovely daughter, Charlotte. I told the guard you had also come to visit Yolanda. She's been here six months, but she's never received any visitors."

The child's curly hair flowing down her nape formed ringlets. Julia teased the golden loops, and the child squealed with delight. She extended her hand for Julia's drink, gulped it in one go, and handed back the empty can. Yolanda looked mortified. "She's hungry," Julia offered. "The food here is not good for her."

"Don't they offer any special food for children?" Emily asked.

"No," Yolanda spoke for the first time.

"But ..." Emily had a puzzled expression on her face, "how can they imprison children? I mean ... it's not right. They should aim the punishment at those who perpetrated the crime."

"My child has lost weight," said Yolanda. "She cries the whole night."

Emily looked like she was about to cry herself. "Where's her father?"

Yolanda averted her face.

"I'm sorry," Emily said softly. "I didn't mean to pry."

"She was born in this country," Julia said, caressing the child's brown skin. "She belongs to this country."

People continued to arrive. The woman in the queue who had asked Emily if she was a lawyer the previous day was back. When she saw Emily, she gestured and paced the space between their tables.

"Hello," she said in a friendly manner. "Are you a lawyer?" She asked in a strong West African accent.

"No, I'm only visiting my friend."

"But you can still help me. It regards my mother. These people will listen to you. They don't listen to us."

"I'm afraid not. You need to speak to a solicitor, I'm—" Before Emily could continue, the woman pulled up a chair and positioned herself next to her, ignoring the rest of them.

"My mother is old and her health was beginning to fail. My brother and I arranged to bring her to this country so she could get better medical facilities. We paid an agent to obtain a false French ID. She entered the UK via France but was arrested at Dover, lo! She was sent to jail for nine months. Nine months, lo! How could they imprison a grandmother? They would never do that in Africa. These people are heartless. My mother almost died in jail. When she was released, she was advised to apply for asylum. Her application was rejected, and she was brought here. Three months now. They plan to deport her next week. You have to help me, lo!"

"Look, she's not a lawyer," Kagaba said. "Please leave."

The woman shot him a killer look, sucked her tongue, and stood up. "Give me your number," she said to Emily.

"Leave her alone!" Kagaba yelled. One of the female guards walked over and asked if everything was alright.

"Is okay," the West African woman answered before strolling off.

Emily began walking the width of the room with Julia.

Kagaba was left alone with Yolanda; Charlotte was playing in the play area.

Yolanda's mouth loosened and words spilled out. "I used to work as a teacher in Cameroon before getting married. Unfortunately, my husband died after just a year, leaving me to raise our only daughter. Then my late husband's people forced me to become the fourth wife to his older brother. He had HIV and my fear was that I would die and leave my young daughter alone. Luckily, when I tested, I was negative and that's when I made plans to escape to the UK."

She paused. Her lips were dry and cracked, and her braided hair had come undone. She could be in her mid-thirties, probably younger. Her nails were chipped, and she chewed on them until they bled.

Then Yolanda gripped his hands. "Ask your white friend to help me." She held his eyes in a steady, fierce gaze. Her grip was firm; her rigid fingers dug into his flesh. He winced, tried to pry her hands off but failed. "Will you ask her?" Her eyes were red, burning.

He nodded and swallowed. She loosened her grip and smiled, retrieving a sheaf of papers she had hidden in the pockets of her cardigan and thrusting them into his hands.

"Those are my deportation papers. They've placed me on fast track."

Kagaba found his voice. "What's that?"

"It means that my child and I will be deported in the next two days. Your friend will help me, yes?"

"She's not a lawyer ..." he began, but the look in Yolanda's eyes stopped him.

"I can't go back to Cameroon."

He did not say another word. He began perusing the papers she had given him. Some minutes later, Emily and Julia returned, and he stood up, ready to leave.

"I need a change of clothes," Julia said to him, looking down with disdain at the crumpled shirt and worn-out jeans she was wearing. "These were given to me by a charity that organizes visits to the center."

Kagaba remembered Julia's love for beautiful clothes—he would go to her house and pick up what she needed. "Just a few things; I'll give you a list. Ask Ochola to give you the key. He called me yesterday to say he was still busy with his research."

At the door, Yolanda said to them, "Thank you very much for coming to visit us." Charlotte was jiggling colorful toys she had picked out from the play area. She pushed up her little hand, asking Emily to take it.

"She wants to go out with you. We're not allowed outside. She refuses to play with the other children."

Once outside, Kagaba gulped the fresh air, happy to regain his freedom. But his mind remained on Yolanda, her story, her child. Had Julia planted her on them? Did Julia know everything already, and had she planned for Yolanda to meet them?

This is how they would get him if he was not careful, he kept thinking. Even if he changed his name. He recalled being fingerprinted at Heathrow. That's how they get to know your real names, by running your fingerprints through their database.

Emily wanted to buy sanitary towels for Julia from a nearby shopping mall. She had been bleeding since the day she was arrested. The house nurse had examined her and concluded it was because of shock. "I've advised her to see a doctor," Emily continued, "she might become anemic. Perhaps I'd better buy some for Yolanda."

"I don't think she needs them."

"Why's that?"

"I read from her deportation papers. She's four months pregnant."

Kampala

1

Daisy was almost seven months old when Ajuna received a text message from Ama: *bringing Ssenga J. 2 ur house 2day.* She did not believe Ama until she and Kato turned up at her front door later that evening, with a beaming Ssenga Jovia in tow. Ama lugged a colossal black travel bag, and Kato a gunnysack of fresh food, vegetables, and fruits. Ssenga Jovia had a hen in her hands.

"I bring a name for the baby," Ssenga Jovia said.

"She already has three," Ajuna objected. Her own mother had added to the list, but it was "Daisy" that had finally stuck.

"That one is a mere pet name." She handed Ajuna the hen and said it was to authenticate the special name, Akiiki. "It was our late mother's. It's an honor for me and my brothers." Ajuna laughed and said she would eat the hen on the baby's behalf and the infant would taste it in the breast milk.

"No, no. You have to keep that hen until it lays its first egg."

"And I shall cook the egg for the baby?"

"No, you rub the egg under her armpits. That will prevent her developing a sweaty smell and no hairs will ever grow under her armpits."

Ama and her husband did not stay long as they were rushing to pick up their kids from school. Ajuna received Ssenga Jovia with mixed feelings. She wondered how long she was planning to stay. How would they get on? Where was she going to sleep? Was she upset with Ajuna for having failed to take the baby to the village, as she had promised to do when Daisy was born? She had a valid excuse; excuses: busy with work, still struggling to find a good nanny after the one she had hired soon after Daisy was born had run away; anxious about making the trip—alone—after what had happened the last time she visited Kagaba's home.

Whatever the case, she was grateful that Ssenga Jovia had come at the right time. The demands of looking after Daisy were beginning to weigh her down. It was lucky the university was still on recess.

She partitioned off a sleeping area in the living room using a makeshift drape and installed a mattress on the floor, but Ssenga Jovia refused to sleep "in the doorway." So Ajuna removed the laundry baskets and suitcases from her bedroom to create room for a mattress.

The black bag was too big to fit in the wardrobe. She asked Ssenga Jovia if she could empty it of its contents and squeeze it under the bed, but Ssenga Jovia said the bag contained very important things and she preferred it to be kept on top of the wardrobe instead.

Daisy's cot was at the head of the bed, and when Ajuna woke in the night to feed her, she had to step over the mattress. Soon, Ssenga Jovia took to getting the baby out of her crib. If Ajuna dozed off and Daisy was still crying, Ssenga Jovia would lay her on the mattress next to her, give her a cuddle and together they would drift off back to sleep.

In the absence of her mother, and the house cleaner who she had finally sacked, Ssenga Jovia soon assumed the role of nanny, cook, and cleaner. She carried on her roles with such ease and amazing competence that it left Ajuna astonished at the abilities of such an elderly and, recently, poorly woman.

Following Ssenga Jovia's arrival, Ajuna spent less time caring for Daisy. Ssenga Jovia bathed, fed and put her to sleep. She took time to prepare her bath, adding ointments she had carried from the village that smelled like honey. Daisy's skin became smoother, with a radiant sheen.

Ajuna had introduced formula, and Ssenga Jovia had quickly learned how to prepare it. She held Daisy expertly while feeding her and sang her lullabies to lure her to sleep. It was rare to hear Daisy cry. If she was hungry, she would stick her thumb into her mouth; if she wanted to alert her minder to a wet nappy or any other baby-related discomforts, she would just roll her eyes placidly and Ssenga Jovia would take the cue. Her hand was like magic. The only chores Ssenga Jovia could not do were washing and ironing Daisy's clothes because she did not know how to use the machine and the steam iron.

Ajuna returned home one time to find Ssenga Jovia had fastened rattles on Daisy's right ankle, insisting their sound would speed up Daisy's movements so she could walk sooner. Another day she had tied a beaded string round her waist, supposedly to give Daisy a future waistline. Rather than object to the superstitious paraphernalia, now a part of Daisy's dress code, Ajuna found them intriguing.

When Jane came by one weekend and found Daisy wearing "amulets," she teased Ajuna. "You've now turned Daisy into a proper bushman."

On more than one occasion, Ajuna would catch Ssenga Jovia gazing at Daisy, or tenderly planting quick, soft kisses on her cheeks. "This child looks like her father. See," she commented one day, as she straightened out Daisy's fingers, which had curled into fists, like a cat's, "even these nails are her father's."

As the bond between Daisy and Ssenga Jovia flourished, so did the relationship between Ajuna and Ssenga Jovia. She felt closer to Ssenga Jovia than her own mother. Every afternoon Ssenga Jovia prepared African tea for her, brewing tea leaves, milk, honey, fresh ginger, and budalasini together and filling a one-liter flask. Ajuna barely finished a mug, but that never deterred Ssenga Jovia from her tea ritual.

"You really don't have to do this," Ajuna repeated, like a mantra, each time Ssenga Jovia placed the flask and mug in front of her.

"Yes, I do. You have looked after me well, my daughter. Even my pressure is now gone."

After putting Daisy to bed, they would sit in the living room and talk till late, as Ssenga Jovia sipped her favorite Bell beer, and Ajuna a glass of red wine.

Ssenga Jovia did most of the talking; narrating stories from the village about people Ajuna did not know, except a few, like Father Bonaventure.

"He almost died just weeks before I came here. He developed a problem in his stomach. He was taken to hospital, and the doctors said his case was too complicated for them. They even did an operation, but his problem only became worse. His mother is my good friend, and she came to seek my advice. I took her to meet a prophetess who prays for people to get well near my home. This prophetess was visited by the Holy Virgin Mary and the Virgin Mary handed her a rosary. So, she prayed for Father Bonaventure, and he is now healed."

Ajuna remembered Ama telling her another version of the story. After visiting the prophetess and failing to see any improvement, Father Bonaventure had come to the National Hospital, where he was diagnosed with bowel cancer and started on chemotherapy. Maybe that's why he was feeling better now.

It bothered Ajuna that neither Ssenga Jovia nor Kagaba were keen to discuss the mystery surrounding his birth mother. "How was Kagaba as a baby?" she put the question to her tentatively one evening, hoping to use her answer as a precursor to open up a more serious discussion.

"He was peaceful and quiet as a mouse. He would fall asleep in the middle of a bath. That's where his daughter gets her good behavior. I told you already, she's going to turn out exactly like him. She's going to be tall and beautiful ..."

"Were you already living with Kagaba's father when he was born?" Ajuna pressed.

"Yes, I ... I ..." she hesitated before saying, "I did not go far in school. When our mother died, I was only eleven and, being the only girl in the family, I was forced to drop out of school so I could care for my brothers and father. Mr. Nathan is the eldest and then follows me. Tomas' father is the youngest.

"So, when Mr. Nathan became a teacher, he moved out of the family home and invited me to go and live with him. Kagaba was born about that time, and I started caring for him until he was sent to boarding school.

"Then he married Ama's mother. That's when I moved out of my brother's house."

"Why?" Ajuna had always wondered why Ama and her mother did not live with the family; why Kagaba's father took so long to marry Ama's mother.

"Mr. Nathan was not sure whether to marry Ama's mother or not. Many people had warned him against her."

"But they already had a child together. Ama?"

"Yes, but why marry a woman who had failed to give him another child? When she moved into our house after their marriage, I did not get on well with her. I got married myself and left. But we could not have children. My husband had a problem. He was a good man, though. We lived together until his death many years later."

Ajuna had learned from Kagaba that most of Ssenga Jovia's and Ama's mother's arguments were about him. Ssenga Jovia was suspicious of Ama's mother, claiming that because she was a quarrelsome woman, she was bound to mistreat Kagaba if he was left in her company without supervision.

And Ama's mother accused Ssenga Jovia of witchcraft. After the birth of Ama she had tried to have another baby but had suffered three miscarriages. The herbalist said she had a fire in her womb that chased away the babies before they were due. That someone who did not wish her marriage, someone of Ssenga Jovia's height, complexion and long hair, had done bad medicine on her.

Once in a while, Ajuna would buy a phone card so Ssenga Jovia could speak to Kagaba. Ssenga Jovia would ask him when he planned to return. "You've been gone one year now. Haven't you finished your studies yet? Haven't you made enough money? Come back and see your beautiful daughter. Come and find your wonderful wife. These two are more important than what you are doing in Bulaaya. Besides, your father and I are not growing any younger."

Ssenga Jovia was right. A year was too long for Kagaba and herself to have been apart; for Kagaba not to have met Daisy yet. She had confided in Jane about her suspicions over Kagaba's infidelity, threatening to end the relationship altogether.

"You don't have proof of your allegations, Ajuna," Jane had pointed out.

"I know him well, Jane. There's no way he would buy such presents for Daisy and myself without a woman's assistance. He would never get our sizes right, to start with. But everything he sends is perfect: the sizes, colors, quality of the handbags."

"That doesn't prove anything, Ajuna. It could be a female colleague or friend helping him."

"I can see you are bent on defending him. But there is more. I think he is also lying about the jobs he does. Jane, a whole year and he hasn't come any closer to achieving any of his goals? No proper job; no school; we haven't cleared the debts he left behind!"

"What does he say when you talk to him?"

"Naturally, he denies everything." Ajuna felt they were increasingly growing apart; like she was putting her own life on hold. She wanted Daisy to grow up bonding with her father.

Ssenga Jovia planned to return to the village in two weeks, but Ajuna asked her if she could stay a little longer as she had not yet found a good nanny.

"It's my pigs that I am worried about. There isn't much farming in the village anymore," Ssenga Jovia would say. "The seasons have changed, and we no longer know when to prepare the garden, when to plant, or when to expect the harvest. When the rains come, they flood everything; the sun is so fierce that it dries up all the crops. This hot sun can go on for three months.

"We have never experienced anything like this before. The trees are finished in the forest. People cut them down to sell firewood so they can use the money to buy food from the market. The market is now our garden. The rivers have dried up and we have to walk long distances to fetch water for drinking. As for the cattle, they are thin, like this finger. The money I get from selling pigs is what I use to buy food. But it's very little, and you saw how I looked when I first came, my daughter. The flesh was falling off my old bones. You have looked after me well. You don't shout at me or behave like some other educated women. I wish I could stay longer, but I must now return to my home."

Ajuna suggested that before she returned, it would be good to visit Ama and her family. Ama had been promising to come to the apartment and bring the kids, but she was hopelessly busy working two jobs, dropping and fetching kids from school, and tending to her husband's extended family.

In two weeks, she hoped she would have found a nanny. The university was due to reopen. She was looking forward to returning to the department, all the same, and to the stuffy office she shared with Dr. Tindi.

2

When Dr. Tindi came back from the UK, his utterances at the monthly departmental meeting had caused a stir.

"The way you describe that meeting, my! As if it was a village council gathering rather than a university meeting?" Jane later said to Ajuna.

"Right?" From Ajuna's experience, conflicts between academics tended to simmer beneath the surface; the aggressor choosing their words carefully, to minimize hurt. But what transpired during the "Dr. Tindi versus Head of Department" meeting that day was like a public spectacle.

Dr. Tindi had just returned from Cambridge, where he had spent four years earning his PhD in Geography. Ajuna started teaching in the department during his absence and was meeting him for the first time. During the meeting, he sat huddled in a corner at the end of the table, smiling politely at staff members who expressed good wishes on his return. But he did not contribute to the discussions.

As Ajuna walked back to her office after the meeting had ended, Dr. Tindi fell in step with her. "I don't think we've met," he said. He was short, dark skinned, and dressed in a bright-colored African shirt over a pair of denim jeans and a baseball cap, worn backward. His brown-rimmed bifocals made him look cute, rather than bookish, which Ajuna liked. For shoes, he had on sneakers. He looked about forty.

"Dr. Tindi?"

"Oh, so you've heard," he broke into a loud guffaw. By that

time, they had reached her office. She opened the door and he followed her in.

"Listen," he took the only chair in the office and started fanning himself, using a pamphlet on the desk. Ajuna opened the only window in the office, but the room remained humid and hot.

"Let me tell you the story about this 'Dr.' thing. When I returned from Cambridge," he began, "my family was very excited and proud of my achievements. And my father announced to everyone that I had become a doctor. I did not want to contradict my father and in a way he was right. From that time, the title stuck. My uncles in the village still believe I can treat their fractures, cancers, and coughs," he hooted with laughter and Ajuna laughed with him.

He was funny and open-minded, she thought, and smart. She had imagined a conceited, domineering, condescending bastard, because of his insistence that he be referred to by his full academic title. Instead, she was drawn to his good looks and charm. A few days later, she bumped into him at the university canteen. He asked if she could join him for a drink. He was not in a rush to go home, he revealed; and neither was Ajuna. Kagaba had been gone for nearly three months. She found him knowledgeable and comfortable to talk to.

The rumor mill reported that their head of department was threatened by Dr. Tindi's return. She imagined Dr. Tindi would undercut her authority and take over her position. She had also refused to allocate him an office. His former office was occupied by two new tutors. It was also true, though, that the department was in dire need of office space—everyone was forced to share.

That's why Ajuna offered to share hers with Dr. Tindi. The truth, though, was that she enjoyed his company. Squeezing an extra desk in her tiny office did not feel like a burden.

The office issue was to become the department's watershed. At the next staff meeting, Dr. Tindi suggested that some of the newly introduced courses be scrapped. In his opinion, they were useless and not worthy of the students' money and time. He also wanted the teaching hours reduced from twelve to eight, and staff's part-time pay doubled. "What we earn for teaching the part-timers is a mere eight pounds an hour. That's what our brothers and sisters in the UK earn for cleaning toilets at Heathrow."

His sweeping ideas did not go down well with the head, who promptly accused Dr. Tindi of overstepping boundaries and told him to "take his proposals back to the UK."

"These are simply my opinions," Dr. Tindi shot back.

"Well, nobody asked for your opinions, *venerable doctor*."

The quarrels continued. The staff were divided on the matter.

"Shia! Who is he to come from the UK and tell us what to do?"

"Just because he went away for a few years?"

"He imagines he's better than us who stayed?"

"Let the man speak! You can't criticize anyone at this university without becoming sworn enemies. No one ever speaks their mind."

"He's a fresh breath of air."

Ajuna got on well with her female boss. She could not accuse her of malice as some of her colleagues did, claiming that, on several occasions, she had used her position to block their career advancement by delaying endorsements of their documents for promotions, or applications for further studies.

When a lucrative project was awarded to the department involving foreign students, the head put Ajuna at the helm of it and the extra income enabled her to buy her current car.

But she found herself siding with Dr. Tindi, where many of her colleagues took the H.O.D.'s side. To be fair to Dr. Tindi, long before he returned the university's image was already flagging, tainted by exam malpractices, forgery of academic transcripts, and misappropriation of funds.

"Look, Ajuna," Dr. Tindi said one time when they were having a drink, "I have two hundred students per lecture, from eight in the morning to ten in the night, including Saturdays and public holidays. I use a microphone to shout out my lecture and some students have to perch on windowsills because of lack of space. That's in addition to supervising three doctorate students. When will I do my own research, writing, and publishing? Am I not at risk of becoming an academic pariah?"

"You ask too many questions, Dr. Tindi."

"I am a professional student, I guess, and was born with questions on my lips."

He decided to take up the office issue with the Faculty Dean. The dean listened and promised to have a meeting with the head, but nothing happened. Dr. Tindi then wrote to the Vice Chancellor, threatening to stop teaching if his grievances were not addressed. The VC's response was swift. He summoned the head and Faculty Dean, and when the meeting ended, the head emerged with puffy, red eyes. This information was relayed to the staff by the VC's secretary. The head did not report for work the following day, and instead wrote to Dr. Tindi telling him to take over her office, and her job, if he so wished.

He was eventually given back his office, but he refused to move, saying he was comfortable where he was. More positive changes soon followed, with lecture allowances increased, and even tea and biscuits introduced.

Ajuna was happy that Dr. Tindi had chosen to stay with her in her airless office. On evenings when they both could afford the time, they would drop by the canteen for a drink. They would chat until past nine. Dr. Tindi would insist on walking her up to her flat. He lived outside the campus accommodation but said very little about his family. The only information he volunteered was his married status.

The first time Ajuna met Dr. Tindi's wife, a few months into their office-sharing arrangement, she reaffirmed her belief in the adage that opposite poles attract. He walked into the office with her and said by way of an introduction: "Lorna, this is where I live, and this woman here," he pointed at Ajuna, "is my neighbor. Ajuna, this is my wife, Lorna."

She laughed at his joke and said to Lorna, "I'm very pleased to meet you. Your husband is right. At times it feels like we live in this office. This place is a madhouse. We spend less time at our actual homes."

Lorna's face remained deadpan. She was dressed in a drab, shapeless, long dress with a wide neckline that exposed her beige bra. Her feet were in sandals; her calloused hands carrying a tattered handbag, its faded color impossible to tell. "I'm glad to meet you, too," she said humorlessly.

It was impossible to imagine she had ever been young, or a teenager, or that she would age and become an old woman. She appeared complete. How could such a handsome, witty man be married to her? Did they have children? Were they married-married, or simply cohabiting? She felt great disappointment and a tinge of jealousy toward Dr. Tindi for having chosen this woman.

Dr. Tindi said nothing after his wife left. Ajuna debated whether to pry, but decided to let it pass.

Dr. Tindi's penchant for cheering up things and making it seem like every problem had a solution drew Ajuna closer to him. Their friendship blossomed. She shared with him even the most intimate information—he made it so natural, so uncomplicated. He knew much more about her than she did about him.

After Daisy was born, Ajuna's cravings for sweet things continued for several months. Dr. Tindi surprised her one morning when he dropped by her apartment with a food box containing freshly baked pancakes.

"Where did you find these?" Ajuna could not hide her joy. The pancakes were wrapped in flamed banana leaves, reminding her of the pancakes they used to enjoy as children in primary school. She took a bite. "These are extra sweet; the baker must have used *real* sweet bananas; just what I need. Thank you."

"No problem."

Ajuna marveled at Dr. Tindi's thoughtfulness. He could have overheard her when she called Jane asking where she could buy pancakes to feed her sugar craving. He might even have ordered the pancakes from the village. They were authentically delicious.

When she lost her cool with Kagaba because she suspected him to be cheating on her, and after he told her the "all-important job interview" with a Mr. Masego had been postponed, which she did not believe, she had sought solace from Dr. Tindi.

"I don't believe him. Why is he keeping things from me?"

"Calm down, my lady."

"Something is going on."

"Let's talk about this on Monday, okay?"

On Monday, before Ajuna could raise the issue again, Dr. Tindi announced, "I went to church yesterday." He was beaming, like he had accomplished something major.

"I didn't know church was your sort of thing?"

"Occasionally, I do go to church. You could refer to me as secular. But my dear wife is devout and so is the rest of my family. I don't want to be left out of this 'social movement' thing. Besides, I fear what my wife might do in my absence, so I trudge along. Wives, or girlfriends for that matter, should not be left on their own for long."

Ajuna ignored the intended innuendo, knowing he was making a joke, and asked instead, "So what happened at your church?"

"Two things. Do I start with the bad or the good?"

"The good."

"Okay. It was after the service had ended and we were standing outside, mingling with the other faithful. The pastor came to talk to us, and I asked him, 'Pastor, what's going to happen to the offertory we made today?'"

"It's an offering to our Lord, son," he replied.

"Yes, I know, but how do you ensure that He gets it?"

"I toss it up to Him. He takes what he needs, and the rest returns to me."

" Get serious for once!"

"God is serious business."

3

On the Sunday that preceded Ssenga Jovia's departure at the start of December, Ajuna woke up early to prepare Daisy and to assist Ssenga Jovia to pack a small bag, as she planned to spend a few days with her niece and her family, before returning to her home. It was perfect timing. The university had been shut, just a few weeks after reopening, because of a strike by students over tuition increment, but everybody knew there were other grievances. The students complained that lecturers were cutting too many classes; there was a need to expand lecture rooms and restock the main library.

When three meetings between the University Council and Students Guild failed to resolve the matter, a fourth one, chaired by the head of state himself, was convened. He ordered the Council not to increase fees, but the Council defied him. The students reacted by destroying property and burning some lecturers' vehicles.

It could take up to two months to reopen the university, which worked in Ajuna's favor. She would use the free time to look for a nanny and train her.

They arrived at Ama's house about midday. Ajuna had not visited them since Kagaba's departure, a year earlier. She was surprised at how much their neighborhood in Kisaasi suburb had transformed. Their three-bedroomed bungalow, which used to stand out, was now dwarfed by newly constructed, imposing edifices. But the mud-and-wattle shacks, rundown houses, and semi-complete structures remained. The road leading from the main tarmacked highway to the house was still like a cattle track.

This was the thing about Kampala city: the rich and the poor lived side by side. Some of the dilapidated homes belonged to the original inhabitants of the land, who had sold off chunks of their plots to the new breed of Kampalan elite; the shacks, on the other hand, were constructed by the many fleeing the crushing destitution in rural Uganda.

Ama was in the kitchen and Ajuna knew they were in for a sumptuous meal. Kato was watching a football game with his sons as he drank from a can of imported beer and snacked on roasted groundnuts. Ajuna had hoped he wouldn't be at home. Her discomfort about his corrupt ways had never gone away, even when Kagaba was more forgiving. The time when she had walked in on him and Ama falsifying his project's accounts still made her shiver whenever it crossed her mind.

When they entered the living room, Kato muted the volume on the TV and froze the images. The boys snorted and screeched. "Dad, you can't do that!"

"We have guests," Kato replied, but Ajuna could see on his face the disappointment of missing minutes of the match between Manchester United and Arsenal. He was wearing a Man-U T-shirt inscribed with *No. 10 ROONEY*. Ama shouted a welcome from the kitchen.

"Greet the visitors," Kato said to his sons. Culture did not permit him to touch hands with Ssenga Jovia because she was an in-law. He bowed respectfully.

The boys sulked and looked like they were about to throw a tantrum.

"Greet the visitors and I will switch the TV back on," their father persuaded.

Two of them jumped to their feet and scurried to greet Ajuna, their hands extended.

"Hello," they said in unison.

"Hello David," Ajuna replied, taking his hand in hers.

"I'm not David. I'm Dan."

"I'm teasing! But you're all grown up. You're now competing with your older brother in height and size. How old are you now?"

"I'm ten and David's twelve."

"And how's school?"

"Fine."

The third boy remained hovering behind, unsure how to proceed.

"Come on, Eric, come and say hello," Ajuna prompted.

"Who is he?" Ssenga Jovia asked Ajuna.

"That's Musana's son—my brother's," Kato replied. Eric had a slight resemblance to his cousins.

"And where's your sister?" Ajuna asked Eric.

"Eva? We sent her to boarding school last term," Kato replied.

The boys retreated to their seats and looked up at their father, wondering why he wasn't switching on the TV again as he had promised.

"You haven't greeted Ssenga Jovia," their father reprimanded.

They sprang to their feet once again, extending their hands.

"Good afternoon," they said together again. Ssenga Jovia smiled back and looked down at Daisy who was sleeping in her arms.

"She doesn't understand English. Greet her in Luganda," their father urged.

They turned their faces away.

"Ah, these kids," Kato said. "They don't want to learn their own language. We communicate to them in Luganda, but they refuse to speak it." He switched back to the TV images and put up the volume. The boys clapped happily and settled back in their seats.

Ama walked into the living room wiping her hands on her apron. She hugged Ajuna, then took Daisy from Ssenga Jovia's arms.

"This child is growing like a weed!"

Daisy woke up and started crying. Ama handed her to Ajuna. She pulled Ssenga Jovia to her feet, throwing her arms all over her body.

"My child, you will make me fall. You have too much energy," Ssenga Jovia sighed.

"You are welcome to my home, Ssenga Jovia, welcome," Ama purred. "Girls, come here and greet our visitors," she called her two daughters who had been in the kitchen helping her with the cooking.

"Greet Ssenga Jovia," Ama commanded the moment the girls appeared, in the same manner her husband had done. Daphne, the older of the two girls, approached and stood in front of Ssenga Jovia.

"Kneel," her mother thumped her from behind. "I will smack you until you learn you cannot greet an elder while standing. This is the trouble with raising our kids in the city. They never get to learn about our culture."

The girl looked like she was going to cry but nonetheless went on her knees and mumbled a greeting. Her younger sister, Doreen, followed, and afterwards took Daisy from Ajuna and disappeared back into the kitchen. She came back moments later with two glasses of fresh butunda juice.

"Daphne," their mother called again. "Come and take Ssenga Jovia's bag to your bedroom. Have you tidied it up? What? Are you sulking now because I asked you to vacate your bedroom for our visitor? Ssenga Jovia," she turned to address her aunt, "you should take these girls back with you to the village and teach them some manners. Daphne has the manners of a goat.

"Come to the kitchen," Ama continued, standing up. "Let the men watch their silly game." Ssenga Jovia moved to sit at the balcony with Daisy and Doreen, while Daphne went to prepare the room where Ssenga Jovia would sleep.

Ama cooked as she talked. She grumbled about the soaring food and fuel prices, exorbitant school fees, and how big-headed Daphne had become. She blamed her bad behavior on the influence of Musana's daughter, Eva. That's why she had sent Eva off to boarding school.

"Don't you think you should have consulted Musana first?" Ajuna queried.

"He would never approve. And you don't know that girl! She is only fifteen but has the body of a mature woman. Men are already eyeing her. Suppose she became pregnant? She is safe in a boarding school where they keep them locked up.

"Daphne will join her next term. We're waiting for her to sit her final exams first. We'll inform Musana after she has joined. We don't want him to feel like we're discriminating against his children. After that, Doreen will follow; I will have the three boys to deal with. I think boys are easier than girls."

"It seems Musana loves his daughter very much?" Ajuna inquired.

"Loves or spoils? Too much love is not good for a child. I don't understand why he doesn't love the boy as much. He sends Eva expensive gifts and gives the boy and my children nothing.

"Last school holiday, it was Eva's birthday. Her father wanted us to invite her whole class and to videotape the celebrations. Of course, I refused. There was no way I was going to make my own children feel inferior because I would never match Musana's extravagance.

"I told him if he wanted a party for his daughter, then he should send enough money to have birthday parties for all the children, including Eric. It's not good to favor one child against the others. It affects their mental well-being. Look, Ajuna, I'm trying to raise these kids as if they were sisters and brothers, and not cousins. Musana is miles away."

"What about their mother? Does she ever check on them?"

"She's only been here a couple of times. She's still struggling to sort out her life. She has been living in Rwanda, but she's back now. Mbu, once she is settled properly, she will take her children. I don't believe it, though. These children don't even know her. She abandoned them to us when they were infants. They are happy here."

Ajuna could see Ama was trying her best. Kagaba had told her how Musana regularly sent money for the children's upkeep. It seems Kato never mentioned the money to Ama. Musana had also bought the car Ama used for school runs.

"How is work?" Ajuna asked, wanting to bring Ama back to the present.

She shrugged. "Sometimes I wonder why I'm still working in that forsaken place. Most doctors have quit and have set up their own private clinics. But," she laughed, "the things that happen in that hospital! Listen to this: A mother came in yesterday with a boy of about seven, who had a serious bacterial infection. The doctor examined him and sent him to the Injection Room. He looked at me and asked if I was going to give him an injection, and if it would hurt. 'Yes,' I said. And do you know what he said next?"

"No."

"Here. Take my pocket money, and then you can tell my mother that you actually gave me the injection."

Ajuna laughed at the indignant expression on Ama's face.

"Can you imagine a boy of seven trying to bribe *me*? It only shows how rotten our country is."

"Corruption is everywhere," Ajuna remarked, glancing at Ama, hoping she might make a connection between the hospital incident and her husband's corrupt tendencies. But the irony seemed lost on her.

4

Dr. Tindi came by Ajuna's apartment to pick up a textbook she had borrowed. Ajuna was preparing to go to the market, not because she needed to replenish her food stocks—she had done very little cooking since Ssenga Jovia left, preferring to buy takeaway—but she felt the urge to get out of the house. She had been waiting for the plumber since morning and it seemed he wouldn't be turning up, after all.

She had even attempted to do some reading and preparation for lectures for when the university reopened, but Daisy kept disrupting her: for a nappy change, or to get her toy from the table where she could not reach herself, or just to be held and cuddled. She had to admit she was not used to giving her daughter the full attention Ssenga Jovia had gotten her used to.

Dr. Tindi offered to accompany her to the market.

"Oh! Are you sure?" She was surprised but delighted by his offer. She had missed him, she realized. Since the university closed, they had not seen each other.

"I'm not doing anything else today, unless you mind?" he looked at her.

"No, no," Ajuna shifted her gaze. When she looked up, he was still gazing at her, a noticeable glint in his eyes.

"Where's your mother-in-law today?" he asked before they set off.

"She's not actually my mother-in-law. She's Kagaba's aunt and she's visiting with her niece."

"Ama?" he surprised her by asking. She didn't think he

would remember her, having met Ama only once when they ran into her at the bank. Dr. Tindi had lost his ATM card and had asked Ajuna to rush him to the bank to cancel it.

"And how's little Amala-Daisy?" He made it sound like it was one name.

"She's not that little anymore. Eight months and already toddling. I'll wake her so we can go before the sun gets too hot."

Daisy was still sleepy as they got into the car. She started to cry when Ajuna tried to buckle her in her car seat. She clung to her blouse, refusing to let go; when Dr. Tindi tried to take her, Daisy screamed like she'd been pinched.

"Perhaps you should drive so I can carry her," Ajuna teased Dr. Tindi. He had bought a car at the beginning of the year but failed several driving tests. She enjoyed poking fun at him about his lack of driving credentials.

"A man with powerful qualifications and you can't drive a mere car?"

"I'm a faithful believer in the written word."

"And what's that got to do with learning how to drive a car?"

"Everything. I love words. I can kiss words. If that stupid driving instructor had handed me a written manual, instead of shouting out his instructions, 'Now engage gear number one, now two, now three, now the brakes, accelerator …' I'd have passed the first fucking test. I find it hard to process things verbally."

As they waited for Daisy to calm down before driving off, she tried the plumber's number again, just in case he turned up when she was away.

"It's still off."

"Who's making you upset now?"

"It's the plumber. He had promised to be here at eight sharp, today, Saturday. And now look, what time is it?"

"Did he mention the year?"

"Don't start."

"I'm trying to be helpful. What I mean is, he might still turn up."

Ajuna put Daisy in her car seat and got behind the wheel.

Nakawa food market was already buzzing with activity when they arrived. Most stalls were manned by women selling garden-fresh foods, vegetables, and smoked fish. The women were engaged in a contest as they chorused endearments to potential buyers: "Mummy, uncle, daddy, auntie, sis; jangu ogule. Bei raisi, bei raisi." The one who shouted loudest got the most customers.

Muscular men ferried sacks of foodstuffs from delivery trucks parked on the street outside the market. Others pushed overflowing wheelbarrows, their shirtless torsos heaving with the effort. "Fasi, fasi, fasi," they edged out anyone who obstructed their path.

Dr. Tindi remained in the car with Daisy. Ajuna didn't take long, knowing the car would be boiling hot in the afternoon heat. She bought some vegetables, fruits, meat, and sweet potatoes.

"Everything is so expensive these days," she grumbled as she got into the car. "I wonder how the ordinary person is surviving. I mean, there are people out there who earn very little—less than what I've just spent—as their monthly salaries. How do they manage?"

"They are magicians."

"Guess you're right. You need a magic wand to survive in this country."

After the market, she stopped at Shoprite to buy some groceries. At the counter, Dr. Tindi pulled out his wallet and, before she could object, handed over the money to the woman at the counter.

"Payment for the lift to the bank," he explained, "and to the pharmacy the other week, and to the dentist's last month. Fuel prices have been rising."

"Okay," she said, but when he insisted on pushing the trolley to the car while carrying Daisy on his shoulder, she protested and took the trolley from him.

"Consider me your faithful minion."

"I don't want a minion. I don't *need* a minion."

"Yes, you do. Now shut up and drive us to Fido Dido for an ice cream. My throat is cracked from this heat."

They drove along Kampala Road looking for a parking space. Being a Saturday, town was abuzz with shoppers, wedding entourages, and university students on a day out.

"Poor urban planning," Dr. Tindi whined, as she turned a corner to a parking slot she had spotted. "Everything's crammed in the town center: offices, boutiques, salons, banks, restaurants."

She tried to slot coins into the machine, but it spat them out. A parking attendant approached. "It's dead, madam. But you can give me the money and I will take it to head office on Monday." She gave him a few coins. He held out his hand for more.

"Eei! Banange, how much is it now?"

"Two thousand, madam, and then you can park for as long as you want."

Downstairs was already filled with families, so they proceeded upstairs, which was quieter but windowless. A fan was in motion, its metallic blades giving the room a cooling effect.

Dr. Tindi sat Daisy on top of the table and fed her ice cream from his tub with a wooden spoon, but she spilled most of it on his shirt. He wiped it off with a napkin without any fuss. Some of it landed on Ajuna's blouse. Dr. Tindi reached over with a tissue, dabbed at her blouse.

"Thank you," Ajuna placed her hand on top of Dr. Tindi's. He rubbed it gently.

What was happening to her? She did not want to remove her hand to break the magic.

By the time they returned to the apartment, Daisy was asleep again and Ajuna carried her straight to the bedroom.

The weather was becoming sultrier—it never used to get this hot, even in December. After changing into a pair of cropped linen shorts and a pink camisole, she made melon juice which they took on the balcony. The heatwave made it impossible to engage in proper conversation.

Ajuna was fighting off the urge to doze. She went back inside and, careful not to disturb Daisy, stepped out of the shorts and tied a lesu loosely round her waist.

By the time she returned, Dr. Tindi had been knocked out by the immense heat. He was shirtless, his head tossed back in light sleep, his glasses lying next to his feet. She spread a mat on the floor and placed her head on a cushion. Soon, she was snoring.

"Amala-Daisy is awake," she heard Dr. Tindi say. She cocked her ear but heard nothing. The wailing came minutes later.

"It's this heat," she said, getting up. "I pray the rains will soon arrive."

A little while later, Dr. Tindi followed her into the bedroom.

"I decided to give her a bath first," she explained as she came through the bathroom door.

"Hello, Amala-Daisy." He tickled her naked feet and Daisy erupted in loud shrieks.

"I'll find some clothes." She handed her over to him. She rummaged through the basket for a pair of shorts and when she tried to get her back, Daisy turned her head away and rested it on Dr. Tindi's shoulder.

"I'm sorry Amala-Daisy," he pinched her cheeks, "but I have to leave now."

"Are you leaving already?" The disappointment in her voice was evident. "I was about to start supper."

"It's nearly seven. I really must be getting home."

"It doesn't look like seven at all! The sun is still bright and hot. But thanks for … everything."

"No problem." Dr. Tindi tried to hand over Daisy, but she clung to him.

"This child really loves me."

"She's attracted to all men. Whenever she's in male company, she treats me as a total stranger. You should see her with Jimmy, my brother."

"I see. So, it's not about me." Dr. Tindi's face fell in mock regret. He sat on the bed with Daisy and continued stroking her wet hair.

Ajuna remained standing, unsure what to do next. The realization dawned on her slowly. *Dr. Tindi is in my bedroom, sitting on my bed. Daisy on his lap.* How did this happen?

Dr. Tindi looked at her, his eyes radiating emotion. "I better go."

A thrill swept through her body. "Of course."

Dr. Tindi stood up and placed Daisy in her cot. She did not protest. Instead, she started playing with the teddy bear hanging by a string over the crib.

He stretched out his hands. "Come here."

She obliged. He folded her in his arms; kissed her on the mouth. Ajuna started crying. He touched her face, wiping away her tears.

She buried her head in the crook of his shoulder, sobbing silently. He did not show surprise at her tears. He did not ask why she was crying. They stayed in that position—Ajuna blowing her nose, Dr. Tindi stroking her cheek with the back of his hand.

He led her to the bed and they sat down, their legs touching. He placed his hand on her naked thigh where the lesu had come undone. Ajuna closed her eyes, feeling his hand traveling to her breasts, his breathing coming in short, quick gasps. His hands fumbled with her camisole. He swung to his feet and flung off his own clothes like they were burning him.

His manhood was thick and beautiful, his thrusts forceful. When they finished, he remained on top of her. He held her buttocks firmly from underneath, and she clasped his compact, muscled body close to her, surprised by its lightness. He started moving once again, exploring her, his thrusts gentler.

Their breathing rose and fell, rose and fell, in a harmonious duet.

5

Ajuna woke before Dr. Tindi did. When she tried to remove her hand from under his cheek, he clutched it, murmuring something before he opened his eyes.

He wasn't startled to find her lying beside him. He turned to face her, then grabbed her naked body and held her close. Shortly, he got out of bed and padded to where he had tossed his clothes near the window. He had a pert bum, solid, like the rest of him. He looked shorter naked.

Ajuna watched him as he dressed, enjoying the silence. When he was fully dressed, he sat on the bed and took her hand in his. His signature playfulness was gone, replaced by a countenance she had not seen before. Was it regret? Yearning? Love? Minutes ticked. He said nothing. She said nothing.

"I'll call you," he murmured. "Come and close the door so someone doesn't come in and carry you away—both of you."

Daisy was awake in her cot; had she witnessed everything? He peeped at her. When he waved at her she did not cry. Ajuna got out of bed, picked up Daisy, and went to lock the front door.

She returned to the bedroom and placed Daisy on the bed, thinking about Dr. Tindi and what had just happened. I have cheated. We have cheated. Would Kagaba ever get to know? They were still engaged. They had a child together. What about Dr. Tindi's wife? She had gathered that Lorna was studying for a bachelor's at an upcountry university, where she had also rented a house. He must be lonely. That's why he seemed to enjoy her company as much as she did his. Was he a serial cheater?

If Kagaba had not left, no, if he hadn't given her reason to suspect that he was being unfaithful, it was possible her relationship with Dr. Tindi would have turned out differently. Dr. Tindi filled the gaps. He was present. Excuses for cheating? Maybe not.

She glanced at her watch. It was past 9 pm. She did not want Dr. Tindi to call her. It was wrong. He might say he was sorry it had happened. He may want to come to her apartment again. She had to face him in their shared office when the university reopened.

The memories flooded back: the food market, him paying for the groceries, feeding Daisy ice cream and sitting on the balcony making casual conversation about her potted flowers that had withered because of the drought. They had spent a perfect day together and it felt right. Daisy had never met her own father, and she was already bonding with Dr. Tindi.

Ajuna switched off her phone and turned on the TV. He should not call her. She gazed at the pictures on the TV lazily until sleep stole her.

She was awoken by Daisy's whimpering, and she pushed a breast into her mouth and went back to sleep. When she opened her eyes again it was morning. She had forgotten to pull the mosquito net over the bed and the little bastards had feasted on her naked arms and Daisy's legs and face. She massaged the red bumps on Daisy's body, hoping they would not result in a bout of malaria. She remembered what Dr. Tindi once said, "If you think size doesn't matter, try sharing a bed with a mosquito."

She shouldn't be thinking about him.

A dull ache had settled between her thighs. It had been more than a year since Kagaba had left.

Her stomach grumbled. She should get up and prepare some milk for Daisy before she wakes; and a cup of coffee and toast for herself. Perhaps she could also boil an egg and make some fresh juice. But she lingered in bed, wondering whether to drive to the university canteen instead and pick up some breakfast, but being a Sunday, she might not get the full breakfast.

The newscaster on the TV was announcing a breaking news story on the seven o'clock news. A fire had broken out at a primary boarding school outside the capital and twenty pupils had perished in the inferno. One of the pupils had forgotten to extinguish a candle after studying for the end-of-year exams. Again! A similar incident had occurred at another school the previous month.

Ajuna was about to get out of bed when the presenter announced that the fire had happened at Mount Saint Theresa College, an exclusive private school for girls.

She sat up. The images on the screen showed throngs of distraught, grieving parents. The cameras shifted to show the Minister of Education talking to a group of journalists who were already at the scene; then the Minister of Health; a few minutes later, the Vice President, whose daughter attended the same school.

Chaos reigned. The headmistress had gone into hiding, fearing reprisals from the parents who were baying for her blood, accusing her of neglecting her duties. When the fire happened, the little girls were alone in the dormitory. The house matron had taken the night off.

A group of onlookers had gathered, and some were rummaging through the kids' property that had survived the fire, trying to find what to steal. Heavy security detail, including Katyusha multiple launchers mounted on army Jeeps, had escorted the Vice President. Soldiers wielding submachine guns were everywhere, as if they had come to fight the fire with their ammunition. There was no sign of the fire brigade.

A few policemen trying to secure the scene looked overwhelmed by the army. Angry parents surged forward, cutting through the yellow tape as they tried to enter the dormitory.

The cameras kept moving back and forth, before finally focusing on one parent who was speaking in Luganda, tears streaming down her face. There was something familiar about her and Ajuna wondered where she had met her before.

The children's charred bodies looked like blackened metal as they were loaded into the police vans. Ajuna groped for Daisy's little hand. Her eyes filled as she felt the pain of the parents who had lost their little angels in such a horrific manner. She wished she could offer comfort to the parent speaking in Luganda.

Her pain turned into anger. Such a wealthy school could afford a generator for power cuts. She searched for her phone so she could call someone, Dr. Tindi or Jane, to pour out her frustration. When she found it, she realized it was still switched off and hurriedly turned it on.

About ten missed calls jumped off the screen, six or seven from the same unknown number. She dialed the strange number first, although she never usually called back numbers that she did not know.

Kato answered on the first ring. He was at the National Hospital's mortuary. The police had phoned him at four in the morning and in the confusion that followed, he had forgotten his phone at home. He was now using a Good Samaritan's phone, who was also at the mortuary to retrieve his child's body.

Eva, Musana's daughter, had died in the fire. Kato could not give the news to him on the phone. He wanted Ajuna to call Kagaba, who would, in turn, break the news to Musana in person.

Ajuna slumped back on the bed, her body numb. Now she remembered the woman on the TV. It was Kato's sister, Kate, who had once accompanied her to hospital when she was still pregnant with Daisy. It was because of her wig that Ajuna had not recognized her.

Someone was banging on her door. She ran and threw it open, clasping Daisy to her breast.

It was Kalayi.

"Ama called me," she was sobbing. "I tried reaching you, but your phone was off."

Moments later, Jane's car came to a screeching stop in front of the apartment. She jumped out and banged the door shut behind her. "I've heard. Have you called Kagaba? We tried reaching you, but your phone was off."

A raving Ama arrived in her car soon afterwards.

London

1

Kagaba called Musana three or four times. All his calls went unanswered. Was he at work? Should he call Sharon? But his instructions from the people in Uganda on how to break the terrible news were clear: Lure him to the bedroom; use a metaphor, don't mention the word "death." Invite a few friends to be around you when you tell him—it's Sunday afternoon there, isn't it? Many of your friends will be at home. Do you have a priest or pastor friend? Invite him as well.

They were unaware that he and Musana did not live together anymore, and many of their friends would be working anyway.

"I need to talk to you urgently, where are you?" Kagaba said when Musana finally answered.

"I'm busy. What do you want to talk about?"

Kagaba could hear female voices in the background and Musana's speech was slurred. "I'd prefer to talk face to face. Where are you? Can you come to my house?"

He was with Sharon and her friends at the River Nile Bar in Tottenham. He was busy, he insisted, and having a good time. Tomorrow was a bank holiday, and he was taking the day off. "Look, if it has to do with Julia, I don't want to get involved."

"It's not about Julia. It's about your daughter, Eva. Can you please come to my house?"

There was no response.

"Hello?"

"I'll come right away."

With Musana on his way, Kagaba started panicking. Did he already sense his daughter was in danger? Had he been too rushed?

Musana got to East London in just under an hour. He must have taken a cab. Kagaba had no choice but to hand him the news bluntly.

For a long while there was no reaction from him. He sat on the bed, motionless, his eyes closed, his mouth twitching. Then a bawling erupted from his body. Musana started hitting his fists on the table and throwing things against the wall: a shoe, a broom, a glass. At one point, he grabbed Kagaba by the shoulders and shook him till he became dizzy.

"Why me?" he shouted. "What has God got against me?"

He paced about the confined bedroom, puffing, shaking, and tried to call Kato over and over, but his phone was permanently engaged.

"Call your sister," he barked. "Why did Ama send my daughter off to a boarding school without consulting with me first? How did she die? Was she the only one who perished in the blaze? Where was the fire brigade? Was the fire caused by an arsonist or was it an accident?"

It took almost an hour for Musana to calm down. Kagaba later phoned Sharon to tell her what had happened and to ask her to come over and comfort Musana. Three hours later, she still hadn't showed up. When he called again, her phone was switched off.

Toward midnight, Musana finally started talking sense. He would call the Home Office to check on the progress of his permanent-residence visa application the next day.

But the following day was a bank holiday, Kagaba reminded him, so it would have to be Tuesday. He insisted that he had to get his passport back so he could travel to Uganda for his daughter's funeral. He would do anything to expedite the process, even if it meant paying more money so his application could be fast-tracked. He finally got through to Kato and instructed him not to make any funeral arrangements until he had confirmed his travel date.

Musana called Sharon again. He wanted to borrow money for the ticket. Betty, one of Sharon's friends with whom they had been sharing drinks, answered. She promised to pass on the message.

Kagaba tried to persuade Musana to get some sleep, but he wouldn't hear of it. He wanted to talk about his dead daughter.

"Did you ever meet her? She had her mother's big eyes, but also looked like me. When I was about seventeen, I had an accident while riding my father's bicycle. I injured my member, and my balls hurt like hell. I only told Kato, because I was too embarrassed and scared to tell our parents. Kato got some herbs which I applied, but I ended up with an infection. My member was swollen for a long time; afterwards, I became desolate because I was afraid of approaching any girl. You understand what I mean?

"I tried having sex with a girl once, but nothing happened, even after the swelling had gone away. Then I met my first wife, Eva's mother. Only a few months later, she became pregnant. It was a miracle! I had believed I would never become a father."

He started sobbing. "How could this happen to me?" He was exhausted. Kagaba wished he could stop, but he continued.

"But then I got problems at work when money went missing. I wanted to please my woman and give her everything she asked for. I was a fool, of course, not to realize that I would have to pay for my involvement in the missing money. I became stressed and my problem returned. My wife was impatient, and I suspect she got involved with another man. She conceived our son, and I left for the UK when the baby was just a few months old. I'm not sure if he's mine. But I have no doubt about Eva. She even looks—*looked*—like me."

He closed his eyes. After a short while, he lay on the bed

and Kagaba thought he had fallen asleep but then he sat up suddenly and turned to him.

"This muzungu woman you've been moving around with ... she seems interested in you."

"You mean Emily?"

"Don't waste the opportunity."

"What do you mean?"

"You are lucky she wants you—just go for it, man. Marry her and sort your papers. You will bring your woman and child over after you get your citizenship."

"Uh?"

"Don't say I didn't advise you. If you want to survive in this country, you've got to be smart. Sort your papers. It's not good for your wife and child to be alone in Uganda while you are here. Marry the muzungu. Forget Julia. She's only wasting your time. She has no papers so she's of no use to you."

"Musana, I know you are hurting. I don't think we should be discussing this ... this ... issue at this point."

"Don't waste this opportunity, my friend," he spoke in a hushed tone. "Look at me. If I had sorted my papers, all this wouldn't have happened. I would have brought over my children ages ago. Think of your daughter."

Kagaba stood up. "You need to get some rest, Musana, it's almost morning."

On Tuesday, Musana called the Home Office. He was informed his application would take between three and six months to be processed. If he wanted to withdraw it, he would have to write to the office, specifying why, and providing proof. He would get an answer within ten working days.

"My child is dead!" Musana roared into the phone. "Do you think I would make up such a story?"

He decided to go to Croydon to speak to one of the officials himself. Kagaba was torn between accompanying Musana or going to visit Julia at the center to take her a change of clothes as he had promised. He decided to accompany Musana. His situation was more critical.

At the security check, they were asked if they had an appointment to see an official. Musana explained why he needed his passport back. They were then directed inside the glass building with its long, winding corridors. The immigration officer who attended to them had his face shielded behind a sliding window. He spoke through a small, black microphone that looked like a reading lamp. He gave them the same information as the man on the phone. "When you write asking to get back your passport, it means you're officially withdrawing your application. Which means you'll forego the initial payment you made with your previous application. When you reapply, you'll have to pay a fresh fee," he explained.

"But that's not fair!" Musana cried.

"It's your choice to withdraw your application before it's processed. We always advise applicants not to make any immediate or unnecessary travel plans."

"But how could I have predicted that my daughter was going to die?" Musana was yelling at the top of his voice, hitting the protective shield with clenched fists.

The officer pressed a button, and two bulky men appeared and apprehended him.

"Leave me alone, you bastards! Have you ever lost a child? Have you ever ..." He tried to push them off, but they were too strong for him. They began leading him to the back of the building and Kagaba followed. He caught up with one of the men and tapped him on his shoulder.

"Please, don't arrest my brother. He's distraught. He's just lost his daughter. Please," Kagaba was begging. The man did not speak. He continued pushing Musana forward, until they reached an isolated outer building. He used one of the keys from a bunch dangling by his waist to open the door and shoved Musana inside. He banged the door shut and the two of them strolled off.

The door was designed with iron bars lined in columns to let in fresh air. Musana pressed his face close to the bars and stared outside, his eyes dull and empty. He was shivering in the December winter chill, all anger drained out of him. Kagaba was reminded of the time Musana knelt on the motorway to beg a white woman not to call the police when they were driving from the airport.

Eventually, the officer who had attended to them came over and beckoned to Kagaba.

"Your brother acted inappropriately."

"Yes, but please forgive him. He has lost his child and he's not thinking straight."

"We're going to let him go now, and I'll arrange to have his passport posted to him. That might take a few days, but please advise him not to make any further contact with this office."

When they returned to the house, Musana did not say anything. As the day progressed into evening, he slumped further into depression.

Kagaba called Kato, who complained that the vigil was costing him too much. The child's mother had turned up with about twenty relatives at his house after the National Hospital had released the body to him because the mortuary was full. More relatives were pouring in from the village after learning of the tragedy. He had to pay a mortician to come to the house to treat the body daily. Ama was still hysterical, blaming herself for the child's death.

Sharon turned up at about eight with her two female friends and they chorused their condolences: kitalo! Musana just looked on, still unable to speak.

"Kitalo nnyo!" Kagaba replied on his behalf and the women handed him mabugo to help pay for some of the funeral expenses. A few more people came that evening to pay their respects and bring mabugo after word had spread. Some brought food and drinks and stayed till very late into the night.

Nambozo, Musana's sworn enemy, brought freshly cooked

food: matooke, sweet potatoes, chapatti, smoked beef in groundnut sauce, and nakati; enough to feed at least twenty people. As she handed Kagaba some money for mabugo, she said, "Musana's anger toward me is misdirected. I'm not a police informer. For me, I know my heart is clean and I have no ill feelings toward him. I work very hard for my money and because some people are lazy, that's why they think I get paid by the police. One day, he will realize the truth."

Ochola also turned up and brought with him plastic chairs that they squeezed onto the landing and into kitchen. Kagaba was still angry with him for giving Julia the cold shoulder when she was in trouble.

"Did you get my message about Julia being arrested?" He could not help bringing up the subject.

"Yes, I did, but—"

"So, you do not care about her?"

"I care about my sister, but I have been away in Scotland for two weeks now. It has to do with my studies. I called Julia and explained."

Yes, of course, Julia had told Kagaba about Ochola calling her. Kagaba was getting mixed up himself. He hadn't slept much in the past days and had been reporting late for work. He prayed Musana's visa issue would soon be resolved, so Musana would travel for the burial and life would go back to normal.

When she was leaving, Sharon called him aside. "Musana has lied to me on a number of occasions, and I've always forgiven him," she said. "But this time, I cannot pretend that it's okay to be treated like some heap of rubbish. He's been in touch with the mother of his children and, apparently, he has been sending her money. He's even planning to bring her over. Well, tell him he can find himself another sucker. I'm done with him. All his belongings are in my car. Come and fetch them. I only came because death is death, and it can happen to anyone. But I don't want to see him ever again."

The following day, Pastor Moses dropped by to pray for Musana. They locked the bedroom door and emerged two hours later.

"Pastor Moses is confident my passport will be returned within five working days. But he has to offer more prayers, and he will dedicate the next two days. He has asked for a little financial consideration. Pay him from the money you collected as mabugo."

"How much?" Kagaba asked.

"Two hundred pounds."

The passport was delivered to Sharon's house a week later, as Pastor Moses had predicted. By then, Kagaba had collected enough mabugo to buy Musana's ticket. Sean contributed too. Kagaba did not give Musana the angry message from Sharon.

Musana bounced back to life on learning his passport had been returned. He called the travel agent to confirm his booking, and Kato to arrange the burial date. He phoned all the people who had come to offer their condolences and even those who had not, thanking them for their support. Lastly, he called Pastor Moses. "I told you," Pastor Moses boasted, "I got a vision about your passport. More people should respect me now."

Early the next day, before going to work, Kagaba left Musana packing to go pick up the passport from Sharon's. He was trying to shield him from Sharon's anger. He wasn't sure how Musana would react if Sharon told him off. He might get arrested again. When he returned to the house, Musana had already called a cab to take him to the airport.

"But your flight is at midnight," Kagaba said to him. "You still have the whole day."

"I don't want to take any chances."

The cab arrived in minutes. It was while he was on his way to the airport that Musana called Kagaba to say he had checked his passport, and it had been sent back with no visa.

There was no anger in his tone, even when knowing he could never re-enter the UK.

He had overstayed his visitor's visa by nine years, but he would have no trouble departing the UK. "That's the beauty about this country," Musana concluded. "No one asks to look at your passport when you are exiting."

Kampala

1

Ajuna joined the mourners at Kato's house only on the second night, after leaving Daisy in Dr. Tindi's care. He had come to the apartment after learning of the child's death and stayed the night. When Ajuna arrived, the compound was swarming with people. A fire was burning in a corner. Had the person who died been an adult, the fire would have been lit in the center. It would burn for four nights for a male, three for a female.

The fire kept the men warm at night as they drank beer and told jokes to cheer up the bereaved family. Women and children occupied the house and had placed their mattresses anywhere they could find a space. During the day, they cooked and served the continuous flow of mourners.

Ama was inconsolable. Ssenga Jovia was by her side, dabbing at her swollen eyes with a cold compress. Ajuna joined them and a group of several women in the living room, where the coffin had been placed. The women had formed a choir, and they were singing one sorrowful hymn after another. The dead child's mother looked composed, framing her cheek with her hand, her eyes blank. She was neither singing nor crying. Ajuna murmured, "Kitalo." She did not respond.

After about three hours, Ajuna slipped out of the room to join another group of women in the backyard. She recognized Kate, who had been talking to journalists on television the day of the fire. Ajuna walked up to her to give her condolences but she was weeping as she narrated her story of the day the child died. She didn't seem to hear or even recognize Ajuna.

"I had come to the city to ask my brother to finance my hair salon business," she sobbed, "and then the fire happened, and I rushed to the school, hoping the police had made a mistake and that the child might still be alive. What I still don't understand is why Kato allowed his wife to send away Musana's child to a boarding school. Isn't this house big enough for even ten children? What will they tell Musana? Ama is now crying like she's hurting a lot, but she is only pretending. Why didn't she send off her own children to boarding school as well?"

"She was planning to send Daphne to boarding school," Ajuna heard herself say. "And she was going to inform Musana."

"Why are you defending her?" Kate burst out, turning to Ajuna, her eyes red from crying.

"It's the truth, Kate. Ama couldn't have predicted what happened. She loved Eva."

"Who is she?" one of the women whispered.

"She is Ama's sister-in-law," Kate replied. "Let her say what she wants. Me, I will never forgive Ama." She resumed her wailing, calling Musana's name, the dead child's name, lamenting how Eva had died so young.

There was no point in continuing the discussion, Ajuna decided, so she headed back home. Kate was too angry to see reason. She prayed Kato would protect Ama from the family's wrath.

That night, after putting Daisy to bed, Ajuna and Dr. Tindi made love. It felt right. Afterwards, she lay in his arms, feeling safe.

When Daisy woke in the night, Dr. Tindi warmed her milk and fed her. In the morning, she made breakfast as Dr. Tindi played with Daisy in bed, and they did not go out thereafter. Daisy had caught the flu and Dr. Tindi made vegetable soup and persuaded her to eat some. She had refused her bottle and even breast milk.

As they lay side by side on the bed after a light lunch, she asked him, "What about your wife?"

He was silent for a long time. She was about to repeat her question when he said, "There's something you need to know, Ajuna."

She sat up, sensing the seriousness in Dr. Tindi's tone. He gently pushed her back against the pillows and when he started talking, it was in a somber voice.

"Something terrible happened a year after we got married. My younger brother came to visit us and only Lorna was at home. She showed him to his room, but when she went to call him for lunch he was not there. The bed was undisturbed.

"I was working as an urban development officer then, in Kabale. I returned from work in the evening. We searched everywhere for the first few days, and we went to the police, but we never found my brother. We've never got to know what happened—he simply vanished.

"At first, I thought he had skipped the country because of debts. So I paid a private detective to check out the airport, the borders with Rwanda, Kenya and the DRC, but that search yielded nothing. In any case, he would have confided in me if something was bothering him. We spread the search to the next three, four, five towns. We interviewed every possible witness.

"My parents accused Lorna of having something to do with his disappearance. She was devastated. It destroyed our marriage, Ajuna. Lorna withdrew into herself. She lost interest in everything, including me. She dropped out of her nursing course and spent months locked up in the house. I didn't know how to help her, so I took the easy option. I applied for a scholarship and, when I got it, I fled to Leeds for my master's. When I returned, Lorna had gotten worse. She had even attempted to take her own life. I ran away again to Cambridge for four years. I am back now and still …"

Ajuna closed her eyes, not knowing what to think. She felt

guilty for having judged Lorna. She felt stupid that she had not detected Dr. Tindi's unhappiness. She had been fooled into believing that he—always laughing, always cracking jokes—was immune to the cruel side of life.

"He was a focused, hardworking young man and about to complete his undergraduate studies in electrical engineering," Dr. Tindi resumed. "He had a great future ahead of him. It's been ten long, painful years and there's no day that passes without me thinking about him."

He touched her face. "You're crying?" he sounded surprised. "I'm sorry I've depressed you with all this heavy stuff. You're dealing with so much already."

"Don't be silly," Ajuna said, wiping away her tears. "I am so sorry for having missed your suffering all this time. What was your brother's name?"

"Raymond." He got out of bed and began dressing.

"Are you leaving?"

"I'll come back if you stop being sad."

He sat down on the bed again, pulled her close to him, poking a finger in her ribcage. She giggled as she pushed him away. He tickled her and she laughed aloud. "Is that your other job? To make people laugh?"

"I don't always succeed. Since my brother's disappearance, I vowed not to dwell on things. Life is far too short."

"Has there been someone else?" The question was out before she could stop herself.

"You mean have I cheated on my wife before? Yes. There was someone during the last two years at Cambridge. We were serious, but it was too complicated. She wanted me to remain in the UK and I could not. I wanted children and she did not."

"White?"

He nodded. "Ajuna, I know what you must be thinking." He turned to face her. "You think I'm only using you to deal with my own pain and broken marriage. That's not true. My wife and I have had no sexual life for at least ten years. But that's only part of the reason why I enjoy being with you. There's another incentive; something much more important than sex."

"Which is?"

He did not respond.

After he had left, Ajuna turned to her own thoughts. She had never dated a married man before. During her undergraduate days, there was a lawyer who she believed she was in love with. They went out for a couple of months, but it wasn't working. He wanted to possess her; he wanted marriage even before she could complete her bachelor's. She had to call off the affair.

Eva's death seemed to have brought Kagaba and her closer again. When they spoke the day after she died, Ajuna had cried, and he had comforted her. They had spoken in hushed tones late into the night. He was worried about Ama, and Ssenga Jovia. She had promised to go to the vigil and make sure they were fine. He had sounded distraught, and she was worried about him. How was he managing to keep Musana calm? How were they managing with food? Were they also holding a vigil in London? She urged him to keep warm, to drink plenty of hot tea so he wouldn't fall sick during the winter. It felt like old times, when he had just left, before she had suspected him of infidelity, and before she had cheated on him with Dr. Tindi.

Dr. Tindi. He made her feel more romantic; sexier. He texted her love notes. *My abandoned Pumpkin*, he would write when he had failed to keep an appointment, or *My sweet kitten*. Kagaba always wrote her full name on the notes he left her on the dining table. "For Gods" sake," she complained once, "there's only one Ajuna in this house." After that, he used all three of her initials.

When she eventually told Kalayi about Dr. Tindi she said, "You did not even cheat on that banker who treated you so badly. You don't love your prince anymore?"

"I do, Kalayi. It's complicated. Dr. Tindi is … different."

"You mean present? I think you love him as well. Ha! I can see how happy you look, sis. I've never seen that cheerful glow on your face before. You can keep them both, you know," Kalayi chuckled.

As she had expected, it was Jane who asked the hard questions. Did Kagaba know? Was Dr. Tindi's wife aware? Would there be a divorce? What about Daisy? How would all this affect her? Ajuna hadn't thought through any of the questions.

Ajuna skipped the burial because Daisy's flu had got worse. Dr. Tindi insisted on representing her and so he traveled with Jane, Kalayi, and Tal to Mityana for the burial.

Ajuna went to visit the family after they had returned to Kampala. Ama, Kato, Musana, and the dead child's mother, Mama Eva, were gathered in the living room. At first Ajuna imagined they were having a family meeting, but only silence filled the room.

Ama started to cry when she saw Ajuna. Kato was instantly by her side, his hand draping her shoulders. It must be difficult for Kato, Ajuna concluded, to be seen taking his wife's side against his brother's.

Musana and Mama Eva sat together on the opposite settee, staring into nothingness. Ajuna offered her condolences to Musana. He only nodded a brief acknowledgment. Ajuna pondered what Musana and Mama Eva's relationship was like now that Musana had left the UK for good. They appeared to be back together. Maybe Musana and Mama Eva would soon rent their own house and move out of Kato and Ama's home.

The atmosphere was stifling. After thirty minutes, Ajuna excused herself and moved outside, where a few mourners remained.

"Thank you for everything," someone said behind her. It was Mama Eva.

"Hello?" she said cautiously. "What is your name, by the way?" Ajuna asked, looking for an opening.

"Solange," she smiled, revealing a dimple on one cheek. Her front teeth were stained. Maybe that's why she did not smile or speak as much, but when she did, her eyes exuded cheerfulness.

"Thank you for supporting Ama," she spoke while looking at her feet. "She is a good woman. She looked after my children. I blame myself for Eva's death. If I hadn't left my kids behind, this would not have happened."

"Why did you leave them?" Ajuna asked gently.

Solange blew her nose and continued to speak without looking up. "It was their father. He was using them to bargain with me to stay. 'If you leave me, you will never see your kids again,' he would say. But I had to leave."

"Was he violent?"

"No, he was not. He was a good father and husband, but …"

Ajuna waited.

"He had a problem."

"The money that went missing?"

"No. I mean, yes. But that's not why I left. He had another problem." Solange was not ready to continue the conversation, and they returned to the living room.

Ajuna had already planned to take Ssenga Jovia back with her. Her blood pressure had shot up again in the past few days because of all that had happened during her visit to her niece. She was still talking about returning to the village in the coming week to spend Christmas at her home, but Ajuna managed to convince her to stay on for at least another two weeks. She wanted her to see a doctor before she returned to the village, and to recover from the ordeal she had endured at Ama's house.

PART THREE

2009

London

1

As the new year began, Kagaba was determined to turn his life round. He had never been stopped and asked to present his papers, but who knows. He could end up incarcerated like Julia. Caged as an animal, unable to return to Uganda, or live freely in the UK.

His hotel cleaning job was not renewed for the new year when the passport owner had withdrawn his services. Kagaba tried but failed to negotiate with him in the absence of Julia. He would survive on the little savings he had put aside, he convinced himself. His hopes of getting a proper job hinged on meeting Mr. Masego. He would chase Emily to set up a meeting again.

With extra time on his hands, Kagaba returned to the removal center to visit Julia. Kagaba waited in the reception room for over thirty minutes while the guard went to fetch her, wondering what was going on. Was she unwell? Or did she not want to see him because he had not been in contact for a while?

Emily had offered to stand surety for Julia's bail application but had failed to put together all the requirements in time: a letter from her employer, pay slips, bank statements, proof of address, certificate of good conduct, and so on.

He hoped Julia's solicitor appointed by the Home Office had arranged a new date for her bail hearing. Then she would be released into Emily's care but still be required to report to an immigration center daily. If she complied with all her bail conditions, she would be allowed to apply for asylum and life would return to normal. She could get a proper job and she could continue remitting money to Uganda to assist her family. Would he and Julia go back to being just friends?

When Julia finally emerged through the strong room, his worst fears were confirmed at once. Her eyes had lost their color: they were pale, anemic. Her shoulders were diminished, her collarbones jutting out, like sticks.

Weeks later, when Julia's lawyer interrogated him to build up a case for her bail, Kagaba would struggle to remember his reaction when he saw Julia that day. Did her hands tremble? How many pounds had dropped off her body since the last time he had seen her over two months ago?

Julia wobbled to where he was sitting and collapsed her waif-like body against his chest.

"Are you alright? What happened? Are you sick?"

She shook her head in response. She was dehydrated; her lips were cracked and bleeding.

"Please tell me what's wrong. Are you hungry?" He wished he had bought her favorite Chinese takeaway, the only food she enjoyed outside of her own home-made cooking. He held her weary body against him, fearing to let go in case she collapsed to the floor.

"It's about Yolanda," she whispered.

"Is she sick?"

She shook her head. Her face fell and Kagaba expected the worst.

"Has she been deported? What about her child? Her lawyer didn't help?" Perhaps they were going to deport Julia next. Yolanda's lawyer was the same one representing Julia. Maybe he was not as efficient. After all, he was appointed by the government. He did not care if he won their deportation cases or not. If Kagaba was to be apprehended, this might be the same lawyer the government would appoint to defend him. He started panicking.

"She's not been deported. She killed herself three days ago."

Julia broke down in sobs and disengaged herself from his embrace. Kagaba stood still, unable to react to the horrific news, then Julia spoke again. "After she was denied bail, she told them she did not want to go back to Cameroon; she *could not* go back there. Her other daughter she left behind died due to neglect."

She paused. Kagaba was about to say something when Julia continued. "She hanged herself in the bathroom, with a scarf. Her child has been taken into care, until they find her a foster family," she wept.

Kagaba pulled her shaking body close to his. He felt completely useless, not knowing what to do or say that would comfort Julia. She stood up and swayed on her feet, like a drunk. He put out his hand to steady her, but she shoved him away. He was taken aback by the strength in her disheveled body.

"She was the only friend I had here." Her voice was raised. "My roommate is Ugandan, but we don't even talk. I've been demanding to know what they've done with Yolanda's body. They might have burned her already!" she exploded, hitting her frail hands on the table.

A female guard strode toward them. "What's going on?" she aimed her inquiry at Kagaba.

"I want to go home!" Julia shouted. "I want to go back to Uganda. Leave me alone, you killers!"

There were fewer guests than usual, but Kagaba felt their nervous stares. A second guard appeared from somewhere within the reception room. Julia got hold of a chair and flung it at him. It missed his head narrowly and smashed against the door. The guard tried to take her by the hand, but she kicked at him.

The female guard spoke into her walkie-talkie in a fearful tone, and two broad-shouldered security guards arrived in moments. They looked from Kagaba to Julia, wondering who was causing trouble. As if to put their indecision to rest, Julia hurled more insults at the men, calling them murderers, cannibals. She lashed out at them as they inched forward to restrain her. She then fell on the floor. The men tried to get her to her feet, but she would not let them. They grabbed her hands and began dragging her across the tiled floor.

Kagaba did not realize he was crying until tears dropped on his shirt.

"She'll be alright," the female guard said. "Was it something you said that upset her? News from home?"

Kagaba shook his head, more tears overwhelming him.

"Is it a marital dispute?"

He shook his head again.

"Tomorrow, we'll send her to the psychiatric unit. She'll be assessed by a professional."

"She's faking it," the male guard said without empathy. "They think it will gain them our sympathy. They believe if they act mad, they will be released. Idiots."

Kagaba tried to speak but the words stuck in his parched throat.

"In the meantime, no more visitors," the female guard addressed him.

Kagaba walked out of the center feeling like he had been dunked in cold water. He wandered aimlessly in the parking lot, still rattled. When the free coach arrived to take visitors to the city center to catch a train back to London, he did not see it. One of the visitors who had come in his car gave him a lift to the train station.

In the night, his phone rang, rousing him from sleep. He was surprised he had slept at all, given the painful scene he had witnessed. Kato was on the line, and Kagaba got concerned. Why was he calling him at that time of the night?

"Hello," his voice was gruff from sleep.

"Sorry, did I wake you?"

"Is there a problem?"

"No, no. Everyone's fine." He paused. "Ama has calmed

down a bit now, and Musana, well, he'll live. He's coping. And I recently spoke to your father, and—"

"For God's sake, Kato. *What is it?* Have you lost your job? You don't call me … it's what, two in the morning in Uganda? To tell me about, about …"

"No, I've not lost my job." Kato sounded nervous. "It's about Ajuna."

Kagaba sat up, grabbed the bedpost firmly. He sucked in his breath, waiting.

"She's well, and so is the baby. It's … she's having an affair, Kagaba. I wish there was a gentler way of telling you. But it's true. I've seen them with my own eyes."

"She has another man?" The question made him feel stupid.

"Yes. They work together at the university. He even came for the funeral. They move together openly. I know this is hard for you to take. But I thought it would be best if you knew, and I didn't want you hearing it from someone else."

After Kato had hung up, Kagaba got out of bed and began pacing the room. He grabbed the clothes he had been wearing the previous day and as he dressed, he trembled. He sat on the chair and tried to recollect himself. Why had Ajuna done it? Was it in revenge over his transgressions with Julia? Why was she being so indiscreet? Who was Dr. Tindi? Was he more handsome, richer, older?

He found a heavy cardigan and put it on over the jumper he was already wearing. Some minutes later he began to calm down. He got out of the house and started walking toward the train station. He felt lightheaded, like he was floating on a cloud. He wasn't quite sure where he was heading, but the idea of a train station made him feel better, as if he wasn't trapped; could escape.

Then he saw a sign near the train station: *Railway Tavern: Beers, Lagers, Wines, Spirits.* How come he had never seen the pub before? And how come it was still open? Maybe it wasn't as late as he imagined.

He opened the door and stepped inside. He wanted to laugh. He had never been to a pub before. All his outings with Julia were to Ugandan-owned restaurants and bars. A pub looked different. It was more like someone's living room, coal burning steadily in the fireplace.

When he entered, people froze. He ignored them, walked up to the counter and perched on a high stool. A waitress wearing heavy make-up, tight jeans and a gauzy blouse asked him what he wanted to drink.

"Whiskey."

The waitress eyed him curiously.

"Give me a bottle of whiskey."

"Which type, sir?"

He thought before replying. "Jack Daniels."

"You have to pay for it first, sir."

He patted his pockets for his wallet. This was a stupid idea. He couldn't afford a bottle of Jack Daniels. With no job to count on, he had to be careful with the little money he had. He should just leave and return to the house.

"Hello, brother."

Kagaba turned to an old man who wore his white hair in long, dirty locks. He was the only other black person in the pub.

"Give my brother a drink," the old man addressed the waitress. "Whatever he wants."

"He wants a bottle of Jack Daniels," the waitress answered.

"Give it to him. How much does it cost?" He spoke with a thick Patois accent. He got out his wallet, counted out some notes, and handed them to the waitress, who counted off what she needed and returned the rest to him.

After the waitress had placed a bottle of Jack Daniels, two glasses, and an ice bucket and ice tongs in front of them, the Jamaican said, "So, my brother, what's eating you?"

Kagaba poured out a generous amount into his glass and another for his companion. He took a sip as he pondered how to respond. Could he trust him? He felt a sense of camaraderie toward this man who had bought him a bottle of whiskey. He wanted to confide in him; he wanted to talk to somebody about his anger. And it felt right to entrust a fellow man.

"It's about a woman, isn't it?" the old man prompted.

Kagaba nodded.

The Jamaican's laugh was deafening. He pulled at his bushy beard, hooted some more. "Tell me about it, brother. Women! I know all about them."

Kagaba raised his brow.

"My missus threw me out of the house last year. We had been married nine years, two kids. I had a good job and was almost done with paying off the mortgage. Then she filed for divorce, claiming irreconcilable differences. She got the house and the kids, and I got to pay alimony and child support. What remains at the end of the month, I bring here—to buy a friend a bottle of whiskey. A man's got to be happy," he chuckled. "What's your missus done?"

"Cheated."

He laughed again, tears rolling down his face.

"What's funny about that?"

"Drink your whiskey. Forget about her."

Kagaba downed more whiskey until his head spun. He went to take a pee. While he was washing his hands, he peered at his face in the mirror above the sink. His eyes had turned red. His head felt heavy, as if it did not belong to him. As he walked back to the counter, he caught the eye of one of the women on the sofa and she gave him a small wave. He waved back and she smiled. A few people were swaying their bodies to the music of The Beatles.

"Why didn't you get another woman?" he asked the Jamaican when he returned to his seat. He had stopped drinking and was nodding off. Kagaba had to repeat his question.

"That was my third marriage." His eyes were glassy. He was no longer laughing. Kagaba patted him on the shoulder. It felt better to comfort someone else.

The woman who had waved at him walked up to them, her slim body attired in a tight, short leather skirt, black jacket and stockings. She had red high heels on. She pushed her large breasts close to Kagaba's face. "Hello, handsome, come and dance with me."

Kagaba slid off the high stool without hesitation, almost falling on his face. The woman steadied him. He knew he couldn't dance, but tonight he was oozing confidence. He waltzed with the woman to Phil Collins' "Paradise"; when she squeezed his buttocks he squeezed her thighs. She leaned in, burying her face in his chest. He laughed. It felt funny to be holding a white woman. She wriggled her hips to the rhythm of the music; thrusting her big breasts into his chest.

"I love you," his voice was husky, a whisper.

"I love you too, babe," she hissed back.

Wetness soaked his pants. "I want to fuck you."

She grinned. "That will be a hundred quid an hour, for a black man."

"Huh?"

"You heard me."

She had stopped moving her groin against the bulge in his trousers. He pulled her to his body and tried to kiss her. "Flip off," she shoved him with her elbow. He staggered but did not fall. She strolled off without another glance at him.

He scanned the room. It appeared no one had witnessed his embarrassment. At the bar, the Jamaican was resting his head on the counter. Kagaba nudged him on the shoulder, and he opened his eyes.

"What?"

"I'm leaving. Thanks for the drink." He felt clear-headed. The whiskey had evaporated.

"No problem. Come back tomorrow. I'll be here and you can drink on me."

It was eleven in the morning when Kagaba opened his eyes. The house was eerily quiet.

He drank water and forced a spoonful of baked beans and potatoes into his mouth. Everything tasted stale. He would never touch whiskey again.

Ajuna!

In his drunkenness, he had composed several texts to her—*I hate you, you cheat. I never want to see you again. I am demanding full custody of my daughter; I don't want your bad behavior rubbing onto her. I know about you and your new man. I will crush his legs when I return*—but he never sent her any of the angry messages.

He imagined meeting Dr. Tindi. He would say to him: Thank you very much for taking care of my family while I was away. But now I am back, and your services are no longer required. Now please, leave!

If Ajuna refused to take him back, he would return to the village and live with Ssenga Jovia as he used to as a youngster, when he had basked in her unlimited love, a time only marred by loneliness because Ssenga Jovia did not have any children he could play with. When the solitude became too much, Tomas and he would spend their afternoons shooting weaverbirds with the catapults that Tomas had been so good at making.

He drank another tumbler of water. His behavior with the woman in the bar the previous night had been despicable. He felt like cutting off his head whenever he thought of what he had said and done. Her purple lipstick had stained his shirt.

In the evening, he returned Emily's call. He had left a message on her voicemail about Julia's condition and what had transpired at the center the previous day. She must have called back when he was sleeping off his hangover. But she wasn't answering, and he decided he would call her later that night.

His mind returned to Ajuna. His stomach churned like a boiling pot as he envisaged *him* making love to her beautiful body. He closed his eyes, but the same image kept flashing through his mind like a light—the whole evening, the entire night, refusing to let him sleep. He did not feel anger toward Ajuna anymore. It's *him* he wanted to maim, kill, destroy. For snatching his woman when he knew he was thousands of miles away and could not defend his territory.

Kampala

1

Eva's death had cast a dark cloud on the Christmas celebrations. Ajuna hoped the new year would usher in new beginnings for everyone. She had bought supplies and other gifts for Ssenga Jovia to take back with her: sugar, rice, soap, paraffin, a carton of long-life milk and another of matchboxes, a pair of bedsheets, a blanket, and a piece of fabric, which she could make into a dress.

Ssenga Jovia thanked her excessively, saying no one had ever given her so many presents. Ajuna had decided this was the right moment for Daisy to visit the rest of her father's family, so she would accompany Ssenga Jovia. Her departure would be a relief of sorts. She would be sad to see her leave, not least because she hadn't found a nanny yet, but her situation had become complicated because of her involvement with Dr. Tindi.

He had kept away since Ssenga Jovia's return to the apartment and their only form of communication was by phone. Ajuna yearned for him. The bed felt empty without him beside her. His good humor and physical presence was something she had come to take for granted in the last few weeks. She wished the university was not on strike; they could then have met in the office they shared.

Kalayi and Tal's engagement party was on Saturday. They had pushed it forward because of an impromptu business trip Tal had to make to Turkey. They had invited Jane, and Ajuna and her "new man," as Kalayi referred to Dr. Tindi. It was Kalayi's idea to have a formal but modern engagement occasion; not the traditional kwanjula Kagaba and Ajuna had had. They had not invited anyone from the village.

Ajuna woke up on Saturday morning not in the mood for a party. She hadn't finished packing and preparing to leave for the village the next day.

She was anxious about the journey. It would be Daisy's first trip. Ajuna hoped she wouldn't get sick. Should she carry bottled water, and a gas cooker to boil water for drinking to protect Daisy from diarrhea, or should she buy water treatment tablets instead?

At nine months, Daisy should be eating solids already; but Ajuna was struggling to introduce her to matooke and sweet potatoes, or beans and rice. Daisy only ate cereals, pureed vegetables and fruit, which would require refrigeration and a blender.

She hoped Kagaba's people would not perceive her as a city woman who looked down on them. To compensate, she would carry a couple of bitenges so she would look decently attired— no short skirts or jeans.

And would they be able to tell she was cheating on their son?

Jane and Dr. Tindi were keen to attend Kalayi's party and Ajuna didn't want to let them down. Besides, she had never been to Kalayi's new home, and this would be her opportunity to visit. She would leave Daisy with Ssenga Jovia, who was happy to resume her nanny duties.

She picked up Jane at her house near the Business School campus and they met Dr. Tindi at the City Square. She was still in low spirits, and she was getting more irritable as the day progressed. She could not explain it; not even seeing Dr. Tindi for the first time in three days lifted her morale.

Kalayi and Tal lived in Ntinda, an affluent part of the city east of the university. Ajuna stopped at a gas station to refuel but realized she had forgotten her purse at home—another sign of anxiety.

"Oh no!" she groaned, looking at the fuel gauge.

"What is it?" Dr. Tindi peered to see where Ajuna's finger was pointing.

"The tank's empty and I forgot my purse."

"I thought 'E' stands for Enough?" Dr. Tindi laughed and Jane laughed with him.

"It means Empty, you moron." Ajuna was smiling and beginning to feel relaxed.

Kalayi's new home was one of eight units in a newly constructed complex, encircled by a high brick wall with coils of razor-wire running the length of the symmetrical fence. A wide, automatic gate opened at the touch of a button after the visitors identified themselves on the intercom.

"I didn't even know such technology existed in this country," Dr. Tindi marveled.

"Bushman," Ajuna teased.

She could see Dr. Tindi had made an effort to impress their hosts. He had a new haircut and, instead of his usual trademark jeans, T-shirts or kitenge shirt, and sneakers, he was wearing a white long-sleeved shirt, black trousers, and black shoes.

"Some people live in pure opulence." This came from Jane as she admired the blue-marble balcony.

"I wonder how much they pay in rent." Dr. Tindi put his head through the car window to take a better look at the apartments. "What does this Tal chap do?"

"He's a hustler." Ajuna uttered the word with conviction, as if that would explain everything.

"I see." Dr. Tindi sounded defeated.

Inside the house, the wall-to-wall carpets were extravagantly thick and plush, as were the leather sofas. The oil paintings on the walls were modern and abstract, clearly very expensive. There were more guests than Ajuna had anticipated, and her anxiety returned.

Kalayi was exuberant, laughing effortlessly and greeting all her visitors with a warm embrace. She was dressed in white linen slacks, a rose-pink cotton shirt, and red sandals. Her engagement ring must have cost a fortune.

"Tal bought it in Dubai." Kalayi twirled the gold carat.

"It's Cartier!" Jane mouthed.

Kalayi had hired a catering service who served and replenished the drinks and eats. It was like a wedding party.

Ajuna stole a look at her sister, not knowing what to make of her new life. Gone were the hard times when she was jobless and miserable and had to squeeze in the same bed with Ajuna in the sparsely furnished university apartment. Being Tal's woman had changed everything.

Tal was mingling easily with his guests. He wore a glittery brown suit with a matching yellow shirt, gold cufflinks, and a bowler hat, as if unaware of the sizzling January heat. He came to where Ajuna's group were seated and introduced them to a couple of his friends: "This is my sister in-law. She is a professor at the National University, and these are her colleagues. They are all professors."

"We are not ..." Ajuna began, but Tal had already moved on, showing off his acquisitions to his guests as he conducted a tour of the apartment.

Ajuna's appetite, like her morale, had taken a dive and she declined the food Kalayi offered her.

"Your sister might think you're snubbing her food," Jane tried to persuade her. "She might even think you're not happy for her, or that you're jealous of her achievements."

"Nonsense." Ajuna did not want to get into an argument. "Of course I'm happy for her. She finally has a home of her own. She's not my responsibility anymore."

"Then eat something!"

"She's watching her height," Dr. Tindi said with mock seriousness.

Ajuna chuckled, once again feeling the tension leave her shoulders. She tried some of the food.

"I can see why you fell in love with him," Jane commented after Dr. Tindi had moved away to talk to a cluster of men standing by the balcony. He seemed at ease in their company, like they were old friends. "He's good for you."

"You're right," Ajuna agreed. "He's funny and sensitive and easy to get along with. You should see him with Daisy. He rarely loses his head, and he handles difficult situations very well, including my moody and grumpy episodes. And he pays the bills."

Ajuna told Jane bits of his sad story. "I really think he's a special person."

"A special, married man, who's good for an engaged woman—married—actually, if we're to talk culturally. A perfect love triangle. But, hey, I'm not judging. I'm sure you'll do what's right by you. You're two mature adults."

The party atmosphere had failed to raise Ajuna's spirits, and when Dr. Tindi returned and suggested they leave, she agreed.

The three had decided to stop by Ajuna's flat for a drink. At the university main gate, they were stopped by security. Dr. Tindi wound down his window.

"Good evening, sir," the man said to him. "Where are you going?"

"Ajuna lives here," Dr. Tindi snapped, pointing at the windscreen. When the security checks were introduced during the strike, all staff cars were allocated stickers for easy identification.

"Okay, but I have to check your boot, sir."

The security man used a torch to look inside, even though it was only seven in the evening and the sun was still shining. In a few seconds, he walked back and asked Dr. Tindi. "Do you have a gun, sir?"

"No, but we have a bomb."

The security officer smiled at the joke and waved them through.

"Their job is to check for ammunition, not ask if you're carrying any. The administration should just abolish the stupid checks." Ajuna was feeling an unexplained anxiety to get back home.

Ssenga Jovia was soaked in sweat when they got to the apartment. She was slumped on the sofa, oblivious to Daisy's wailing, her toys scattered all over the living room.

Jane rushed to Ssenga Jovia's side and checked her pulse, then started to undress her. "Bring some water, quick!" she shouted to Ajuna. Ajuna was trying to calm Daisy, who had turned hysterical after seeing her. "Put the child down!" Jane commanded. But Ajuna did not. Jane turned to Dr. Tindi. "Bring a cushion, something to pillow her head."

Dr. Tindi dashed to the bedroom and came back with two pillows. "Here, let me help." He cushioned Ssenga Jovia's head and stretched her out on the sofa. It would be futile to call an ambulance. Only a few private hospitals operated any, and they were always busy and far too expensive.

After Jane had removed Ssenga Jovia's red scarf and most of her garments, her breathing improved. When she regained some energy, Dr. Tindi helped her to the car and reclined the front seat so she could lie down. Ajuna got into the driver's seat. Jane stayed behind to mind Daisy.

Ajuna called Ama as they set off, but she did not answer. When Ama called back, Dr. Tindi answered Ajuna's phone. She could sense the hesitation in his voice as he gave her niece details of the sick woman's condition. Did Ama know about them?

Ama said she was in the village attending a wedding and would return to the city the next day, but she called a nurse friend at the National Hospital who assisted them to jump the long queue at the Emergency ward and have Ssenga Jovia assessed.

Ssenga Jovia's blood pressure had gone through the roof, the doctor informed them. He recommended that they retain her for observation. The medicine he had prescribed was not available at the hospital; Dr. Tindi rushed to a nearby pharmacy to buy it, leaving Ajuna alone with Ssenga Jovia.

Ajuna sat on Ssenga Jovia's bed and took her hand in hers.

"I'm sorry, my daughter," she spoke like her tongue had gone flaccid, and she could not muster enough energy to lift it.

"Sorry for what, Ssenga Jovia?"

"I shouldn't have stopped taking my medicine. But when I was at Ama's house, everything got disorganized after Musana's child's death. See now, all this trouble I'm causing you." She said that since that morning, she had been feeling unwell, but she had not wanted Ajuna to miss her sister's party.

Dr. Tindi returned and Ajuna paid a nurse to keep an eye on Ssenga Jovia during the night.

"Good night, Ssenga Jovia. I'll be here first thing in the morning."

She smiled and said, "Bring Daisy to see me."

"I will," Ajuna answered, though knowing child visitors were not allowed in hospitals.

"And don't tell Kagaba about my illness. It will only alarm him. In any case, I will be out of here tomorrow and we shall travel to the village the next day. My pressure is nothing new. It must have white hairs by now. And thank you, my daughter, thank you for looking after me. You are a good woman. You made me eat Christmas and even the New Year in the city!" she chuckled, "but tomorrow I should return to my home."

They got home after ten and Jane left soon afterwards. Dr. Tindi spent the night. She had missed his firm body against hers. She was glad she was no longer feeling agitated. Perhaps she had simply been missing the romance.

The following morning, they were at the hospital before eight. Daisy remained in the car with Dr. Tindi as Ajuna went up to the ward. The plan was to bring Ssenga Jovia back to the apartment and then go out for lunch. That would give her the quiet she required to recover from her ordeal.

The moment Ajuna entered the hospital room, she knew something was wrong. A different nurse from the one who had been on duty the previous night was standing by the bed, closing Ssenga Jovia's eyes.

"She just slipped away," the nurse said when she saw Ajuna. "This morning, she got up and washed herself. Then she took some tea, and afterwards she said she wanted to rest. When I came back a few minutes later to give her medication, she was gone."

At first, Ajuna felt no panic, no pain, just numbness, and a sense of disbelief. Her legs became unsteady as she paced the short distance between the door and the bed. She touched Ssenga Jovia's cheeks; they were still warm. Her lips were slightly moist and open. *She was sleeping, not dead.*

Her head was slumped to one side, resting on her shoulder. The nurse brought it back to the center of the white pillow and pushed her chin straight up. Her right hand had fallen off the mattress and was dangling, almost touching the floor. Ajuna lifted it gently and laid it on her side. She felt for her pulse. Only last night, it had been racing like a fast train, but it was still now. The nurse took both her arms and crossed them on her chest, like in prayer. Her chest did not heave up and down; there was no air to power her lungs.

The nurse wanted to pull the white sheet over her face, but Ajuna stopped her. *She was not dead!* The nurse left the room.

Ajuna sat on the bed with the corpse. When her phone started ringing, she stared at it like it was something foreign. It was Dr. Tindi, telling her Daisy wanted to feed.

The nurse returned, telling Ajuna to bring some clothes to dress the body before it became stiff. Ssenga Jovia was still wearing the hospital gown.

Later, after they had returned home, she let Dr. Tindi do the hard part. He called Ama and Kato. Within a short time word of Ssenga Jovia's death had spread, reaching Kagaba an hour after his beloved aunt's death.

Ajuna pondered what clothes Ssenga Jovia would have wanted to be buried in, and for the hundredth time since it happened, she wished Ama was present. She felt like an imposter—she was not related to the dead woman by blood, and yet she was making all the important decisions.

She retrieved from the top of the drawer in the bedroom the black bag she had squeezed in there when Ssenga Jovia first arrived. She started removing the clothes, neatly pressed and folded. She chose a long blue dress Kagaba had sent her as a Christmas present. Ajuna had never seen her wearing it. As she unfolded the dress, something fell from it and landed on the bed. It was a khaki envelope. She hesitated before opening it. She did not want to intrude on the dead woman's privacy.

It was a photograph.

There was no mistaking who the woman in the picture was—Ssenga Jovia as a teenager. Her hair was long, reaching her shoulders. She was holding an infant, who could not have been more than three months, close to her chest. Had it not been for the shape of his nose, for its distinctive sharp tip, its narrow, well-shaped nostrils, its smooth blackness, she would not have recognized the baby in the photograph.

But because she knew a similar nose—her daughter's—she identified who the baby was. It was the way Ssenga Jovia held the baby—one hand cradling the infant's cheek, her eyes gazing at the baby's face with great tenderness—that gave away the rest of the mystery: only a mother could cuddle her baby the way she did.

Ajuna knew then. She knew without being told. It had been obvious all this time, the writing clear on the wall, and she had missed it. Ssenga Jovia had made hints. "It's Kagaba who sustained me during those difficult years after I realized I could not have children with my husband." The close bond with Daisy, whom she considered "her own grandchild" was finally explained. But who, then, was Kagaba's father? It couldn't be Mr. Nathan.

She folded the envelope and put it in her handbag. She put the dress in a bag, along with Ssenga Jovia's red scarf, and headed back to hospital.

Ama had arrived and Kato was already making arrangements for the funeral. Ajuna handed Ama the dress and returned to the apartment to be with Daisy, whom she had left in Dr. Tindi's care. She sat on the bed for a long time after Dr. Tindi had left, crying silently for the loss of her second mother, and contemplating her stunning discovery. Did Kagaba know?

2

There was no wake for Ssenga Jovia. Ajuna traveled to the village for the funeral with Daisy and Jane in Tal's powerful Land Cruiser. Kalayi drove them. Dr. Tindi kept away.

Ssenga Jovia was buried at her brother's home, which was unusual, given that she had been a married woman and therefore should have been buried at her marital home. Ama had explained that her father had made the decision, perhaps because Ssenga Jovia's husband had died so long ago. Many of the mourners, though, came from her late husband's village.

Ama's mother, Amooti, appeared sad at the death of her former archenemy and took charge of everything. Time had healed their differences and bitterness. Ama, who had never let the bickering and bad blood between her mother and aunt affect her relationship with the dead woman, was devastated, and Kato and she sponsored most of the funeral expenses, even when Ajuna knew they were still struggling to deal with Eva's death, just a month prior.

Musana and Solange traveled together. Ajuna saw them seated in one of the smaller tents under a mahogany tree and went over to say hello. Solange was crying, her head on Musana's shoulder. Perhaps the funeral reminded her of her daughter's death. Musana's face portrayed sadness too. Both had never met Ssenga Jovia, but they came to show their solidarity with Kato, who had lost an in-law, and to Ama, notwithstanding what had happened between them.

Ajuna had carried along the gifts she had bought for Ssenga

Jovia, not quite sure who to hand them to. She gave them to Amooti, who said they would put the blanket and bed sheets in the coffin. The other items, shoes and clothes, would be given to the person chosen to stand in the dead woman's place.

"Who will that be?" Ajuna was intrigued. Officially, Ssenga Jovia was childless, yet culturally, every adult must have someone to carry on their name after they died.

"Ama. She was her favorite niece."

Mr. Nathan looked withered as he read a short, sorrowful speech. He described his sister as the rock of their family after their parents passed away. There was no mention of the lies that had dogged her life. After he finished his speech, he read out an email from Kagaba. He expressed his deepest regrets for not having been with the family to bid farewell to his aunt, whom he referred to as his best friend, his great love.

He doesn't know, Ajuna concluded.

Later that evening, after Kalayi and Jane had returned to the city, Tomas came to inform Ajuna that Mr. Nathan wanted to speak with her. Ajuna had decided to spend the night. She felt that her close relationship with Ssenga Jovia and other marital responsibilities obligated her to stay behind and condole with the family. Besides, she wanted to talk with Mr. Nathan.

Tomas had vacated his quarters for Ajuna and Daisy. When Mr. Nathan came into the room, he sat on a stool in the corner. He looked more tired and older. He asked about Daisy and said how pleased he was to finally see her and hold her in his arms. He said she looked so much like her father, that she had inherited his pronounced forehead and pointed nose.

"I know everything," Ajuna said, before he could continue.

For a moment, he looked confused.

"I know she was Kagaba's mother," Ajuna said.

Mr. Nathan gave a small nod, frowning. "She had a brief affair with the pastoral man I had hired to look after my two cows." He spoke softly, not looking at Ajuna. "I should have sensed something was going on between them." He looked up

258

to meet Ajuna's eyes, his own portraying regret. "He wasn't right for her."

"Why?"

"He was a foreigner. We did not know his ways. We did not know anything about his family. We worried that he would take her away to his homeland. When I found out about the affair, I chased him away. I did not know she was already pregnant.

"Our parents were already dead, so I hid her in the house until the baby was born, then declared that I was the baby's father. I told our neighbors and relatives that the baby's mother and I had separated when she was already pregnant, but that I did not know at the time; that when the baby was born, she abandoned him to me and that my younger sister was helping me raise him.

"That's the story everybody believed all these years. Until a few years ago, when Ssenga Jovia wanted to come out with the truth. She wanted to tell Kagaba that time when she tried to come to the city but the bus conductor ruined her trip.

"I have explained everything in this letter. I want you to post it to Kagaba with the fastest means."

Ajuna left in the morning. She wondered if she would ever return to this home. Perhaps for another funeral, or when Daisy was a big girl and demanded to know her roots.

She would make a copy of the photograph and send it with the letter by courier. She would frame the original and keep it for Daisy, for when she was old enough to understand the complexity of her father's family history.

London

1

Kagaba spoke to Ajuna a few days after Ssenga Jovia's funeral. It was an awkward exchange punctuated by heavy silences, unlike the conversation they had had the day after Eva died. He thanked her for caring for Ssenga Jovia; for attending the funeral. Ajuna put Daisy on the phone and she babbled a few baby sounds, which made them both laugh, easing the tension somewhat.

The affair with Dr. Tindi had remained unvoiced. After he had failed to send her the angry messages he had composed on the day he learned about it, he had called Jane and poured out his heart: how disappointed, broken, devastated, frustrated he was because of Ajuna's actions.

Kagaba knew Jane must have talked to her friend afterwards, and he had waited for Ajuna to come back fighting, denying the affair or trying to justify it.

But she did not. If she had, he would have been convinced that she still cared for him. He would then have explained his involvement with Julia. She would forgive him, and he would forgive her, and everything would go back to being normal between them.

The telephone conversation soon dried up and, before hanging up, Kagaba asked Ajuna to send him Daisy's most recent pictures so he could see for himself how much she had grown.

When the courier man knocked on his door a few days later and asked Kagaba to sign for his parcel, he at first imagined they were the photos Ajuna had promised him. But the parcel was small and contained only two letters: one from his father and a note from Ajuna. He opened Ajuna's first. Between the two folded sheets was a photograph. It was faint-colored and looked like it had been copied from an original version. *I thought you should have this,* said the note, but the rest did not make much sense. Until he read his father's five-page letter, scripted in fine handwriting, as usual, like an artwork. It was dated 10 January 2009. The day Ssenga Jovia died.

Several valves in his head burst open, letting out a gush of mixed emotions: confusion, bitterness, anger, disbelief. His father, no, his *uncle*, was begging him to understand and forgive his past mistakes. He was also asking him to return to Uganda for the sake of his daughter, so she would not grow up without a father, too.

What cheek! They had let him grow into an adult without telling him about his real father and now they wanted to lecture him about his responsibilities to his daughter. In the mad anger that seized him, he must have thrown a glass against the fridge; he only heard the crash as the glass exploded into a thousand pieces.

He called Ajuna, but her phone was engaged; most likely she was busy talking to her lover. He ripped the letter into two pieces, but then thought better of it and pieced it together again with sellotape. He needed to read it again.

He called his father, his *uncle*. "Is this true?" he screamed into the phone.

They had done it for him, Mr. Nathan answered in a feeble voice; they thought it best to keep the truth him from. They were protecting him. It was all done in good faith.

Kagaba was thrown into renewed fury. "You did it for *me*? What a load of rubbish! You should have told me the truth, and then let me decide whether I wanted to live the lie or not." He raged on until his credit ran out.

Ssenga Jovia: his own mother! So that's why she hadn't accompanied him to the kwanjula ceremony because, customarily, the groom's mother was not permitted to participate in her son's traditional marriage.

Ssenga Jovia: his mother. So that's why she had once let slip that his nose was like his father's; because she knew who his *real* father was. He was about ten years old. He had fallen off his bicycle and hurt his face. His nose was bleeding. "This long nose of yours," she had said teasingly. "One thing your father gave you," she had added as an afterthought, like she was talking to herself.

Ssenga Jovia: his mother. So that's why he spent all his vacations at her house; that's why she fussed so much about his well-being. That's why she sometimes referred to him as "Mutabani wange." My son.

He went to buy more credit and called Ama. "So, you're not my sister after all. You're my cousin. I have no sister or brother, or perhaps I do, from my absentee father. Did you know about this? Tell me the truth."

Ama said her mother had whispered something to her many years ago but begged her never to say anything to him.

"And you kept quiet about it! You betrayed me, just like the rest of them. And even Ajuna knows. What? Can you imagine that? She's the stranger in the family, but she gets to know all the secrets before I do."

He called Emily. He needed to talk to her right away. She had earlier sent a text asking him to call her. But she did not answer.

Finally, the tears came. Tears he should have shed when he first received news of Ssenga Jovia's—*his mother's*—death that Sunday morning.

Emily returned his call around seven in the evening asking him to meet her at a restaurant near her office. He sat on the train, his mind blank, avoiding thinking about anything.

The moment he saw Emily, he dissolved into tears.

"I'm so sorry for your loss," Emily attempted to console him, as she wiped away her own tears. She didn't seem as shocked as he would have imagined or liked her to be. He wanted her to be angry on his behalf. Maybe it was a muzungu culture. He was about to say something, but she interrupted. "Mr. Masego called me from Botswana this morning." She paused, waiting for his reaction.

"That's, uh, great." He forced himself to sound excited, but his mind was still in turmoil. "He has emailed me some documents for you to look at. He believes he has found you a match with a management company in Botswana." Emily was beaming. "Here's all the information you will need to apply," she said as she fished for the documents in her handbag.

Before she could hand them to Kagaba, he said, "I don't think I'll follow up with the job offer anymore. That's what I wanted to talk to you about. I want to return to Uganda and be with my daughter. I don't want her to think I abandoned her. So much has happened in these past months and nothing seems to make sense anymore. Nothing is more important right now than being with my daughter."

"Kagaba, you are not thinking straight at the moment. You must be feeling terrible about what your family did … the lies. But you cannot let this opportunity pass."

"I know what you are saying, Emily, but my mind is made up."

"Look, you have sacrificed a lot already. You cannot return to Uganda without a job."

"I just want to return home." His voice was emotionless.

"Mr. Masego's company will pay for your air ticket to Botswana. You will undergo an interview. I'm certain you will smash it."

"I need to see my daughter."

"I see." Emily sounded deflated. "I'm sorry it took so long to speak with Mr. Masego."

"It's not your fault, Emily, and thanks so much for your efforts, but this is my decision."

The cappuccino Emily had ordered when they sat down

had gone cold and the carrot muffin remained untouched. She put back the sheaf of papers in her handbag.

"Thank you, Emily," he said. She shrugged, with just a flicker of a smile.

They stood up at the same time. She extended her hand first, but he wanted to hug her. The mere shaking of hands would not express his gratitude for her kindness; not only to him, but for her involvement with Julia's case. When he shook her hand, it felt cold.

"When ... will you ... uh ... be returning to Uganda?" Emily avoided looking at him.

"I haven't decided on a date yet, but sometime this month." He was running out of cash.

"I see. Let me know how things go."

"I will." He was still holding her hand.

They started walking to the train station, taciturn, the evening traffic of cars, buses, bicycles, humans mingling to drown out their unspoken thoughts.

He started composing *The Letter* the moment he got on the train. He would tell Ajuna *everything*, so she would know before he returned to Uganda. No more lies about what he did for a living. About Julia. It was going to be a very long letter.

2

On Saturday, Kagaba called Ochola to tell him about his loss. He wasn't feeling as sad or angry, which surprised him. He was pleased he had managed to expunge these two emotions that had beleaguered him for the past two days. His decision to return to Uganda had empowered him. He was still worried about disappointing Emily. But one day, she would understand.

When he spoke with Ochola, he downplayed Ochola's sympathies for his bereavement. He did not mention that Ssenga Jovia was his mother—which lessened the burden of loss. He must have sounded cheerful enough for Ochola to suggest that they meet for a drink. He said he had finally finished his degree, and they would be celebrating his achievement.

They found their way to a pub on Tooley Street. It was packed with a group of youngsters celebrating their friend's birthday. Normally, Kagaba would have preferred a less rowdy place, but tonight he welcomed the boisterous chatter of the revelers.

"Drink a whiskey. This is my major celebration, man!" Ochola offered.

"No whiskey, please," Kagaba laughed as he narrated his experience with the hard liquor months back.

"Coward, I'm going to order a bottle of wine."

Kagaba had not seen Ochola this happy.

"After four years of toiling, I'm finally going home with my degree."

"I am happy for you. I believe you will find a job in Uganda, with a master's in architecture?"

"Architectural Engineering. How about you? You mentioned you'd be returning to Uganda as well? How about the job Emily has been trying to connect you to in Botswana?"

"I've changed my mind."

"About the job, or returning to Uganda?"

"I'm returning to Uganda. I've given the matter enough thought over the past week. It's the right thing to do."

"Right, but not logical. You need a job, my friend, and a steady flow of income once you return to Uganda."

Yesterday, he had posted *The Letter* to Ajuna. He would give her enough time to absorb its contents. He had not mentioned his return. He would wait for her to respond, or react, before telling her.

"Have you visited Julia of late?" Ochola changed the subject.

"No, have you? She had a mental breakdown and was placed in an isolation unit with no visitors allowed; not that she had anyone except me."

Kagaba had not meant to antagonize Ochola, but he couldn't help himself.

Ochola put down his glass of wine. "My sister is a survivor."

"What do you mean? She's been in a very difficult situation."

"Don't get me wrong; that's not why I didn't go to visit her."

"What, then?"

For a while, Ochola stared into his glass of wine. "Did Julia ever tell you about her sham marriage? No, I don't think so. That woman, Nambozo, made the connection. For a commission, of course. I had just arrived in this country and still had my stipend from my scholarship intact. Julia begged me to lend it to her so she could pay the man to marry her so she could get a spouse visa. I lost all my money. The man became violent after the marriage. She had to leave him. I couldn't afford rent, so I moved in with Julia. She was working three jobs and eventually repaid me. So, yes, she's a tough girl.

"But there was more to come. When I was living with her, she rented out my passport to an illegal without my knowledge. If they had caught him, I would have lost my scholarship and had my visa canceled. After that, I told her I would never get involved in her escapades again. This time, after she was sent to the detention center, she wanted me to help her obtain some forged papers that would have aided her release; when I refused, she asked if I could stand surety for her bail. It's very difficult to say no to Julia, so I decided to keep away."

"At first I thought you were lovers."

Ochola chuckled. "I can't blame you. Julia uses me as a front when it suits her. She wants to create an illusion that the suitor is up against some competition. She's always up to some mischief, but she always manages to pull herself out of it."

"And are you actually her real brother?"

"Our mothers are sisters, but my father is from the north."

They polished off two bottles of wine and Ochola ordered more. The teenagers had started dancing and Ochola pulled Kagaba to his feet and they joined the celebrating teens on the floor. "We came to celebrate, not to mourn." They swayed to the hip-hop music, the teenagers clapping encouragingly.

It was late when they left the bar. The street was still abuzz with tourists speaking in foreign languages.

"Bonjour," Kagaba shouted to a group of about five. "Are you from France? I'm from Uganda and my name is Kagaba." He was addressing them in broken French from his secondary-school days, the wine impelling him, and the tourists laughed good-naturedly. Ochola fell into hysterics and linked his hand in Kagaba's, then started to chant tunelessly, "I'm going back home, I'm going back home with my degree, I'm ..."

Kagaba joined in as they swayed in the middle of the street. Cars hooted at them, but Ochola responded with the victory sign. They had lost track of time; the bright streetlights, the multitude of tourists and heavy traffic, and the shops still open all made it look like it was early evening—but it could just as well have been midnight. Finally, they collapsed on the cold metal bench by the bus stop, breathing heavily, teeth chattering in the freezing, winter wind.

"Did Julia tell you about the father of her child?" Ochola was shouting.

"Yes," Kagaba shouted back.

"And how he was deported? What she didn't tell you was that she was with him that day. It has never been clear how Julia managed to escape arrest. I told you, she knows all the tricks to survive in this country."

The trains had stopped running.

"You can crash on my couch," Ochola offered. "We'll take a cab. I don't like those night buses, they take forever."

Kampala

1

With the funeral over, and Ssenga Jovia gone forever, life was beginning to regain some form of normality. Dr. Tindi spent fewer nights with Ajuna. He had fallen behind with his marking load and wanted to catch up before the university reopened in two weeks. The government, once again, had successfully blocked the University Council from increasing tuition. The students were happy, but the lecturers themselves would soon be striking because their salaries hadn't been increased as they had demanded.

Ajuna had not even started marking. Even if she worked day and night for the next two weeks, she would never finish even half of what awaited her. She had decided to put her PhD on hold until things stabilized.

On a personal front, her life was in meltdown. Her washing machine had broken down and the plumber was charging too much to repair it. The cost of a new one was beyond her means. Her laptop's battery had come to the end of its life after five years of use. Daisy had come down with malaria but, after two nights in hospital, she was beginning to show signs of recovery. A new nanny, not half as good as Ssenga Jovia, had started work only a week earlier. Daisy detested her and Ajuna was wary of leaving the two together when she resumed work.

The girl was only sixteen, not fit to work. Her mother was a friend and neighbor of Ajuna's mother. Their father had died, leaving the family destitute. The girl's mother was worried that her daughter would soon become pregnant, given that she was not going to school anymore. Ajuna's mother had begged and begged: "Please, take her to the city to save her from an early pregnancy and marriage. You don't have to pay her. Just keep her safe. She's good with babies. She is the eldest child in her family and helped raise all her siblings."

Ajuna relented. She was training the girl in every aspect, including hygiene. She was not sure how long she would keep her, though. She needed to find a proper nanny.

Once again, the university had delayed paying their allowances for teaching part-timers and supervising foreign students and, without the additional income, Ajuna could not survive on the miserly university salary. The top-up she had gotten used to from Kagaba had dwindled without proper explanation from him. Was it because of his discovery of her affair with Dr. Tindi? Or was he not working anymore? Soon she will need to ask him for some financial assistance. Even if he was upset about her infidelity, he was still Daisy's dad. Moreover, Daisy's first birthday was approaching. She wanted to do something small, just a celebration. Surely Kagaba should support her?

She turned to Kalayi for a soft loan to clear the hospital bills. "You should quit," Kalayi advised her. "Go to America and teach there, or get a scholarship to the UK to complete your PhD and don't come back. What are you still doing in this stupid country with your big brain?"

Dr. Tindi hadn't made it to hospital when Daisy was admitted, so he came to the apartment following her discharge from hospital. He looked tired and subdued.

"Most of the essays are a disaster," he complained. "These students can't spell, let alone construct a decent English sentence—and I'm talking about graduate students. That's even more reason they should pay us more. I swear, if my salary is not increased this year as the government keeps promising, I'll go back to the village and start a turkey-rearing project."

"And I'll get a scholarship to the US to complete my PhD; and you will never see me again."

"No, you wouldn't!"

"Honestly? I think I will. Otherwise, I don't see how I can ever complete this degree, given all that's going on around me. I've never gotten round to submitting even the first chapter. But, well, I guess, no, I wouldn't leave. I don't think I could survive those winters."

"And the loneliness."

"And I wouldn't want Daisy growing up in a foreign country."

"Anyway, how are you both?

"Alive!"

I'm sorry I couldn't make it to the hospital."

He had brought a takeaway from Nando's and ice cream for Daisy. They ate on the balcony and Daisy managed a spoonful of her favorite vanilla. She had developed mouth sores—an aftereffect of malaria. Mosquitoes were buzzing about; the heavy rains had created dangerous breeding grounds for the parasites. Ajuna hoped Daisy wouldn't get re-infected.

Daisy fell asleep a few moments later, but Ajuna knew she wouldn't sleep for long and didn't bother to carry her to the bedroom. The fever had stolen her sleep. Ajuna felt exhausted herself. She hadn't slept well ever since Ssenga Jovia's death.

"When I'm sleeping, I see her," she said to Dr. Tindi. "She comes and sits on my bed. She holds Daisy and feeds her, but she doesn't talk to me."

"Keep the window open at night. To free her spirit."

"They say people know when they are about to die. Is that why she carried that photograph with her? Maybe she was going to show it to me before she left for the village. She didn't want to carry her secrets to the other world. The day before she died, I was feeling grumpy and nervous. I almost didn't go to Kalayi's engagement party. I think it was a sign that something bad was about to happen."

"I don't remember any signs before my brother went missing, but the remorse I felt afterwards almost destroyed me."

"Did you blame yourself?"

"Yes, in a way. If he hadn't made that trip to visit us; if I had canceled the meeting that day and picked him up from the bus park as he had requested; if I had returned home earlier; if I had gone to the police sooner."

"How did you overcome it?"

"I'm not sure I did. Isn't it strange how life seems to be about regrets? If this; if that … *If you can keep your head when all about you / Are losing theirs and blaming it on you, / If you can trust yourself when all men doubt you, / But make allowance for their doubting too …*"

"Is that a poem?" Ajuna asked.

"Yes. It's titled 'If.' It was written by a British poet, many, many years ago. His name was Kipling. It's very inspirational and elegantly written. I had memorized all of it and used to recite it to myself during those difficult years; its message sustained me."

"You should have been a poet; all that humor should be put to good use."

"*I am* a poet."

"Seriously? Have you written any poetry books?"

"Yes."

She eyed him with skepticism. "How many?"

"Two."

"Where are they? How come you've never shown them to me?"

"They are still here," he pointed to his head. "One day, I'll put my ideas on paper. I would love to write about my brother. Even after all these years, I still believe he is out there, somewhere. Sometimes I imagine I'll just bump into him on the street, or I'll return home after work and find him waiting for me. That day when I told you I had gone to church, it was to mark the tenth anniversary of his disappearance."

"You said two things happened, but you only told me the joke, the good thing," Ajuna remembered.

"Lorna had prepared lunch for my family afterwards, but all my relatives turned down her offer, including my parents. That was the bad thing. They still blame her for their son's disappearance and me for not doing enough to find him."

He stood up to leave, saying he had to return to his marking, but promised to call later in the week. Ajuna did not urge him to stay. He was hurting, she could tell, and had failed to turn on his usual charm to dispel memories of his brother that still lingered.

On Sunday, Ajuna went to Kalayi's house to pay back the money she had lent her and to see their mother, who had come to visit. She planned to leave Daisy at home, in part because she was still weak with fever, but she also wanted her to get used to the maid. But Daisy cried so much that she didn't have the heart to leave her.

She carried basketfuls of laundry so she could use Kalayi's washing machine.

Mayi looked radiant as ever and Kalayi was the perfect hostess. Kalayi had bought new items for her use: a mattress, bed, sheets, and towels. Tal was away on a business trip in Dubai.

Ajuna asked about their father.

"He's not been feeling too well," Mayi replied.

"Who's looking after him now that you're here? How long are you staying?"

"A month," Kalayi answered with authority. "Mayi deserves a holiday, Ajuna. I have a big house all to myself and I can afford to look after her. You should be pleased for her."

"I am. I'm just concerned about Father. That's all."

"He doesn't want to come to the city, as you know. I had invited them both."

Ajuna said no more. If she had space at her apartment, she would have persuaded their father to visit to take a "holiday," as Kalayi put it. He would never be impressed by Kalayi's ultra-modern apartment or with Tal's pompous ways. Perhaps that's why he had turned down the invitation.

Mayi complained. She hadn't seen Daisy since she was a baby. "You should visit us more often," she grumbled. She tried to take Daisy from Ajuna's arms, but Daisy pulled away. "Look, this child doesn't even know me."

"It's been busy for me, Mayi; with Ssenga Jovia's death, trying to find a maid, the university about to reopen."

"The child is all grown. You should find time, Ajuna, to visit us. Look at her," Mayi threw back her head to take a closer look at Daisy. "She is going to be a tall woman."

"Like her dad," Kalayi added. "In fact, she looks like Kagaba in everything. Ajuna, there's nothing of you in this child."

"She has my eyes," Ajuna protested.

"Come and visit us soon," Mayi persisted.

Kalayi had hired two maids who she insisted wear uniforms while on duty. One cooked and washed and ironed, and the other kept the house immaculately clean. Their boss was kept busy with her two businesses: a hair salon and a supermarket. One of the maids offered to iron the clothes after Ajuna had washed them in the machine.

After lunch, Mayi went to take a nap. Daisy, who had surprised Ajuna by finishing her food, had also fallen asleep. Kalayi carried her to the spare bedroom and Ajuna followed.

Ajuna was shocked to find the bedroom decorated as a nursery: an expensive, large crib, various colorful toys, a Moses basket, a swinging baby chair, and many other baby items she could not identify or know their use.

"Last month I thought I was pregnant," Kalayi explained before Ajuna could ask. "But it was a false alarm. I'm getting impatient," she said as they went back to the living room. "I've been with Tal for more than a year, and nothing has happened."

"Don't be dramatic. You're still young and there's still plenty of time."

"I'm not young. I'll be twenty-four next month. I want to get over with kids' stuff and focus on something different. I want four kids, and I want to be done by the time I'm thirty. I've discussed it with Tal. We're going for IVF."

"Now that's over the top."

"I've already seen the doctor at the Women's Fertility Clinic. It will cost about nine thousand dollars."

Ajuna let out a small whistle. "But is this something you really want to go through with? I mean, those tests and procedures are quite intrusive."

"I told you I want to finish with this baby business. There are other things I want to do with my life. I want to travel and see the world. I might even go back to school and earn a university degree."

"Life begins at forty."

"Don't give me that crap. I want mine to begin at thirty, so don't even try to talk me out of this."

"Sometimes things don't always work out the way you would have wished. You have to allow for the gray areas."

"Ah, there you go again. Don't you start, big sis. Life should not be philosophized but lived."

"What about marriage? Wouldn't you rather get that out of the way first?"

"I told you, I don't want any more delays. I want to give Tal a baby boy. He wants a boy. The other kid is a girl. After that, we can talk about marriage."

"I see."

So that's what all this was about. "Where's Tal's other child now?"

"With the mother."

Ajuna creased her brow in surprise.

"I mean Tal's mother. You think I'm stupid?" She began to sob.

"Kalayi, I'm sorry. That's not what I meant."

"No, it's not that. Suppose I don't get another chance. After the ... I mean after what I did? I am worried."

"Trust me, you will." Ajuna took Kalayi's hands in hers.

"There is no need to rush or panic." The doctor who performed the abortion had assured them that Kalayi would have no problem getting pregnant again.

"I don't want to wait anymore. Tal doesn't know anything. But he might get suspicious if it takes too long."

"You will be fine, Kalayi." Ajuna pushed herself to sound confident. She hoped the doctor was right. She pulled Kalayi into an embrace, and Kalayi rested her teary face on Ajuna's shoulder. Her body was shaking.

They stayed like that for a while, not speaking, until Kalayi stopped quivering. Ajuna gave her the money she had borrowed but Kalayi would not take it.

"I don't need it. Keep it. Tal takes care of everything." But Ajuna insisted and lied that their allowances had been paid and she could afford to pay her back.

"It's your pride, isn't it? You don't want to take anything from your younger sister." She looked like she was about to cry again. "You looked after me when I needed you and now you won't accept a little help from me. You're like Father; he won't take any money from me, either."

"Alright," Anjuna said, and put the money back in her bag. "Thanks, Kalayi."

2

Dr. Tindi did not call her as he had promised. Ajuna waited another few days before phoning him. He answered promptly.

"Great minds ... I was about to call you." He was his jocular self once again and Ajuna felt pleased.

"Really, what about?"

Because he had started off in high spirits, she did not expect the news he gave her.

"Lorna is back. She's abandoned her course, again, and she's not in good shape, Ajuna. We've been to see a psychologist."

She said nothing.

"Are you there?"

"Yes."

"The psychologist has recommended counseling and a number of tests."

She made no comment.

"But I have some good news. I've been allocated an office in the new Lule Building; when we resume, I'll have my own space. Ajuna, are you alright?"

"I'm fine. I'll see you next week then."

"I'm not sure I'll make it the first week. I'll be accompanying Lorna to hospital and all that.

"And ... I think I forgot to mention ... my application for a postdoc at the University of Cape Town has been accepted."

She took a moment to respond. "I see. So, you will be leaving."

"Yes ... How's Amala-Daisy?"

She didn't answer him immediately.

"Ajuna, are you sure you're alright?"

"She's good," she said eventually.

"Great. I'll call you sometime this week. I have to let you go now. Bye."

Jane came the next day and found Ajuna furious.

"He's been having an affair!" She was still dressed in her pajamas, her eyes puffy from crying.

"Who's having an affair, Ajuna?"

Ajuna reached for the envelope on top of the table. "Here, read for yourself."

But Jane did not take the envelope. Ajuna started sobbing again. "How could he?"

"Ajuna, please calm down and tell me what's going on." Jane's tone was reassuring but firm. She took the letter and opened it. There were about five typed sheets, stapled together; but Jane's attention was caught by the dog-eared page and the few lines at the bottom, which Ajuna had circled in red ink: *Julia was a mistake. What happened between us meant nothing. You and Daisy mean the world to me.*

"I see." Jane handed the letter back to Ajuna. "You long suspected he was cheating. Anyhow, we're not canceling our tickets for tomorrow's gig." Jane planned to take Ajuna out to a live performance. Jane knew Ajuna needed a break after all she had been through.

"I'll pick you up at eight? The show starts at ten."

"I don't want to go."

"You'll feel better if you go out." Jane stood up. "I'll see you tomorrow."

In the morning, when Ajuna got out of bed, the heavy cloak of despondency had lifted. For the first time since receiving Kagaba's letter, she was feeling upbeat.

So, he's been seeing another woman. Not wanting to give herself time to think about what she was doing, she retrieved the letter from under her pillow, found a matchbox in the kitchen, and set the letter on fire. The smoke filled the small kitchen and she opened the window and the door to let it out.

London

1

Kagaba didn't know what to expect as he waited for Julia to come through the reception area. He had only spoken with her by phone the previous month. All he knew was she was now out of the solitary unit and was being allowed visitors. She said she was still waiting to hear back from the judge regarding her bail application.

Julia had lost her vim. Her skin was pale; her small eyes did not sparkle. But she was dressed in clean clothes and her hair was neat. Nearly six months in this place had taken their toll on her.

She sat across from him, resting her elbows on the table. He had come to say goodbye. He wasn't sure if it was necessary to tell her all the news that had happened since his last visit: Ssenga Jovia's passing and his discovery that she was his mother; Musana's daughter's death and how he had left for Uganda for good; his breaking up with Ajuna. He was still waiting for Ajuna's response to *The Letter*. That she had received it, he was not in doubt; he had sent it via courier.

In the end, he said nothing. It all sounded too much for Julia's fragile mental state. They sat in comfortable silence, stroking hands until she started speaking.

"When Yolanda was being deported, they assigned her two kanyamas to escort her on the plane to Cameroon. On the first day, as they were about to board the plane, she started yelling and kicking at the two strong men. She fell on the floor and when they tried to lift her up, she sank her teeth into their hands. The pilot refused to carry a disruptive passenger.

"The second time, they shackled her and put handcuffs on her wrists. As they boarded the van to take them to the airport, she hit her child on the head with the handcuffs. They had to rush the little girl to hospital and abandon the trip to the airport.

"That night, Yolanda killed herself. What do you think happened to her body, and to her unborn child? Did they burn her? It's taboo to bury a pregnant woman before removing the fetus."

Kagaba had let her talk without interruption, in fear of upsetting her again.

"Why did she hit her own child?" he asked finally.

"She had already decided that if they were so determined to return her to Cameroon, then she would spare her child the misery, and Yolanda could not return to Cameroon herself as she had sold all her mother's land.

"My lawyer called this morning," she said as an afterthought, looking up. Her small eyes were sharp and distinct, like the first time he had met her at Musana and Sharon's party.

Kagaba held his breath, not wanting to say anything. "And?" he prompted, when Julia seemed like she wasn't going to tell him.

"I was granted bail."

Relief washed over him. He wanted to lift her high up in the air and dance in circles in the heavily guarded reception room.

"I'll be released in a few days." She had a small, teasing smile on her face. She was enjoying his shocked reaction to the good news.

"And where will you go?" Her bail conditions, as Emily had explained, required that she be released to her surety and continue reporting to an immigration office until her case was resolved. He had let Emily down. He wondered if she would still be interested in helping Julia.

"Come back with me to Uganda. I'm leaving this month." Kagaba's sudden proposal surprised even him.

Julia laughed, looked away, like she did not believe him.

"I'm serious. You have a university degree. I'm sure you can find a job."

She shook her head vigorously.

"It's doable, Julia, this place is not good for you. I mean the UK."

"No."

"What do you mean no? Listen, Julia, if—"

"Stop!" she hissed. "Listen to yourself. You're not making any sense. My life is here now. I've lived in this country for ten years. I wouldn't know what else to do with myself. My daughter doesn't even know me; besides, I don't have the confidence or the skills to handle an office job. All these years, I've worked as a cleaner and carer. The university degree you refer to is useless to me."

Kagaba was still holding her hands. He turned them over, so the palms were facing him.

"You can return," Julia added, unclenching her hands. "This country wasn't really for you. I sensed it right from the beginning. I could see you wouldn't last long. You even refused to dance. You're just like Ochola. I'm glad you're leaving. I'm sure you'll be happy back in Uganda."

"What about you? Are you going to find another job?"

"I'll be fine," she spoke with optimism. "I'll apply for asylum. Within a year, everything will be okay. I called Emily to let her know about my bail. She will help me with everything. Go." She pushed him gently, grinning.

"Will you keep in touch? Will you let me know how you're getting on?"

"Sure," she laughed boisterously, like she used to before all this happened. "And I hope you work things out with Ajuna. You still love her. I know that."

She hugged him for a short while. "Take care. Thank you for looking after me. You're a special person."

With a quick step, he walked through the door and got back home earlier than he had anticipated. It was nearly eight in the evening, but he did not feel like eating or watching TV.

He lay on the bed. In a few weeks, he would be on the plane to Uganda. Like Musana, he wouldn't have trouble leaving the country. But he would never be able to return.

Back home, he would have to face his deceptive family, cope with Ssenga Jovia's eternal absence, deal with Ajuna's infidelity, meet his daughter for the first time. He had to figure out where he would stay for the first days. He hadn't told anyone yet about his planned return.

He dozed off, woke up, slumbered in again. He was sinking into a deep, black pit of nothingness, the pounding in his head escalating.

2

A thunderous bang woke him. Heart racing, he jolted up in bed. A faint glow was streaming in from the window. What time was it?

Bang! Bang! Bang! He jumped out of bed and reached for a towel he had thrown on floor to wrap round his waist. His head was still pounding. He inched toward the door and, before he could speak, someone yelled, "Open! We're the enforcement agents."

"The what?"

There was more pounding. "Open this door now; we know you are in there!"

He turned the key, but the door was unlocked. It was the signal the intruders had been waiting for. In a flash, the door was flung open. There were two of them, tall and muscular. The one who had entered first wedged his foot in the doorway to prevent him from closing it again.

"Good morning, sir, we're court bailiffs, and we're here on behalf of our client to recover rent arrears." The man flashed his ID, which was pegged on the breast of his blue uniform.

"I ... I don't understand ... I ..."

"Look, sir, we're not here to play games. We're here to recover the money you owe to your landlord. We sent you a letter more than seven days ago." He shoved a copy of the letter in Kagaba's face. "Now, are you ready to pay the money?"

"I think you are mistaken. I am not the—"

"You're not Mr. Musena? Oh, come on, of course you are.

Look," his tone was stern, "please, don't waste our time, and we'll not waste yours."

"You mean Musana?"

"Whatever." The man went on to explain that they had sent several letters to Mr. Musena, demanding payment of rent arrears, which had now accumulated to over six months, but got no response. The direct debit Musana had set up for rent payment at the end of each month had been stopped by the bank because there was no more money in Musana's account.

Kagaba was required to pay the money due—right now, either in cash, or with a credit card. His pleas of mistaken identity fell on deaf ears, his cries of not having any money, in cash, or on a credit card, which he did not even possess, went unheeded.

"Sir, how much can you pay today? We can work out a payment plan; just tell us how much you are ready to pay now."

"I don't have any money. Musana returned to Uganda in December. He lost his child and his visa was not renewed." Words were tumbling out of his mouth, eager to be believed.

"Sir, we're only interested in what you can pay today, and not your stories."

They said if he wasn't ready to pay, they would confiscate any valuable items in the house, which they would resell to recover the money owed. They wanted to know if he owned a car; they scanned the tiny space, looking for anything of value, a TV, a few suitcases, an old computer. The wardrobe was devoid of any designer suits or jackets. Some of his nice clothes were still at Julia's apartment, and Musana had moved his to Sharon's. There was nothing of value to take.

He was then informed that he had to vacate the premises. The landlord was taking back control of his property. He was given two hours to pack up. They would change the locks after he left.

Kagaba was paralyzed. His head was pounding. He was still undressed, with only the white towel sitting loosely around his waist. They said they would wait outside for him to get dressed and finish packing. He did not move.

"Sir, if you don't cooperate, we'll call the police. And please remove all your belongings. Whatever is left behind will be put outside. Our job is to hand the property back to your landlord."

The men stepped outside but did not close the door. The one who had been mostly silent returned and said to him, "You can call some of your friends or relatives to arrange where to sleep tonight, or they can lend you some money?"

He shook his head.

"Don't you have anyone who can help?"

When he did not get an answer, the man started moving out of the room, but Kagaba said to him, "I don't have anywhere to go. I don't have any money. I was planning to return to my country in a few weeks. I have already bought my air ticket. Can't you let me stay for just … just …for …"

The man looked undecided before answering. "It's not up to me. I'm only doing my job." His tone was kind, his voice low. "But surely you must have someone you can call? Problem is, we can't let you back in. You must vacate the premises."

It was not difficult to pack. Once Kagaba checked and ensured that his passport and air ticket were in his rucksack, he threw a few toiletries, some clothes and shoes in one of the suitcases.

He aimed for the park where he used to spend time loafing soon after arriving in the UK. It was nine in the morning and very cold. There was no one on the benches, nor any children rocking on the swings. The drizzle and gusts of wind would keep away many park lovers.

He called Sean. These days he hardly saw him. He worked two jobs. He did not answer. Emily. Straight to voicemail. Had she not said she would be heading to Botswana this week? Ochola. No answer. He was also due to return to Uganda this week. He could have left already. Sharon. They had not spoken since Musana left. No, he wouldn't call her.

The benches were filling up. An old man with a dog on a leash had positioned himself next to him. A woman with a child who would not stop crying sat across from them. Two teenagers, one a boy, the other a girl, in oversized jogging pants and hooded jumpers roamed the park, puffing at large, rolled-up tobacco. The old man's dog barked at them, pulling at its leash.

The wind grew stronger. The old man's eyes became rheumy. He pulled his woolen cap to cover his forehead, turned to face Kagaba, and gave him a toothless grin. Kagaba pulled his heavy coat tight and looked away. The old man started coughing, his lungs wheezing, before releasing brown spittle near Kagaba's feet. Kagaba stood up to move to another bench. The old man pulled something from deep in his trench coat pocket and offered it to Kagaba. A soggy sandwich. "No," he shook his head.

A brief scattering of snow appeared. In April! Temperatures had plummeted to 2 degrees from the readings on his phone. Icy sleet dropped from the sky, covering the grass, trees, benches, swings, his shoes, the old man's trench coat, and the dog, in white. Everything turned white.

Kampala

26ᵗʰ April 2009

Dear Kagaba,
I'm writing to you on Daisy's first birthday. I had hoped you'd call. It's a major milestone, you know, for both of us. Daisy has never met you. She's beginning to say a few words, and she calls me "Mummy," which melts my heart! "But where's Daddy?" I'm sure she wonders. She was beginning to bond with Ssenga Jovia, and she, too, left her.

On several occasions, I doubted myself, questioning whether I would be able to raise and care for Daisy single-handedly. But, hey, we've made it through the first year! I was lucky to have the support of family and friends from day one, I must say. Ama has been amazing, in spite of what happened when Eva died. Mr. Nathan was recently in Kampala to check on the progress of his pension money. He dropped by and brought jackfruit for Daisy. Jane has always been there for us. I'm sad that she's leaving for Canada next month at the invitation of her brothers. They believe she might find an opportunity to teach at one of the universities there. Who can blame her? As for Kalayi, hmmm—you know how she can be like. But she's a great aunt and spoils Daisy with expensive toys. She and Tal are expecting triplets, by the way, all girls! Daisy will soon have a troop to play with.

Job-wise, I'm now the acting Head of Department after my boss resigned to join politics. I put in my application for promotion to Senior Lecturer. If it's approved, I will be confirmed.

A lot has happened since you left us, Kagaba, one and a half years ago. Mistakes were made, as you pointed out in your letter. I know you got to know about myself and Dr. Tindi; but all that is now water under the bridge.

I pray you are well. I have not heard from you for a long while. I imagine things haven't been easy for you as well. Did you finally get a proper job?

Anyway, I hope to hear from you soon, if only to say hello to Daisy.

I will keep this letter brief. I'm sending it by courier to ensure that you receive it.

With sincere wishes for a better future.

Ajuna and Daisy

London

1

At Heathrow, they took the glass elevator to Terminal 3 and joined throngs of passengers strolling leisurely on the polished, brown tiles, trying to kill time before their departure. Others raced by frantically, hoping to catch their flights in time. Duty-free shops selling jewelry, perfumes, wines, and liquor were crammed with shoppers. Kagaba did not remember seeing all this activity when he passed through the same airport when he first arrived in the UK.

"It's a pretty busy airport," Emily remarked, noticing his awed expression.

"I saw a signpost the day I arrived," he said. "But I can't find it now."

Emily laughed. "There're millions of them, Kagaba."

"The one I saw was distinct. It had a unique message about life being a curve. I'm sure it's there somewhere."

Emily shrugged, her attention on the wide screens displaying information about flights. It would be a long flight to Gaborone's Sir Seretse Khama International Airport. Sixteen hours in the air. The first stopover would be in Amsterdam, and the next, Addis Ababa. The layover at Bole International was a killer. Six hours. With a Ugandan passport, Kagaba was exempted an entry visa into Botswana. He would get one on arrival.

"We still have more than an hour to board," Emily revealed. "Can we have a coffee?"

They took the elevator to the ground floor and found a

Costa. June had arrived in the company of an unrelenting heat wave. It was difficult to reconcile the current weather with the snow that had hammered England in April. He recalled how he had nearly frozen in the park after being evicted from his house.

The memory flashed through his mind, and he shuddered. After three unanswered calls, Ochola had finally called back the following morning.

"Sorry I missed your call. Yesterday was crazy. I'm applying for a visa extension. My university persuaded me to stay on and teach. But the paperwork I have to deal with is insane. Then there are interviews and—"

"Can I crash on your couch?" Kagaba interrupted him.

"What happened to your house?"

"Long story."

It took several weeks for Kagaba to recover from the horrific experience of spending a night in the freezing park. His body was jaded, his mind in a whirlwind with everything that had happened in the past months. If it hadn't been for Ochola's kindness and encouragement, he would have completely lost himself.

For the first three or so weeks after arriving at Ochola's, whenever he remembered his near brush with hypothermia, he would feel like his mind was detaching from his body. "Write to Emily," Ochola had encouraged him. "I'm sure she will understand. Tell her you need that job. Tell her everything you've been through since you last met. A fresh start in Botswana is what you need."

And so he did. She would see what she could do, she responded, but she wasn't promising anything. Since she was currently in Botswana, she would speak to Mr. Masego directly. Kato had also been in touch to say he had set up a money-lending business, which Musana was now managing. And if things were not working out for Kagaba in the UK, he could return to Uganda and work alongside Musana.

Kagaba waited to hear back from Emily before calling Ajuna. It had been nearly two months since they had last talked.

"I'm going to Botswana," he started.

"You are?"

"I have been offered a job."

"You have?"

"Yes! Emily's boss … I mean the chair of her board … has connected me to a company."

He was greeted with silence and was disappointed by her lukewarm response to his good news. So much sat between them—he knew that—but this was something to celebrate nonetheless.

"Ajuna," he was already thinking how he would make up for his past inadequacies, for not sending her any money in the past several months, for not communicating. And the presents he would buy her and Daisy once he settled in Botswana: diamond bracelets and earrings and necklaces. Botswana was the world's leading producer of diamonds; it was possible that jewelry there was affordable. And then, the invitation for them to come and visit. He had long changed his mind about going to Uganda. He was not ready to face his family.

"How's Daisy?" he prompted.

"She's good. She turned one year, you know. We had hoped you would at least call, or respond to my letter."

"It must have been delivered to my old address, Ajuna. I swear I did not receive it. I have been living with Ochola since April. I—"

"Who is Ochola?"

"Ajuna, I will explain everything. I—"

She had hung up.

Emily tapped him on the shoulder, bringing him back to the present. "I'm really glad you made this decision, Kagaba," she put down her cup.

"I can't thank you enough, Emily, for your patience. I was stupid. I should never have turned down the job offer in the first place. You had already gone to great lengths to help me."

"No, you were not stupid. You were angry … you were confused, you were wronged, Kagaba. Children should not be lied to. They should have told you the truth about your *real* mother."

Kagaba scanned Emily's face.

"You know Sean and I don't really get along," she continued. "He behaves," she paused, "like the outsider. He believes he is an outsider."

"Was he adopted?" Kagaba was astonished by the connection he had made. "That's why he is different. The ginger hair. That's why he left home early. So, you are not his *real* sister?"

"Yes. But it's me who was adopted."

"What?"

"I was never told, until I was an adult. I love my parents. They have given me everything. But the revelation affected Sean. He started treating me as a usurper. He dropped out of school. He left home."

"I am so sorry."

"It's alright. I never got to know my birth parents. My parents are the only *parents* I've ever known."

"I am so sorry," Kagaba repeated, not knowing what else to say.

Emily did not respond. She pulled out her phone and started scrolling. After a while, Kagaba strolled away and stood looking through the broad, crystal-clear windows. All those planes. Over a thousand of them went through the airport daily; seventy-five million passengers annually.

When he first arrived, seeing a plane in the sky would remind him of home. He would draw a mental picture of himself leaving the UK aboard one of the planes, with money in his pocket, suitcases of presents, an academic certificate from a reputable college. He would plan to arrive on a weekend so that all his family would be at the airport to receive him. This time, Ssenga Jovia wouldn't be messed around by a bus conductor. He would hire a car to bring her and his father and Tomas to Kampala.

Ajuna would have prepared a big party to welcome him back in their newly built house. And he would see his daughter for the first time.

London had changed him. It had tainted his mind with pessimism. It had robbed him of his innocence and left him dry as a bone.

No point dwelling on the past. Better to embrace the promise that lay ahead: a new job as a business analyst at Bacha Consulting in Gaborone. It was one of the biggest private companies in Botswana. He was more than ready to dive in once the paperwork for his work permit was sorted.

He glanced back at Emily. She was still browsing through her phone. So, she was adopted. In Uganda, children who lost their parents or who were abandoned would be taken in by relatives, who raised and cared for them. Emily had never met her birth parents. Her adoptive parents were her actual parents. She had taken on their surname, even though they were not related by blood.

Did it matter? Watching Emily and her parents, one would never guess they were not a blood family. They loved her very much, and she loved them back. Mr. Nathan loved him in the same way a father would love his son—perhaps even more. He was a loved child. As was Emily. It was possible to create a family beyond blood ties.

"It's time to go," Emily announced.

As the aircraft shot higher and higher into the skies, gobbling the thick clouds like a glutton, he dreamed he was returning to Uganda. The compound was filled with merry-making relatives, friends and neighbors of his family. He spotted Ssenga Jovia seated alone under the mahogany shade, dressed in a white tunic with a red scarf wound round her neck.

She smiled when she saw him and walked to where Kagaba was standing on the terrace with Ajuna and his father. His father handed him a rooster his stepmother had prepared to cook for lunch.

Kagaba thanked his father and turned round to say goodbye to Ssenga Jovia, but she was not there anymore. Then he caught sight of her white dress as she disappeared around the corner of the house. He shouted for her to stop; he tried to run after her, but his legs were heavy, as if a brick had been tied to each.

He opened his eyes. Emily was now buried in her laptop across from him. They were about to touch down and the pilot was commanding everyone to fasten their seat belts and switch off electronic gadgets. As the plane began to drop, the desert sand rose up, like a storm, to receive them.

Acknowledgments

This novel has benefited from the input of numerous individuals. I'm grateful to the first readers, who ploughed through drafts, and drafts, and more drafts. What an uphill task! Thank you for holding my hand, for the hugs, for wiping my tears of frustration. With your permission, I will mention you here: Ellen Banda-Aaku, for those endless calls I made to clarify things; Jacob Ross, for telling me "it's not ready, my sister" and "cut, cut, cut"; Otieno Owino, for opening my eyes to why the narrative voice wasn't working at the beginning; Peter Urpeth, whose quiet counsel and wise guidance saw me through those early days of uncertainty; and David Godwin, for listening to the story as it unraveled in my head. You patiently sat through my incoherent rumblings and encouraged me to put words on paper. Thank you for keeping the faith.

I pay tribute to the subsequent readers, who urged me to the finishing line: Lynn Taylor, what a sensitive, eagle-eyed reader you are! Jennifer Nansubuga Makumbi, thank you for the tough love; Fourie Botha, you are an excellent, patient editor! And more.

To Jessica Powers and the team at Catalyst Press, thank you for believing in this novel.

And for G. Always.

Goretti Kyomuhendo is a leading Ugandan novelist and founding director of the African Writers Trust and TUBAZE African Books. She is the author of four novels: *The First Daughter* (1996); *Secrets No More* (1999), winner of the Uganda National Literary Award for Best Novel; *Waiting* (2007), published by The Feminist Press in New York and translated into Spanish; and *Whispers from Vera* (2023). In 2014 she published the *Essential Handbook for African Creative Writers*. She has also published several children's books and short stories. Goretti holds a master's degree in creative writing from the University of KwaZulu-Natal, South Africa, and taught creative writing at the same university. The first Ugandan woman to receive an international writing program fellowship from the University of Iowa, Goretti has been recognized internationally for her work as a writer and literary activist. She has chaired the judging panel for the Caine Prize and also served as a judge for the Commonwealth Book Prize. In 2019, she was featured among the 100 Most Influential Africans by *New African*. Goretti is a founding member of FEMRITE, a women writers' association and publishing house in Uganda, and served as its first director for ten years.